THE COMPLETE
Guitar Course

THE COMPLETE
Guitar
Course

Learn to Play in **20** Easy-to-Follow Lessons

Tom Fleming

Reader's
Digest

The Reader's Digest Association, Inc.
Pleasantville, New York/Montreal

A READER'S DIGEST BOOK

This edition published by The Reader's Digest Association, Inc., by arrangement with Amber Books Ltd

Editorial and design by
Amber Books Ltd
Bradley's Close
74–77 White Lion Street
London N1 9PF
United Kingdom
www.amberbooks.co.uk

FOR AMBER BOOKS
Project Editor: James Bennett
Design: Zoe Mellors, Mark Batley, Keren Harragan
Studio photography: Mal Stone
Picture Research: Terry Forshaw, Kate Green

FOR READER'S DIGEST
U.S. Project Editor: Marilyn Knowlton
Canadian Project Editor: Pamela Johnson
Project Designer: Jennifer Tokarski
Associate Art Director: George McKeon
Cover Photographer: Christine Bronico
Executive Editor, Trade Publishing: Dolores York
President and Publisher, Trade Publishing: Harold Clarke

With special thanks…
To Rick Hessney—for the loan of his Martin guitar (shown on cover) and for his enthusiastic support of the book.
To Chip Lovitt—for lending his keen teacher's eye to the text and music and for his willingness to answer "just one more question."

Library of Congress Cataloging in Publication Data:

Fleming, Tom, 1975–
    The complete guitar course : learn to play in 20 easy-to-follow lessons / Tom Fleming.
        p. cm.
    "Reader's digest" book.
    Includes index.
    ISBN 0-7621-0662-X
    1. Guitar--Methods. I. Title.
    MT582.F49 2006
    787.87'193--dc22
                        2006045420

Address any comments about *The Complete Guitar Course* to:
        The Reader's Digest Association, Inc.
        Adult Trade Publishing
        Reader's Digest Road
        Pleasantville, NY 10570-7000

For more Reader's Digest products and information, visit our websites:
        www.rd.com (in the United States)
        www.readersdigest.ca (in Canada)

Printed in Singapore

10 9 8 7 6 5 4 3 2 1

CONTENTS

Getting Started 8

Your First Chords 26

Putting It Together 40

Lead Guitar 50

More Lead Playing 64

More Chords 72

Power Chords and Overdrive 86

Rock 'n' Roll 100

Barre Chords 112

Fingerstyle Guitar 122

Classical Guitar 136

The Blues 144

Lead Techniques 156

Rocking Harder 172

Getting Funky 184

Country Guitar 192

The World of Guitars 202

Guitar Gear 218

Chord Reference 228

Practicing with Scales 244

Index 253

Introduction

The guitar is probably used across a broader range of musical styles than any other instrument—from classical music and flamenco through blues, folk, and jazz to rock, funk, and heavy metal. The guitar plays a part in all of these styles and is central to most of them. As a beginner setting out to learn the guitar, you may already have a clear idea of the musical path you want to follow. On the other hand, you may have more of a "see what happens" attitude. Either way, this book is for you.

Throughout this book we strive to make learning the guitar fun. Many of the styles we dip into can be a lifetime's study in themselves; our plan is to give you a taste of each one, along with an appropriate basic knowledge of the techniques, chords, and music theory involved so you can decide whether you'd like to explore the style further. The other purpose of this is to help you on your way to becoming a well-rounded musician. While some musicians happily specialize in very narrow areas of music, the most "complete" musicians tend to be interested in all sorts of styles, even if they are not known for playing them. Actually, most great musicians simply can't help it—there's a whole world of endlessly fascinating music out there.

As with any other study, you will be directly rewarded by the time, effort, and patience you put in. Remember, though, that a little practice every day is much more beneficial than a long session once a week. To become a truly good player with natural technique, playing the guitar has to become a normal part of your life. The benefits of this are both physical (stronger fingers, harder fingertips, and so on) and mental. Think of other everyday acquired skills, such as using a knife and fork. You would probably never have gained mastery over these simple tools if you had only practiced once a week!

The guitar has also evolved, more than any other instrument, into many different sub-species. Though they share a common ancestor, the spiky creations favored by heavy rock players and the modern classical guitar seem about as closely related as tigers and domestic cats. The evolution of the instrument is inextricably linked to the many styles associated with it, so we explore this history throughout the book.

Most guitar players will admit that there was one player, or band, who directly inspired them to take up the guitar. Guitar sales figures have always been directly linked to the ascendancy of guitar-playing heroes, from Elvis to Kurt Cobain. Guitar players have held a central place in popular culture for the past fifty years. We explore the lives and styles of many of these greats in this book. Again, you just can't help being interested, and broad knowledge makes for broad musicianship.

Don't forget the most important thing: to have fun!

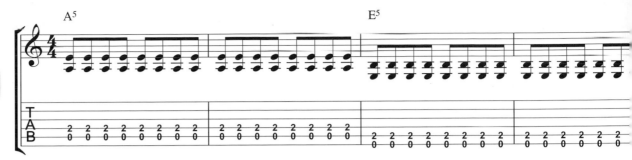

From electric guitars to amps, effects pedals and more, you'll find advice on choosing equipment on pages 202–227.

Simple and easy-to-follow notes and music theory will keep you building your skills.

Throughout the book you will find profiles of some of the world's most famous guitars, such as the Fender Telecaster.

Step-by-step photos show you exactly how to play each note and chord, cutting out the guesswork.

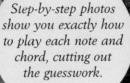

Scattered throughout the book are features on the guitar greats, from Buddy Holly (pictured) to Kurt Cobain.

Getting Started

Choosing a Guitar

Choosing an Amp

Caring for Your Guitar

Changing Strings

Tuning Your Guitar

Welcome to Lesson 1 of the course. In this chapter we'll look at everything you'll need to know to get started, including information on how to choose a guitar or an amplifier (often called an "amp" for short) and what other accessories you may want to pick up while you're shopping. We'll also cover the basics of tuning, holding the guitar, and strumming.

Lesson 1.1: Choosing a Guitar

Your most important purchase will be the guitar. Although some guitars change hands for large sums, it's possible to get started for a modest amount. That said, it's worth going for a quality instrument that will last you awhile. In practice, this means avoiding the very cheapest instruments; in general, you'll be safe with the leading brands.

New or used?

You may be tempted to buy a used instrument. While this can often be a good deal, be aware that many instruments manufactured today are made to higher quality standards than older models. Some of the secondhand instruments available may be up to 20 years old, but guitar manufacturing, particularly at the cheaper end, has made huge leaps forward since that time. There are some "howling dogs" out there on the used market. Even the major guitar makers have let their standards slip from time to time in the past. So unless you're very sure of what you're doing, or you have access to expert unbiased advice, stick to new guitars. In the worst-case scenario—that you end up with a problem—you will at least have some measure of protection.

This advice is even more applicable to amplifiers and other electronic accessories. Used electrical equipment can often perform badly and can even be dangerous. If you do buy a used amp, make sure you buy from a reputable dealer or have it checked by a service technician before you use it.

THINGS TO CONSIDER BEFORE YOU BUY

Size: Your choice of guitar will depend on various factors. Most adults can begin playing with a full-sized instrument. You should go for a smaller instrument only if you have very small hands. However, it's always better to be able to grow into an instrument than to grow out of it quickly. Generally, full-sized guitars are suitable for players age 12 and over.

Type: Since this course covers a broad range of playing styles, most of the information and music in this book can be applied to any type of guitar. Over the next few pages we'll look at the many different types of guitar in greater detail and explain exactly what to look for when choosing a particular type.

The necessary core skills covered in the early stage are the same. Later we'll explore more specialized areas, including fingerpicking (generally, but not exclusively, associated with acoustic and classical players) and electric guitar techniques, including the use of overdrive.

If you're a total beginner, you'll probably find a good electric guitar easiest to play, but it's worth considering all three types—and the musical direction you think you'd like to take—before you decide. It is also important to recognize that the playability of most guitars can be improved after they leave the factory. A good local guitar store will usually make sure that all its guitars are properly "set up," whereas a mail-order operation probably won't.

WHICH GUITAR IS RIGHT FOR YOU?

There are three main types of guitar on the market: electric, classical (also known as Spanish), and steel-string acoustic.

THE CLASSICAL GUITAR

Until recently, most people starting out on the guitar chose a classical, or Spanish, guitar. As the name suggests, this type of guitar originated in Spain and is primarily associated with classical music. If you plan to learn to play classical guitar seriously, you'll definitely need a Spanish guitar. If you plan to play any other kind of guitar music, you'll probably want to move on to another type of guitar at some point, but a classical guitar can still be a good starter instrument.

Popular Makes

Fender
Yamaha
Ibanez
Ramirez
Admira

Pros

- Soft nylon strings are kind to soft hands.
- Available in small sizes for small people.
- Best for classical, flamenco, Latin jazz.

Cons

- A full-sized classical guitar has a wide neck. This can make some chord shapes difficult for players with small hands.
- Not suitable for advanced lead guitar techniques, such as string bending.

What to Look For

- ACTION: This refers to the height of the strings above the fretboard. This should generally be around 1/16–3/16 in. (1–2 mm). The action will always be a bit higher farther up the neck (i.e., closer to the guitar body), but only slightly.

- NECK: Look down the length of the strings (from the bridge). The neck should be straight and should not leave the body at a visible angle.

- SOUND: Good classical guitars are surprisingly loud, with a warm tone in the bass strings and a clear, slightly glassy sound in the higher strings.

Tuning pegs

Nut

Neck
Classical guitars generally have wider necks than electric and acoustic guitars; some beginners with small hands find them harder to play.

Strings
The higher strings are made of solid nylon; the lower strings are made of fine strands of nylon wound with soft metal.

Fretboard

Top/Table

Sound hole

Saddle

Bridge

Body

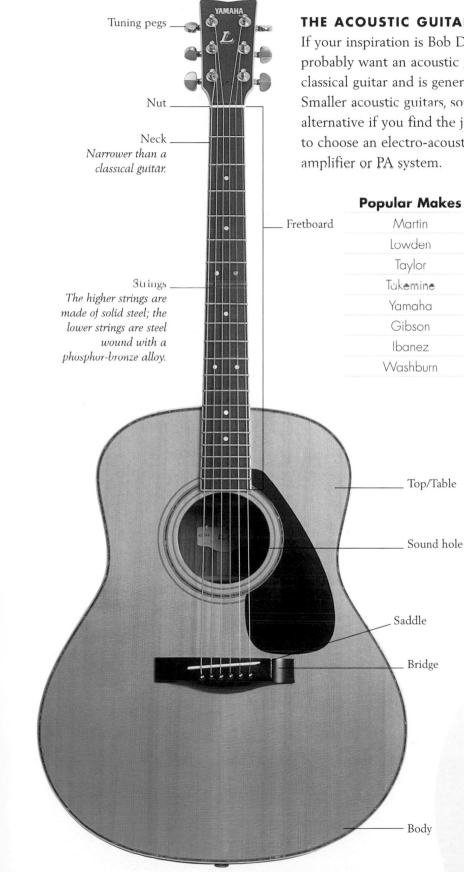

Tuning pegs

Nut

Neck
*Narrower than a
classical guitar.*

Fretboard

Strings
*The higher strings are
made of solid steel; the
lower strings are steel
wound with a
phosphor-bronze alloy.*

Top/Table

Sound hole

Saddle

Bridge

Body

THE ACOUSTIC GUITAR

If your inspiration is Bob Dylan, Paul Simon, or even Elvis Presley, you'll probably want an acoustic guitar. Traditionally, this has a larger body than a classical guitar and is generally called a jumbo acoustic or dreadnought. Smaller acoustic guitars, sometimes called parlor guitars, offer a good alternative if you find the jumbo size just too big. You may also want to choose an electro-acoustic model, which can be connected directly to an amplifier or PA system.

Popular Makes

Martin

Lowden

Taylor

Takemine

Yamaha

Gibson

Ibanez

Washburn

Pros

- The neck is generally narrower than on a classical guitar—better for small hands.
- Best for folk, fingerpicking, easy strumming.

Cons

- Hard, heavy steel strings can hurt soft hands at first.
- Jumbo acoustics can be unwieldy for small people.
- Not suitable for advanced lead guitar techniques, such as string bending.

What to Look For

- ACTION: (see page 10)
- FRET BUZZ: All notes should be playable without buzzing. If any notes buzz, the store technician may be able to cure the problem by spending more time setting up the guitar.
- INTONATION: This refers to how well the guitar stays in tune farther up the neck. This is generally not adjustable on an acoustic, so it's worth making sure the sound is reasonable.

THE ELECTRIC GUITAR

If you aim to play rock, blues, or jazz, you'll probably be after an electric guitar. These come in a bewildering array of types and shapes, some of which are explored later in this book. Most electric guitars available today are quality instruments that should give you years of service. It is often assumed that electric guitars are loud—and, of course, they can be—but without amplification, they can be almost silent. Most of the major manufacturers offer guitar/amp packages that are an excellent deal for beginners.

Popular Makes

Fender/Squier

Gibson/Epiphone

Yamaha

Washburn

Ibanez

PRS

Gretsch

Rickenbacker

Pros

• The best choice for most modern music.

• Light-gauge strings are easy to play.

• Perfect for quiet, unplugged practice.

• Best for rock, blues, jazz, funk, heavy metal.

Cons

• Can be very loud!

• Not always the most subtle instrument in the hands of a beginner.

What to Look For

• ACTION: (see page 10)

• INTONATION: This is more important with the electric guitar, since lead playing often uses the higher reaches of the fretboard. Fortunately, electric guitar intonation can usually be adjusted.

• NOISE: Plug in the guitar and check for crackling sounds produced by turning the volume/tone controls or moving the pickup selector. These sounds can usually be eliminated by using an aerosol electronic switch cleaner.

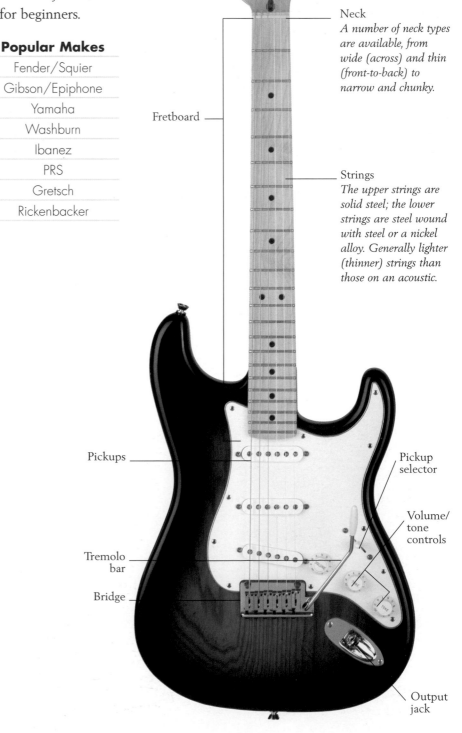

Tuning pegs

Headstock

Neck
A number of neck types are available, from wide (across) and thin (front-to-back) to narrow and chunky.

Fretboard

Strings
The upper strings are solid steel; the lower strings are steel wound with steel or a nickel alloy. Generally lighter (thinner) strings than those on an acoustic.

Pickups

Pickup selector

Volume/ tone controls

Tremolo bar

Bridge

Output jack

Lesson 1.2: Choosing an Amp

Popular Makes

Fender
Marshall
Peavey
Vox
Line6
Crate

If you're buying an electric guitar, you'll need an amplifier. The electric guitar, with its solid body, makes almost no sound until you plug it in. It sounds like an electric guitar only when connected to an amp.

Creating the Sound You Want

In fact, the amp has a greater influence on the sound of the electric guitar than does the guitar itself. This is because it is actually a very different thing from a hi-fi amplifier, which, as its name suggests, amplifies the input signal with *high fidelity*, or accuracy. In other words, the sound coming out should be exactly the same as the signal going in, only strong enough to drive a loudspeaker.

A guitar amp, on the other hand, is actually a very *low-fidelity* device in which varying amounts of distortion and noise have become an inherent part of the electric guitar sound we know today.

Turning any kind of amp up to maximum volume often causes distortion, both in the amp circuitry and the speaker. During the late 1950s and early 1960s, guitar players started to discover that they actually *liked* this sound. Later, amp designers found a way to control the amount of distortion while keeping the volume down.

Until the 1960s, all amplifiers used glass tubes to amplify the signal. Glass tubes are bulky and fragile and get very hot when in use. However, many guitar amps, particularly expensive ones, still use tubes rather than transistors, since many people feel that a warmer, less brittle sound is better.

Gain (distortion) control
Channel selector
Volume (clean channel)
Volume (drive channel)
Headphone socket
Tone controls
Input socket
Handle
Power switch
Speaker
Cabinet

What to Look For

- POWER: Unless you already plan to play with a band, or live on your own, you'll probably want to start with a small, portable, practice amp.

- TUBE OR TRANSISTOR: Tube-based practice amps are rare. Many transistor amps sound fine. If you haven't started playing, ask a sales assistant to demonstrate some amps for you. The most important question is, Does it sound good?

- REVERB: Even cheap amps often feature reverb (which simulates the sound of a large room or hall); this usually results in a smoother, more forgiving sound.

- HEADPHONE SOCKET: This helps to keep the family happy even if you're deafening yourself.

- CHANNEL SWITCHING: Allows quick switching between "clean" and "drive" (distortion) sounds.

Lesson 1.3: Caring for Your Guitar

A good musical instrument can last a lifetime—or more—given proper care. A quality guitar can be an expensive purchase, so here are a few hints to help keep your guitar in top condition.

Cleaning

Use a soft, slightly damp cloth only: Other cleaning materials or detergents may seriously damage the finish. If you want to polish your guitar, use only special guitar polish, which is available from music stores.

Air travel

If at all possible, take your guitar with you into the cabin. Try to be among the first to get on the plane so you'll find plenty of space in the overhead lockers. Since this is one place where a hard case usually won't fit, a soft case is the best idea. If the airline insists on putting your instrument in the hold—check this when booking your flight—use a hard case (ideally, a flight case) liberally covered in FRAGILE stickers. Remove or slacken all the strings. This is because sudden changes in pressure and temperature can cause string breakage and damage if the neck is under tension.

If in doubt, seek help

This book will show you how to undertake certain basic setup and maintenance tasks; others are best left to the professionals. If in doubt, always get help. Most guitar stores will be able to advise you and will request a reasonable charge for maintenance and repairs, especially if you regularly purchase equipment from them. *Never* adjust the truss rod yourself, because this can do serious damage unless you have been trained and know exactly what you're doing.

Extreme temperatures and sunlight

Be careful when playing outdoors. Direct sunlight can damage the guitar's finish, and exposure to extreme temperatures can cause wood to crack or warp. *Never* leave a guitar leaning against a hot radiator or other source of heat.

When changing strings, take the opportunity to clean areas that are otherwise inaccessible.

EXPERT'S TIP:
Electric shocks can kill

Modern guitars and amps are made to scrupulous safety standards, but you can't be too careful. **Never** play with wet hands. **Never** play outdoors in wet weather. **Always** make sure that your equipment is properly grounded (earthed).

Lesson 1.4: Changing Strings

The procedure for changing strings depends on the type of guitar you have. To remove an old string, it's a good idea to slacken the string considerably before you cut through it. This avoids a jolt and the possibility of the end of the string hitting your eye. If you're removing all the strings, slacken them together gradually, turning each one a few times. Otherwise, you can end up with one string pulling unevenly against the tension in the neck (and often breaking as a result).

ELECTRIC GUITAR

1 Electric strings have a ball, or a bullet, at one end. This end attaches to the bridge or tremolo.

2 Feed the string through the bridge/tremolo (the other end first) until the ball end fastens. There are also string-through setups through the bridge.

3 Pass the end of the string through the appropriate tuner post. The thinner (plain steel) strings can be looped through again.

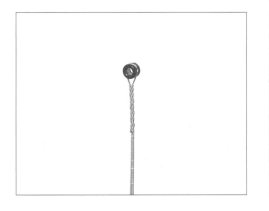

4 Bend the thicker (wound) strings to produce a kink, where they exit the tuner post.

5 Leave enough "slack" so that the string will be tight once it has been wound about five times around the tuner post.

6 Wind the string carefully onto the tuner post, passing through the correct slot in the nut, making sure you go the *right way*—turning the tuning peg *counterclockwise*.

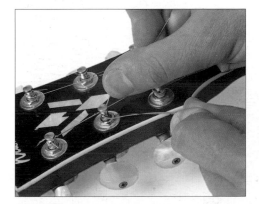

EXPERT'S TIP: String Winder
A guitar string winder is a plastic swivel device with a handle. It has a fixture that fits over the tuning keys, and is very useful because it saves time when tuning, especially if a string breaks during a live performance.

ACOUSTIC GUITAR

1 Steel acoustic strings also have a ball or a bullet at one end. The ball end is anchored to the bridge by means of a plastic or wooden pin.

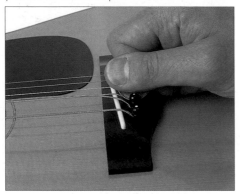

2 Remove the pin—if you can't manage this with your fingers, use a pair of pliers.

3 Hold on to the end of the old string so it doesn't fall into the guitar. Feed the new string through the hole (ball end first) and replace the pin.

4 Pull the string tight so the ball is anchored against the pin. Fasten the string to the tuner post and wind the string in the same way as shown for the electric guitar (see page 15).

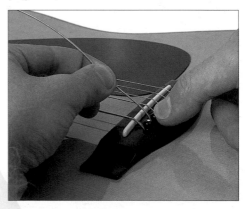

String Suggestions

• Take a good look at your guitar, noting the exact paths taken by the strings before you change them for the first time. You should start by replacing one string at a time so you can easily refer to the other strings as you go.

• Make sure you don't mix up the strings! Most manufacturers label the strings by pitch (note name) as well as by gauge.

• New strings can take awhile to settle in enough to hold their tuning. Half an hour's playing and retuning is usually enough, but the process can be sped up considerably by giving each string a gentle tug, tuning to the correct pitch, and repeating the procedure until the tuning is stable. When the string is fully stretched, tugging should have little effect on the tuning.

• Make sure you use the correct gauge. Sets are usually referred to by the gauge of the top (thinnest) string: A set of "tens" has a top-string gauge of 0.010 in. (0.25 mm). Nines and tens are the most common gauges for electric guitar (twelves or thirteens for acoustic guitar).

• Always trim the string ends neatly, leaving no more than ¼ in. (5 mm) hanging, and bend the end down toward the headstock. Long string ends sticking out at all angles may look cool, but they can be very dangerous if one pokes you in the eye. Make sure the ends are properly trimmed and well tucked in.

CLASSICAL GUITAR

1 Most nylon strings don't have a ball end. Instead, the string is looped through the bridge and held in place by its own tension.

2 Pass the string through the hole in the bridge.

3 Now loop the string back underneath itself, as shown. Then tuck the end back under the string at the back of the bridge.

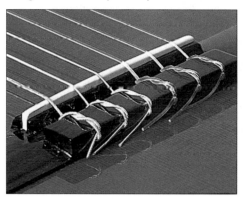

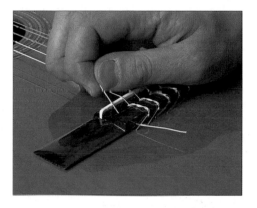

4 Twist the string around itself as it passes over the bridge. This adds friction, which improves tuning stability. Pull the string tight.

5 Tuning is basically the same as for steel strings except that the hole in the tuner post is usually large enough to loop even the thickest string back through.

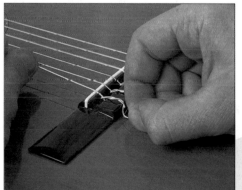

Left-Handed Playing

• About 10 percent of the population is left-handed, but some left-handed players choose to learn to play right-handed (both hands are involved, after all); if you are left-handed, you will probably know instinctively which approach is right for you.

• Unfortunately, there is less choice available in left-handed guitars, particularly at the cheaper end of the market. Some players (notably Jimi Hendrix) have addressed this by simply restringing right-handed guitars; while this can often work well, there are obvious disadvantages—for example, the pickguard and controls will be in the wrong place.

• This book is written using right-handed terminology, but if you're playing left-handed, all you have to do is substitute "right" for "left" and vice versa, and imagine mirror images of the photos of chords and techniques in this book.

Lesson 1.5: Tuning Your Guitar

When to tune

It is absolutely essential that your guitar be in tune. No matter how good your technique, how many chords you know, or how fast you can play, a badly tuned guitar will always sound terrible.

Many studio players check their tuning before each and every "take." Often a slight tweak is all that is needed, but if the guitar has not been played for a while, or after taking it on your travels, more tuning may be necessary.

Which method to use

The good news is that modern electronic tuners are cheap, accurate, and easy to use. Electronic tuners are the best method for beginners, especially those who have never played a musical instrument before. We're going to take a look at three different methods of tuning, however, so you should still be able to get by if you don't have a tuner or the battery dies in the middle of the night.

Whichever method you use to tune the guitar, you need to tune the strings one at a time before moving on to the next. If you have just changed your strings, you may well have to repeat the whole process a few times while the strings "settle in." As we have seen, this can be speeded up by tugging the strings with your fingers. If you are retuning a guitar where the strings have already settled, you should need to complete the process only once, so it's worth making sure you get each string absolutely in tune.

When tuning a string, hold the guitar normally (see pages 22–23), strike the string with your right hand (pick or finger), and make any necessary adjustment by turning the tuning peg with your left hand away from you to raise the pitch or toward you to lower the pitch.

Many guitars hold their tuning very well, but you should still check your tuning every time you pick the guitar up and at intervals during music practice or a performance.

Tuning electronically

Most tuners incorporate both an input socket and a microphone. Simply place the tuner near your guitar or amp in order to use the microphone or connect your electric guitar to the input socket. The display indicates whether the string being tuned has reached the correct pitch. This usually takes the form of either a pivoting needle, a row of LEDs (lights), or both. The string is in tune when the needle reaches the middle point of its range or the central LED illuminates. Additional lights may indicate whether the string needs to be raised or lowered in pitch.

Automatic tuners automatically find the closest note to the incoming signal and assume you are tuning to that note. Manual tuners have to be told (usually by means of a slider switch) which string you are tuning. Some tuners are designed only for standard guitar tuning. *Chromatic* tuners will allow you to tune to any note. Either way, you need to know the names of the guitar strings in standard tuning, from the lowest (thickest) to highest (thinnest):

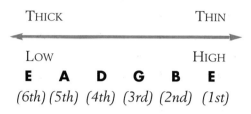

THICK   THIN

LOW   HIGH

E   A   D   G   B   E
(6th) (5th) (4th) (3rd) (2nd) (1st)

There are too many different types of tuners on the market to describe them individually. Consult your manual if you run into difficulties.

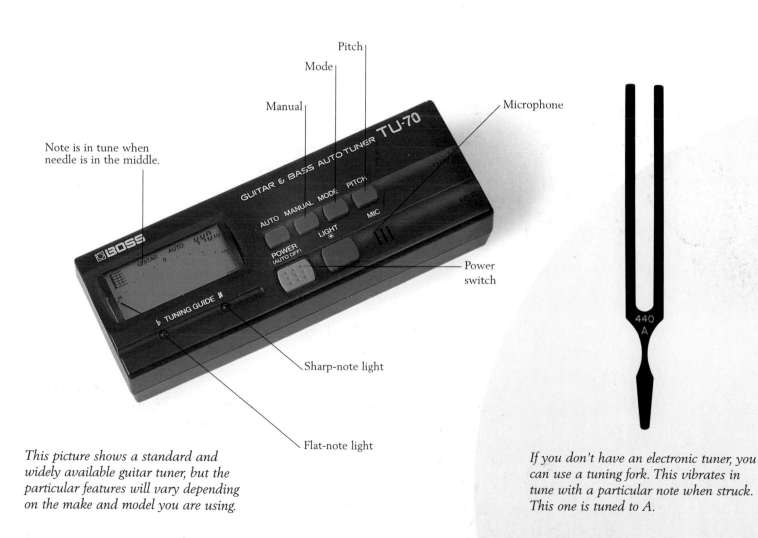

Note is in tune when needle is in the middle.

Manual

Mode

Pitch

Microphone

Power switch

Sharp-note light

Flat-note light

This picture shows a standard and widely available guitar tuner, but the particular features will vary depending on the make and model you are using.

If you don't have an electronic tuner, you can use a tuning fork. This vibrates in tune with a particular note when struck. This one is tuned to A.

19

Tuning to a keyboard

If you have a piano or an electronic keyboard, you can use this to tune your guitar. For those who play piano and read music, shown at right are the notes you need to find on the piano keyboard and how they relate to the guitar strings.

Starting with the lowest string (E), strike the note on the piano, followed by the guitar string, and try to hear whether they are both the same pitch. If they are, move on to the next string. If they are not, adjust the guitar by turning the tuning peg. Using a piano to tune your guitar can be easier if you use the piano's sustain pedal (the rightmost pedal) to let the note ring, freeing your hands to adjust the guitar string.

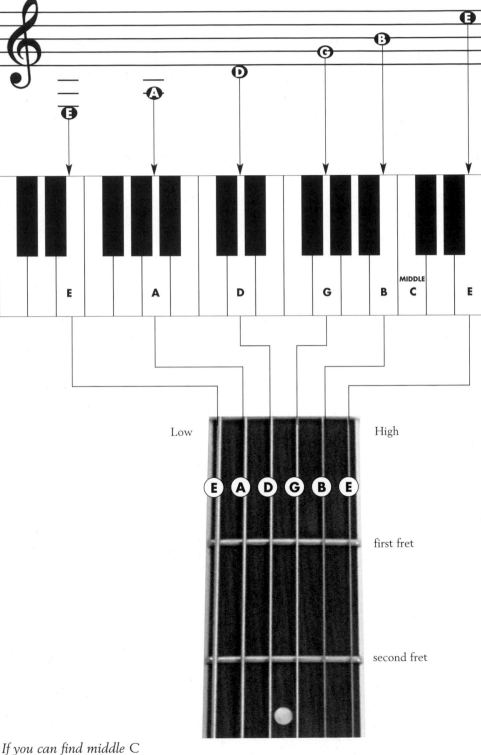

If you can find middle C on a piano, you should be able to tune your guitar to the piano's notes. If you don't play the piano or can't read music, simply refer to the keyboard and fretboard above.

Tuning relatively

If you have neither a tuner nor a piano, you can still make sure your guitar is in tune *with itself*. In other words, the overall pitch of the instrument may not be absolutely right, but the strings will be in tune with one another, so the guitar will sound okay.

A word of warning, though: It's still a good idea to tune to a fixed reference every so often. If relative tuning is used exclusively, the pitch of the instrument may eventually drift a long way from "concert" (standard) pitch. This could result in string breakage (if too high) or a generally poor sound (if the strings are so slack that they start to buzz and rattle). For relative tuning, assume that the bottom (thickest) E string is in tune. You could even use a CD track that you know is in the key of E for this purpose. The following steps ensure that the other strings are in tune, *relatively*, with this pitch.

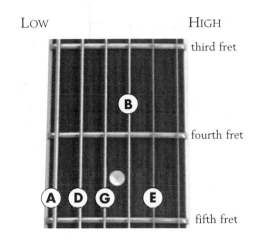

LOW — HIGH

third fret

fourth fret

fifth fret

The notes indicated above should match the open strings in relative tuning.

1 Play the note at the fifth fret on the bottom string; then play the next open string. Adjust the tuner post until the two notes you hear are exactly the same pitch.

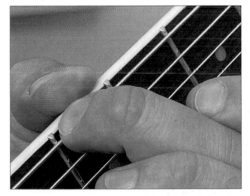

2 Now play the fifth fret on the A, or 5th, string (the one you have just tuned), and tune the next open string (D) to this note.

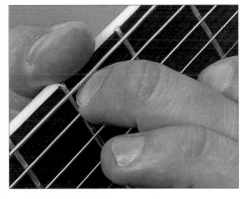

3 Now compare the D string, fifth fret, with the open G string. They should be the same note.

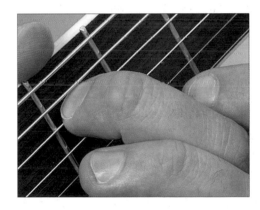

4 The next pair is the odd one out. Compare the G string, fourth fret, with the open B string. They should be the same note.

5 Finally, compare the B string, fifth fret, to the pitch of the open top E string. They should be the same note.

Lesson 1.6: Starting to Play!

Once your guitar is in tune, you're ready to start playing. But before you begin, make sure you're sitting or standing comfortably, holding the pick correctly, and strumming in a relaxed manner.

Holding the guitar

The golden rule here is to make sure you are as comfortable as possible. Generally speaking, if your posture is comfortable and relaxed, it's probably okay. If any part of your body is cramped, tense, bent in an unnatural way, or otherwise uncomfortable, your posture is probably wrong.

Classical guitar teachers are very precise about correct posture and hand positions. (In as far as these are specifically helpful when playing classical guitar, we'll have a look at them later.) Rock and pop playing, however, allows far greater freedom. As with most activities, it's a good idea to keep your back straight.

Sitting

Forget about your left hand for now. Sit or stand with your guitar in a comfortable position. When sitting, most players rest the guitar on their right thigh, as shown in the photograph below left.

Most conventionally shaped guitars fall into place quite naturally. Classical guitarists sit with their left foot on a stool and the guitar on the left thigh (see page 137).

Standing

If you're standing, simply adjust the strap so that the guitar feels comfortable. Most guitars are designed so that the weight is balanced and the standing posture is perfectly comfortable.

Correct seated position   *Too low—shorten the strap*   *Too high—lengthen the strap*

Holding the Pick

STRUMMING

1 Hold the pick between your thumb and the first finger of your right hand. The thumb and first finger should make a "T" shape. Let the pick protrude by about ¼ in. (5 mm). This part will actually strike the strings.

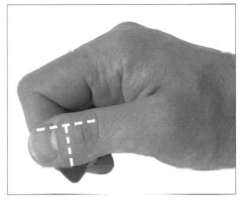

2 Now strum with the pick across all six strings. Try to strike all the strings with the same force. Note starting hand position below.

3 As you strum downward, listen to see if you can hear all the strings. For the moment, the pick should be striking them all. Once this feels natural, try strumming upward between the down-strums.

4 Keep strumming until the action feels really comfortable and natural. When you feel ready, take a deep breath and turn to Lesson 2, where you'll learn your first chords and use them to play your first song.

Helpful tips

In general, avoid wearing the guitar extremely high or extremely low—both can cause unusual muscular pain. If you wear the guitar standing up and then adopt the sitting position already described, the strap should go a bit slack but shouldn't fall off your shoulders. In other words, the guitar should be in roughly the same place in relation to your body, whether you are sitting or standing.

Correct standing position

Accessories

There are many accessories that you may need to buy, depending on your choice of guitar. Some will be essential immediately and may come with your guitar. Others are more likely to be needed by a professional musician.

Picks

Most guitar styles (except classical guitar) are played using a pick, or plectrum. These are usually a slightly rounded triangular shape, made of plastic (sometimes metal), and are available in various thicknesses. Buy a selection and find one that feels right for you. Picks tend to get lost easily, so it's a good idea to buy a dozen at a time and keep them in a tin or jar.

Metronome

This provides a ticking or beeping sound at a precisely defined tempo, helping you to keep perfectly in time during music practice.

Strings

Spare strings are essential. Not only can strings break—usually at the most inconvenient time imaginable—but their sound degenerates over time. Many professionals change all their strings before each gig or recording session. You'll get better value buying a set rather than individual strings; still better if you buy a box of 10 sets.

Electronic tuner

This is by far the most effective way to tune the guitar, at least for beginners. We've looked at tuning to a keyboard and relative tuning on pages 20–21, but both take more time and involve developing your ear to some extent. At this point you just want to get playing quickly, and knowing that your instrument is in tune is a great confidence booster. So it's worth bringing a tuner home with you, too.

Guitar cable

You'll need one of these to connect your guitar to your amp. The plugs at each end are called jack plugs. The very cheapest cables tend to be flimsy and of poor quality. A thick, sturdy cable may cost a little extra, but it should perform well for years.

Strap

If you want to play standing up, you'll need a strap. These come in various materials, colors, and designs—the choice is usually a matter of taste. Note: Classical guitars (and some acoustic guitars) usually don't have strap buttons.

Guitar stand

These can come in quite handy. If you leave your guitar propped up against a chair, amp, or radiator, chances are you'll knock it over and take a chip out of it at some point. Protect your investment with a guitar stand.

Music stand

Don't be tempted to practice music while bent over a desk or watching TV. Whether you're sitting or standing, an adjustable music stand is essential for good, comfortable posture.

String winder

This is useful for winding new strings quickly and easily.

Capo

This handy device clamps across the strings, raising the pitch of the guitar. This is particularly useful when accompanying singers. A capo makes it possible to play a song in a higher or lower key to suit the voice while using the same chord shapes (see page 81 for more information).

OTHER HANDY ITEMS

Pliers/Wire Cutters: Useful for cutting and trimming strings.

Guitar case: If you plan to travel with your guitar, keep it safe in a hard case.

Soft cloth: For cleaning your guitar.

Spare batteries: For tuners, metronomes, and pedals. Most use a single 9-volt battery.

Footrest: Serious classical players sit with their left foot on a special stool. Rock artists wouldn't use one if you paid them. Your choice.

EXPERT'S TIP:
You get what you pay for

Choose accessories carefully from a reputable shop or dealer. When buying electrical equipment, ask for a demonstration in the store. It's worth spending as much money as you can afford on accessories. Some products, such as guitar cables, come with long guarantees. Although more expensive, these are a good investment for the future. Look after your accessories and be sure to keep packaging and manuals (at least for the length of the guarantee).

Your First Chords

Chords
Thumb Position
Strumming Your First Chords
Changing Chords
"Git Changin'"
Tips for Faster Changes
Basic Music Theory

Most guitarists play both rhythm and lead guitar. Rhythm guitar involves playing chords; lead guitar generally involves playing single notes to create a melody. In this section, we're going to get started with chord playing.

Lesson 2.1: Chords

In general terms, "chord" simply means more than one note sounding at once. When playing any instrument capable of producing more than one note at a time, you can play chords in one form or another. A conductor can have an orchestra play chords by giving each musician one note to play.

Chord shapes

Guitarists generally think of chords in terms of "shapes." In other words, though playing a chord may require the use of up to four fingers, this is thought of and memorized as a whole rather than as separate notes. Chord shapes can be notated in a number of ways. For now, we're going to use chord boxes. These give a simple graphical representation of the notes played.

Chord boxes

A chord box consists of vertical lines representing the guitar strings, horizontal lines representing frets, and round dots representing the fingers. Let's take a look at exactly how this works with your first chord, the chord of A. The diagram below shows the symbols used with the A chord:

A CHORD

What the symbols mean

X = **don't play this string.** However, in this particular case, it doesn't really matter if you accidentally play this string occasionally.

O = **open string.** This string should be played by the right hand but not fretted by the left hand. Make sure you don't let your left-hand fingers accidentally get in the way.

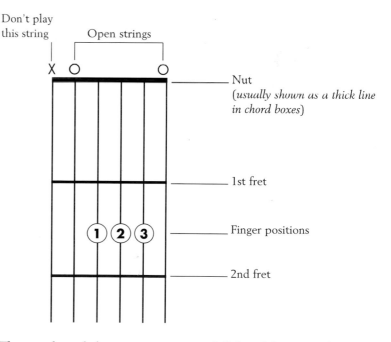

The numbered dots represent your left-hand fingers. The thumb is not counted, so "1" represents the index finger, "2" the middle finger, and so on.

Finger positions in theory

Later in the course, and in other guitar books, the finger dots are not numbered—you have to work out a reasonable fingering pattern yourself. For now, the dots show you exactly where to place your fingers.

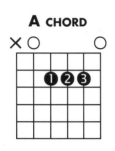

Note that in this chord box, the three fingers are shown in a straight line parallel to the frets. If you try this, you'll soon discover that it's physically impossible. Chord boxes are a quick and simple representation rather than an exact image of the chord being played.

Finger positions in practice

In practice, the three fingers playing the A chord have to be placed diagonally, as shown below.

Use your fingertips

Study the photo and copy the arrangement of the fingers. Make sure that you're using the tips of

the fingers and that each finger is touching only the string indicated. In particular, try to make sure that none of your fingers accidentally mutes one of the strings marked "O" (open). This can happen very easily.

The finger numbering used in this book is shown at right. Once you reach a certain level, you won't need dots to show where to put each finger.

Lesson 2.2: Thumb Position

Since the chord box shows only the fretboard, you may be wondering where to place your left thumb. Depending on the style of guitar you're playing, there are different approaches to thumb position.

FINDING THE RIGHT THUMB POSITION

1 Classical guitarists follow a very strict rule that states that the thumb should remain positioned at the neck's midpoint at all times.

2 Other guitar players adopt a more relaxed approach, with the thumb moving around, as required, and sometimes even being used to play the bottom string.

3 The thumb should always be touching the neck, opposing the force of the fingers. For this reason, it should always be behind the fingers playing the chord.

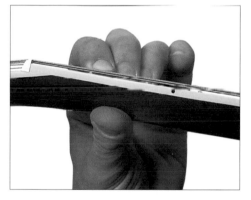

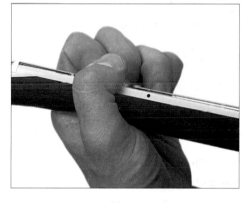

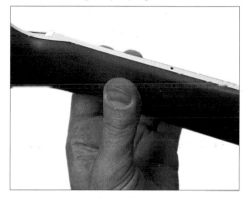

4 **Don't** position your thumb too high up the neck, as shown below. It should always be opposite your other fingers.

5 The thumb can be allowed to move above the midpoint, but **never** below. This ensures that the thumb is always helping the other fingers.

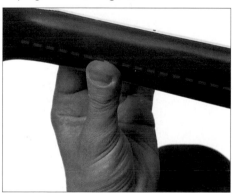

Lesson 2.3: Strumming Your First Chords

Playing the A chord

To put the A chord in context, we need to learn two more very useful chords and start putting them together. Strum the A chord using the pick. Does it sound good? Are all the notes ringing out clearly? If you can hear any muffled strings, try playing them one at a time while holding down the chord shape. If any of the strings sound dead or muffled and is not producing a clear note, you'll probably find that one of your other fingers is getting in the way— try to *feel* the problem through the fingers of your left hand.

However, don't get *too* obsessive about hearing muffled strings at this point.

Improving your chord playing

It's more important to start playing and having fun. As your playing develops and your hands gain strength, your sound will gradually improve.

Two new chords

To progress with this part of the course, you'll need to learn two more chords—the D and the E chords.

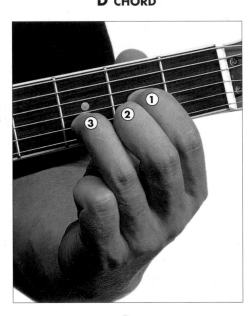

A CHORD

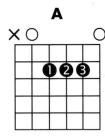

A

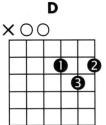

D CHORD

D

E CHORD

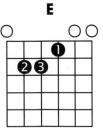

E

Lesson 2.4: Changing Chords

There's a good reason for focusing on three chords in this chapter—a great many songs can be played using just three chords.

Chords and keys

In this case, the chords A, D, and E are the main chords in the key of A and can therefore be used to play many songs in this key—a very common key for guitar-based music.

Changing chords

Before you can put these chords into action to play a real song, you need to get used to going from one to another. As a beginner, getting just one chord shape right can seem like a huge task, while changing chords with any fluency seems impossible. You won't be surprised to learn that the secret, as with so many other things, lies with practice.

To get things moving, try this. Strum the A chord and let it ring. Before moving your fingers, prepare for the D chord by trying to remember where your fingers are going to end up. Try to change them all at the same time, with a minimum of movement, and then strum the D chord, remembering not to play the bottom two strings.

The "bottom" string

Incidentally, the "bottom" string means the string closest to you, which is actually farthest from the ground, but it's the bottom string in *pitch*, producing the lowest note.

Make smooth changes

Now go back to the A chord, listening to make sure that all notes are ringing clearly. Keep repeating this process until you are managing reasonably smooth changes. When you feel ready, add the E chord, remembering to practice both A–E and D–E.

This may take a few days. As with muffled strings, some delay in changing chords is acceptable at this stage and certainly shouldn't keep you from playing songs for real.

Strumming chords

Now let's try these chords with some strumming patterns. Start with the A chord, using down-strums only, counting "1, 2, 3, 4" repeatedly and strumming on each beat. Keep this fairly slow in the beginning. Imagine a leisurely walking pace:

The vertical lines at the start, end, and middle of this example are called *bar lines*. The music written between two bar lines is called a *measure*, or *bar*, and it is a basic unit of time in written music. Most popular music has four beats per measure; hence, the repeated count of "1,2,3,4."

Strumming and changing chords at the same time

Once you feel comfortable playing the chord of A in this steady rhythm, trying changing chords between measures:

Along with changing A–D, remember to change A–E and D–E, too.

Lesson 2.5: Git Changin'

The exercise below will help you practice changing all the chords you've learned so far.

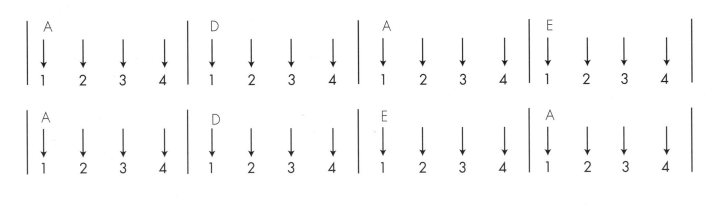

Lesson 2.6: Tips for Faster Chord Changes

Biggest tip of all
Keep practicing!

Think ahead
Try to think about the change before you need to move your fingers. If you are mentally prepared, you are less likely to interrupt the rhythmic flow of your strumming.

Fluid motion
Where possible, move fingers together. For example, when changing from A to E, you'll notice that the second and third fingers play the same fret on adjacent strings in each shape. So when changing from A to E, move these fingers together. Ideally, the chord change should feel like one fluid motion, with the first finger moving to the third string (first fret), while the second and third fingers move across together.

Sliding
Sometimes one of your fingers should not be lifted from the string at all but, instead, should slide between frets on the same string. In

these cases, the sliding finger should lead and the others should follow. For example, when changing from D to E, the first finger slides down one fret while the second and third change position.

When changing between D and E chords, the first finger slides down a fret. Only the second and third fingers come off the strings to move into their new positions in the E shape.

Slide

Elvis Presley

1935–1977

GUITARS: MARTIN, GIBSON

Recommended Listening:

Sunrise

Elvis '56

The Memphis Record

To many people, Elvis Presley is Mr. Rock 'n' Roll.

When the nervous young man with the strange name strolled, guitar in hand, into Memphis Record Service's studio at 706 Union Avenue in 1953, he wasn't setting out to change the course of musical history or to become the best-selling singer of all time. Elvis simply wanted to cut a disc as a present for his mom. His faltering, reedy performance of the ballad "My Happiness" took just a few minutes to capture, and moments later Elvis was on his way with a shiny single-sided 78-rpm record under his arm.

Though there's little evidence of this in the recording, Elvis was already steeped in, and passionate about, the black music of the southern states. At a time when southern dance halls and other places of entertainment were strictly segregated—and radio stations played to either one audience or the other—a white boy from Memphis would have been expected to listen to country stars like Hank Williams. Elvis did love country music, along with blues and Gospel. To combine these separate influences was a daring move in 1954. That's exactly what Elvis did, though, when the studio's owner and Sun Records' boss, Sam Phillips, called him back a year after his first session. Something of this potential must have been evident to Phillips, who had always said that he'd make a fortune if only he could find "a white man who could sing like a black man." Elvis, backed by Scotty Moore on lead guitar and Bill Black on string bass, tried a few "safe" standards before starting to fool around with blues singer Arthur Crudup's "That's All Right (Mama)." Scotty and Bill fell in with a two-beat country backing, Sam rewound the tape, and rock 'n' roll was born.

Though by no means a virtuoso, Presley was a solid player—his acoustic rhythm-playing powering the early Sun sides before anyone thought to add a drummer. But more than this, the image of the most famous singer in the world playing guitar inspired literally millions of people to learn the instrument.

The 1950s saw a phenomenal growth in guitar sales all around the world. Countless teenagers, some of whom would go on to start their own musical revolutions, would never have thought to pick up a guitar without Elvis's influence, direct or indirect. John Lennon, Paul McCartney, and George Harrison are the most well-known examples. As John Lennon famously put it, "Before Elvis, there was nothing."

"Bad Moon Rising"

Words and Music by **John Fogerty**

This country-rock classic uses just the three chords we have learned so far and works very well using just down-strums, though up-strums can be added later.

First of all we'll take a look at the basic chord patterns you'll need to master, before slotting them into the song. This song has been transposed (written in a different key from the original record) to make it playable using the chords learned so far. Later, you will learn about using a capo (see page 81) to make changing key easy. You could use a capo at the fifth fret if you wanted to play this arrangement along with the record.

Here's the verse pattern, which is played four times:

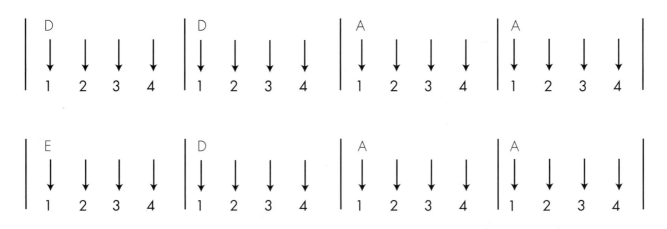

Play this as slowly as you like at first, making sure all the chords are sounding fully. Ideally there should be an even pulse throughout, but don't worry too much at this stage if changing chords introduces a slight delay— this will improve with practice. If you listen to the Creedence Clearwater Revival recording you'll probably notice that the tempo is quite fast; it's better to build up to this speed rather than try it straight away.

After the verse comes the chorus:

This is actually a bit simpler than the verse pattern since there are no changes halfway through a measure. Again, practice it slowly and carefully at first. Throughout the song, try to avoid hitting the bottom string when playing the A chord, and the bottom two strings when playing the D chord.

When you can get around these patterns comfortably, you're ready to slot them into the song.

VERSE 1

```
A       E    D    A
```
I see the bad moon a-rising.

```
A       E    D         A
```
I see trouble on the way.

```
A       E    D              A
```
I see earthquakes and lightnin'.

```
A       E  D    A
```
I see bad times today.

CHORUS 1

```
D
```
Don't go around tonight,

```
            A
```
Well, it's bound to take your life,

```
E      D          A
```
There's a bad moon on the rise.

VERSE 2

```
A    E    D    A
```
I hear hurricanes a-blowing.

```
A        E    D      A
```
I know the end is coming soon.

```
A    E    D        A
```
I fear rivers over flowing.

```
A       E      D          A
```
I hear the voice of rage and ruin.

CHORUS 2   *Repeat Chorus*

VERSE 3

```
A        E    D       A
```
Hope you got your things together.

```
A          E    D        A
```
Hope you are quite prepared to die.

```
A          E    D          A
```
Looks like we're in for nasty weather.

```
A       E    D       A
```
One eye is taken for an eye.

CHORUS 3   *Repeat Chorus*

Lesson 2.7: Basic Music Theory

During this course, we will be exploring enough music theory to make sure that you can get the most out of the songs and other material in the book.

The basic theory

Some beginners may find music theory a bit daunting, but if you understand a few basic principles, you'll be able to work out exactly what's going on and your musicianship will benefit. Understanding theory is especially important if you are using this book without the help of a teacher. Our aim is to develop a knowledge of theory that is *just ahead* of the musical examples in the book. That way, you can concentrate on coming to grips with playing the music at any given stage, rather than struggling to understand what is meant by all these strange dots and lines.

With this in mind, let's start at the very beginning....

Rhythm and pulse

Modern Western music can be thought of as having three components: rhythm, melody, and harmony. All three are important, but rhythm is arguably the most important, and it is the one feature common to almost all music, from all parts of the world and all periods in history. An understanding of rhythm is therefore the most basic part of coming to grips with the way music works.

Nearly all music can be said to have a *pulse*. Put very simply, this is a regular "beat" that defines everything that happens in the

music. When you count "1,2,3,4" before playing or while playing, you are establishing a pulse. If you were to walk in time to a piece of music, your feet would hit the ground at regular times. A metronome produces a tick at precisely defined, unvarying intervals. All these are examples of pulse.

The simplest definition of rhythm is that it, unlike your pulse, does vary. Imagine singing a song while walking in time. Now imagine clapping your hands on each syllable of the song. Your feet would be laying down the *pulse*—1,2,3,4; 1,2,3,4—while your hands would be defining the rhythm, which might be almost as simple or much more complex.

Dividing the pulse

Music is conveyed on the page using a fairly small set of basic symbols. At this point, we'll look at the rhythmic aspects of this; later we'll look at how these symbols are used to notate chords and melodies.

The simplest note to draw is called a whole note.

Count   1,   2,   3,   4

This usually (but not always—more on this later) lasts for one measure. Dividing a whole note in two gives two *half notes*.

Count   1,   2,   3,   4

As you can see, they look exactly like whole notes, with the addition of a vertical stem. Half notes are half as long as whole notes. Dividing half notes in two gives us *quarter notes*.

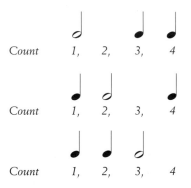

Count   1,   2,   3,   4

These look like half notes but have solid, rather than hollow, noteheads. A whole note is equal in duration to two half notes, four quarter notes, or any valid combination:

Count   1,   2,   3,   4

Count   1,   2,   3,   4

Count   1,   2,   3,   4

Time signatures

One of the first things you'll see if you look at almost any piece of music is called a time signature. This usually consists of two numbers, written one above the other.

$$\frac{4}{4} \qquad \frac{3}{4} \qquad \frac{6}{8}$$

The top number tells us how many beats per measure this music contains. Going back to the idea of counting the pulse, if you try this with a few well-known songs, it should become clear that "1,2,3,4" doesn't always work. Some tunes require "1,2,3." Try humming the well-known tunes listed opposite and see if you agree with the number of beats per measure.

The bottom number in the time signature tells us which type of note is used to convey one beat. Here, whole notes are represented by "1," half notes by "2," quarter notes by "4," and so on.

4/4 time

The most common time signature for most types of music is 4/4. This means four quarter notes per measure. Therefore, each measure can contain four quarter notes, or any combination of notes adding up to four quarter notes. Here's an example of 4/4 time:

3/4 time

Another common time signature is 3/4. Again, one beat is defined as a quarter note, but now there are only three quarter notes per measure, or any combination adding up to three quarter notes. Clearly, whole notes cannot be used in 3/4. Here's an example of 3/4 time:

Counting rhythms

For time signatures using quarter notes for each beat, half notes represent two beats each; whole notes represent four beats each. These should always receive their full count. The important thing here is that each measure must contain the number of beats defined in the time signature; quarter notes and half notes will account for one or two of those beats, respectively.

And that's all the theory you need for now. We'll add a little more in each lesson of the course.

Try setting a metronome to around 80 beats per minute and count through the examples on this page. (One click is one beat.)

4 beats:	3 beats:
• "Hey Jude"	• "Amazing Grace"
• "Brown Sugar"	• "The Times They Are a-Changin'"
• "Sweet Home Alabama"	• "Mull of Kintyre"
• "Addicted to Love"	• "Some Day My Prince Will Come"
• "Bohemian Rhapsody"	• "My Bonnie"

The Origins of the Guitar

The origins of the guitar have been debated by music historians ever since guitar playing achieved mainstream popularity. There is no shortage of possible ancestors. Stringed, fretted instruments appear in various forms everywhere from Europe to Japan and have been recorded as far back as 1900 B.C.

A possible ancestor to the guitar was found in an Egyptian tomb dating back to between 1500 and 2000 B.C., and although it bears a closer resemblance to instruments such as the harp, instruments appeared about 1,000 years later featuring guitarlike proportions and a separately crafted body and neck.

There is little doubt that the guitar, as we know it, evolved primarily in Spain, and it is thought that its immediate ancestors may have been brought to Spain by the Moors, who began a mass invasion of the Iberian peninsula around A.D. 800. They brought with them the oud and the *guitarra moresca*, with an oval soundbox and many holes in the soundboard. However, while such instruments may have influenced its design, the *guitarra latina,* an early lute that found its way into Spain from Europe in the early Renaissance period—is a more likely precursor to the guitar.

Five strings

The sixteenth century saw many important developments in the evolution of the guitar. Throughout fifteenth-century Europe, small, bowl-backed instruments were common, ranging

A young woman is pictured playing a precursor of the modern guitar in this Venetian painting of the Baroque era.

from the *chitarra* (Italy) to the Spanish *guitarra* and the French *quitare*.

In the sixteenth century, these were gradually replaced by guitars with five courses (pairs of strings tuned in unison), tuned the same way as the top five strings of a modern guitar. At the same time, Spain saw the evolution of another instrument—the *vihuela*. While the lute was the preferred instrument of European aristocracies at the time, in Spain it had become associated with the invading Moors, so the Spaniards searched for an instrument that could accommodate the lute's repertoire. Spanish nobles were disdainful of the guitar (a "commoner's instrument"), so they enlarged the four-course guitar and added two lower courses to create the *vihuela*—essentially a guitar comparable in size to modern varieties, with twelve metal frets and courses rather than single strings.

Aristocratic sounds

During the Baroque era (1600–1750), the patronage of the European nobility brought the guitar immense popularity. It is known that King Louis XIV of France played the guitar and regarded it as his favorite instrument. In Venice, Giorgio and Matteo Sellas made ornately decorated instruments, and in France, René Verboam represented the height of French instrument building.

Composers in Holland, Germany, and Eastern Europe began to write for the instrument, and the Spaniard Gaspar Sanz became the instrument's

The popularity of the lute among the royal courts of Europe led to the development of the 12-string vihuela in fifteenth-century Spain.

first enduring composer, creating music which continues to inspire today.

The guitar lost popularity during the eighteenth century, but there were several crucial developments at this time. In Spain, the lower E course was added, while simultaneously French and Italian luthiers began to build instruments with single strings rather than pairs of strings in an attempt to solve tuning and technique problems associated with courses. By the nineteenth century, the Spaniards followed suit.

Other important developments included the replacement of adjustable catgut frets (tied to the fretboard), with permanent frets of ivory and later brass, and the introduction of fan bracing, pioneered by José Pagés and Josef Benedid in the Spanish town of Cadiz. Fan-shaped struts were fixed to the underside of the soundboard to support the bridge, replacing the transverse bar, which had previously done the job.

Standard form

By the nineteenth century the classical guitar, with all of its essential features,

had taken shape. However, it was the Spaniard, Antonio de Torres Jurado, who experimented with the existing construction and dimensions to create the classical guitar in its modern form, standardizing the neck length to 25 in. (65 cm) and increasing the width of the neck to ¼ in. (5 cm) at the nut. He also improved the fan-bracing designs of Pagés and Benedid. These innovations helped to increase the guitar's popularity, and Torres was soon the professional's luthier of choice. At the same time, Frances de Tárrega became the guitar's first real virtuoso, and he established the basic classical techniques that are still used today.

Over the next century and a half, the classical guitar gradually regained its popularity. Thanks to improvements in design, the work of guitarists such as Fernando Carulli and Andrés Segovia (see page 142), along with perhaps the popularity of its steel-strung cousin, the classical guitar is enjoyed and taken seriously by musicians, composers, and audiences, and interest is growing all the time.

Putting It Together

Chords G, C, and Em

Adding Upstrokes

Notes on the Treble Clef

Remembering Notes

In Lesson 3, we'll be learning some more chords and strumming patterns. Though accomplished guitarists end up knowing literally hundreds of chord shapes, you can never hope to memorize more than a few at a time. It's best to learn two or three chords, use them on a suitable song, and with practice, really get used to changing from one to another before you learn more chords.

Lesson 3.1: Chords G, C, and Em

Now that you've become used to the chords of A, D, and E, let's move on to three more chord shapes.

The G chord
Most people find the shape below the easiest way to play the G chord. However, it is useful to be able to play it using other fingers.

The G chord: alternative fingering
The notes of the chord are the same, but fingers 2, 3, and 4 are used instead of 1, 2, and 3. This makes it easier to change to and from certain other chords, such as the C chord. Ultimately, you should be able to use both shapes; it's also a good idea to get your pinky working right away.

G

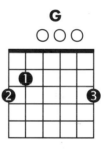

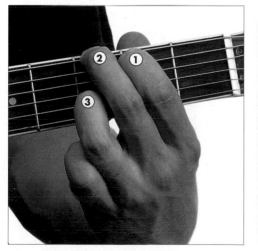

G
(Alternative fingering)

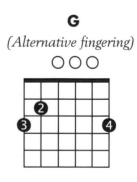

The C chord

The C chord is a bit easier. Take care not to play the bottom E string. This chord often goes with the G chord, so it is important to practice changing between the two. As with the change from A to E, notice that the second and third fingers can move together because they stay in the same formation.

C

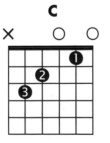

The E minor chord

This last chord is called E minor. It is usually abbreviated to "Em," but you will also sometimes see "Emin" and even "E–." It's an easy chord to play if you've mastered the E chord—simply lift the first finger and let the G string sound open.

Em

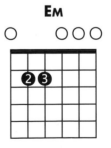

Some famous songs you can play using just four chords (G, Em, C, and D):
"Unchained Melody," "His Latest Flame," "Earth Angel," "Only the Lonely"

Lesson 3.2: Adding Upstrokes

So far, all our strumming patterns have used only downstrokes. It's time to start adding interest with some upstrokes, too.

To start: Play one of our new chords, using downstrokes only, counting "1,2,3,4." Keep this nice and slow—just imagine a relaxed walking pace. You may want to tap your foot on each beat.

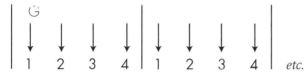

After each beat: Without changing the strumming, say "and."

1 and 2 and 3 and 4 and 1 and 2 and 3 and 4 and...

Make an even rhythm: Each "and" should come halfway between beats.

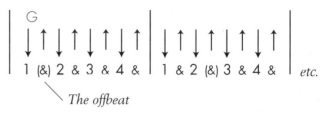

Keep strumming: Now strum upward on each "and." This is called the *offbeat*.

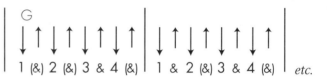

The offbeat

Add variety: For most playing styles, the upstrokes will be lighter than the downstrokes, striking the strings with less force and often hitting fewer strings. An upstroke on every offbeat can also get a bit monotonous.

Play around with various combinations until you feel comfortable. We'll be using some of them in the next song

EXPERT'S TIP: Up and down strokes
The golden rule with these patterns is that no matter which strokes you play or leave out, the right hand should always move downward on the beat and upward on the offbeat. Later we'll be omitting downstrokes, too, and breaking this rule will land you in a mess! If in doubt, imagine that your foot is a puppet attached to your right hand. As the foot goes down (1,2,3,4), so should the hand. Both the hand and foot should be moving upward on the offbeat (each "and").

"Stand By Me"

Words and Music by **King/Leiber/Stoller**

Here's the chord sequence:

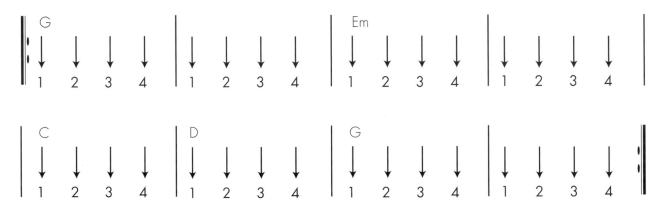

Introducing upstrokes

Once you are comfortable with this sequence using downstrokes only, try to introduce upstrokes. Here's one pattern.

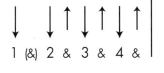

Leaving out strokes

Now try omitting the downstroke on the third beat. This should not affect the directions of the other strokes. The downstroke on beat 3 simply misses the strings.

"Stand By Me" is best known in the version by Ben E. King, who co-wrote the song with Jerry Leiber and Mike Stoller.

INTRO

$\frac{4}{4}$ | G | G | Em | Em |
1   2   3   4   1   2   3   4   1   2   3   4   1   2   3   4

| C | D | G | G |
1   2   3   4   1   2   3   4   1   2   3   4   1   2   3   4

VERSE 1

                G   Em
When the night has come, And the land is dark,

            C   D   G   G
And the moon is the only light we'll see. No, I won't be afraid,

       Em   C   D   G
No, I won't be afraid, Just as long as you stand, Stand by me.

CHORUS

                G   Em
So darling darling, stand by me, Oh, stand by me,

       C   D   G
Oh stand, stand by me, stand by me.

VERSE 2

                G   Em
If the sky that we look upon, Should tumble and fall,

       C   D   G   G
Or the mountain should crumble in the sea. I won't cry, I won't cry,

       Em   C   D   G
No, I won't shed a tear, Just as long as you stand, Stand by me.

Repeat Chorus to fade

Lesson 3.3: Notes on the Treble Clef

In the next step of the course, we'll look at the basics of lead guitar. This involves playing melodies using single notes, not chords. Before we get to that stage, let's prepare the ground by looking at the way notes are conveyed on the page.

The staff, or stave

Most Western music is written using five horizontal lines called a staff, or stave.

The treble clef

Just as a map often features a "key" to the various symbols used, a clef (Italian for "key") is placed at the beginning of each line to identify which notes the lines and spaces are used for.

This is a treble clef and it indicates that the second line up is used to write the note G.

G

Notes

The notes in written music are named after the first seven letters of the alphabet:

A   B   C   D   E   F   G

These note names are repeated—more on this later.

Chords and notes

Music is read from left to right. Notes that are aligned vertically form chords. All the lines and spaces between them are used to place notes.

Chord

Melody

The American Acoustic Guitar

Until the mid-nineteenth century, American luthiers made conventional Spanish guitars strung with gut strings. These were generally similar to European instruments of the time— these luthiers, like most nineteenth-century Americans, were recent immigrants from Europe.

One of these luthiers, C. F. Martin, started manufacturing guitars in New York State in 1833. The company, which is still owned and run by the Martin family, is largely responsible for the standard acoustic guitar designs of the present day.

In the 1890s, many luthiers began to produce steel-string guitars in response to a demand for greater volume from the instrument. Early American folk music was influenced by immigrants from across Europe, and popular instruments included the fiddle, banjo, and mandolin. In this context, the soft tone and low volume of the Spanish guitar do not cut through well.

Dreadnought

The introduction of steel strings enabled an increase in volume and a more cutting tone but brought demands of its own. A standard Spanish guitar neck would soon bend and break under the extra tension exerted by steel strings. Martin strengthened the neck and developed a new system of internal bracing to the body. The large-bodied "dreadnought" shape was

developed in 1916 but did not gain popularity until the 1930s. Once it took hold, however, the shape was quickly established as the standard acoustic guitar.

Martin and others continued to make smaller-bodied instruments, too; these so-called "parlor" guitars retained the Spanish guitar shape and consequently gave less volume than dreadnoughts. Martin dreadnoughts generally carry the "D" prefix before a model number (the D–28 being the best known) and "00" or "000" to signify smaller-bodied instruments such as the 00–18. Both of these types of guitar are also known as "flat-top" acoustics.

Gibson

The other prominent name in early American guitar-making was Orville Gibson. In the late- nineteenth century Gibson took a different approach, evolving a body shape inspired by classical instruments of the violin family. These instruments, which usually feature a curved front and back and f-shaped sound holes, are known as "arch-tops." The arch-top acoustic

guitar, though successful in its own right until the 1930s, is inevitably also remembered for its role in the evolution of the modern electric guitar—early electric instruments were generally arch-tops with a single crude pickup. These early electrics (such as Charlie Christian's Gibson ES–150) played an important part in shaping mainstream jazz guitar sounds in particular, and it is no co-incidence that arch-top electrics are still favored by the majority of jazz players today.

A Martin D–18 acoustic guitar owned by Elvis Presley.

Django Reinhardt

1910–1953
GUITAR: MACAFERRI

Recommended Listening:

Quintette du Hot Club de France:
25 Classics 1934–1940

The history of jazz is full of apparent contradictions. Such was the infectious power and universal appeal of this originally Afro-American style that within 30 years of its birth in the Creole districts of New Orleans, two Frenchmen were able to make their own indelible mark on its history.

Django Reinhardt was born in Liberchies, Belgium, but spent his boyhood and youth in Gypsy encampments near Paris. He learned to play guitar, banjo, and violin at an early age and was soon playing professionally at dance halls in Paris.

At the age of 18, Django's left hand was badly damaged by a fire in his caravan. At first, his third and fourth fingers were so badly burned that they were fused together. Although doctors succeeded in separating them, they never recovered sufficient strength to be of any use to his playing. Determined to be a success as a guitarist, Django managed to develop sufficient strength and speed using just his first and second fingers.

The Hot Club de France quintet formed by Reinhardt and violinist Stephane Grappelli in 1934 was very different from the regular jazz lineups of the time, adding two rhythm guitarists and bass to Reinhardt and Grappelli's lead instruments. Their recordings are instantly recognizable—rhythm guitars pounding away insistently behind virtuosos of their instruments, playing music that is undoubtedly jazz but at the same time very French and strongly influenced by Django's Gypsy heritage.

Django's improvization, fluid by any standard, has an almost supernatural quality when considered in light of his injury. As well as making their own quintet recordings, Reinhardt and Grappelli worked with many legends of American jazz, including Coleman Hawkins and Duke Ellington.

Stephane Grappelli's musical career continued with many brilliant collaborations until almost the end of the twentieth century; Django, sadly, made it only halfway.

Lesson 3.4: Remembering Notes

This is how the lines and spaces in the staff are used to write notes.

It can be easier to memorize the lines and spaces separately. First the spaces, which spell out FACE…

…then the lines, which can be memorized with the phrase "Every Good Boy Deserves Favor"
or
"Every Good Boy Does Fine"
or
"Every Good Boy Deserves Fun"

Extra lines are also used beyond the range of the staff. These lines are called ledger lines and are written only when needed.

Notes written on these lines are named in the same order, using the letters A–G.

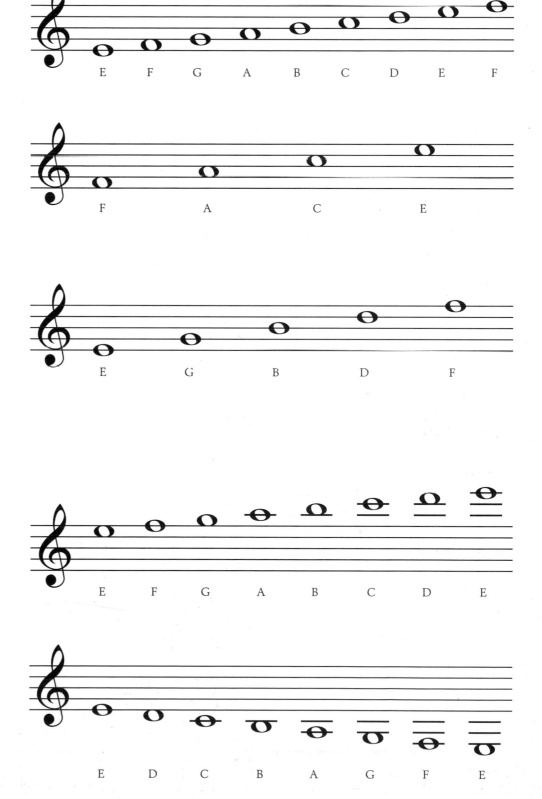

Lead Guitar

The First Position

Easy Tunes to Practice

Scales Practice

Filling the Gaps with Sharps and Flats

More on Rhythm

Thus far in the course, we have been playing chords, or rhythm guitar. As the name implies, the function of rhythm guitar is to provide a rhythmic backing, either to vocals or other instruments playing melodic lines. Now let's look at using the guitar to play the melody.

Lesson 4.1: The First Position

Playing a melodic line on guitar is called lead guitar; most (though not all) of the most famous guitar parts of the last century fall into this category.

Now that you've learned some chords and a little music theory, it's time to start playing some tunes. While the next few pages may seem a world away from "Layla" or "Purple Haze," the basic skills are the same. Developing these skills and adding more advanced techniques will get you to where you want to be in due time.

The first four frets

While lead guitar playing will ultimately take you all over the neck of the guitar, we are going to start by exploring just the first four frets. This is known as **first position**—all the notes can be played without changing the basic position of the left hand.

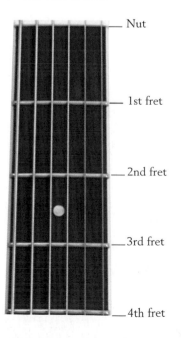

One finger per fret

In practice this means that, for the moment, any notes at the first fret will be played by the first finger, any notes at the second fret by the second finger, and so on.

Standard notation

Guitar music can be written in many different ways. For now, we are going to use standard notation, as explained briefly in the previous lesson. Your knowledge of music notation so far is enough to get you started with the exercises that follow.

Lesson 4.2: Notes in First Position

Learning where the notes are
The chart below shows all the notes in first position that you will need for now, with fingerings and a picture for each note. To begin with, you won't need all these notes at once.

As you work through the course we'll look at some simple tunes using a few notes at a time.

NOTES ON 6TH (E) STRING

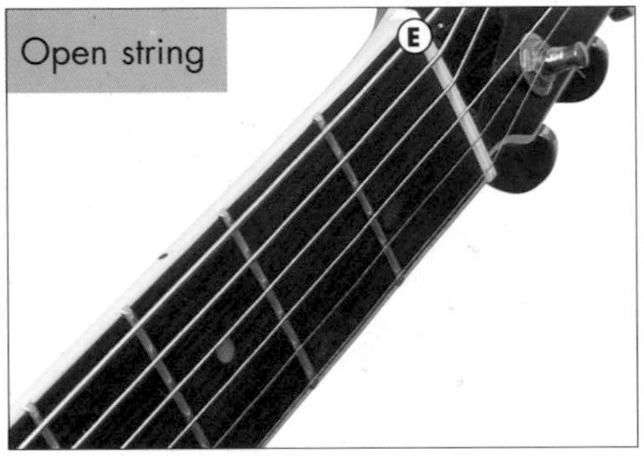

Open string — E

1st fret — F

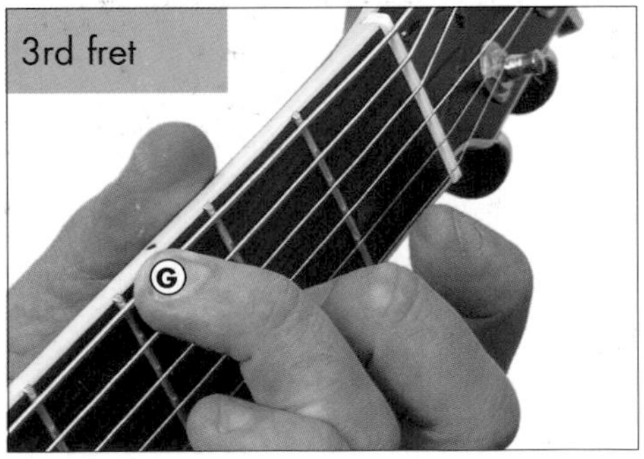

3rd fret — G

NOTES ON 5TH (A) STRING

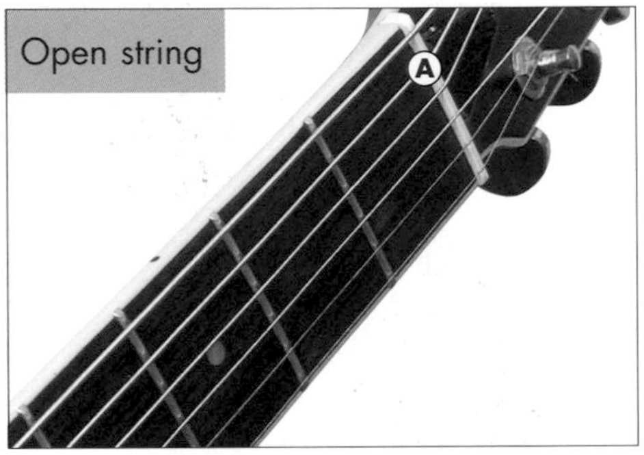

Open string — A

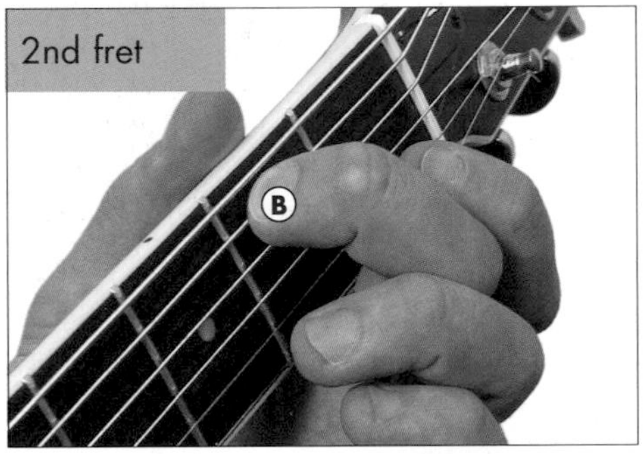

2nd fret — B

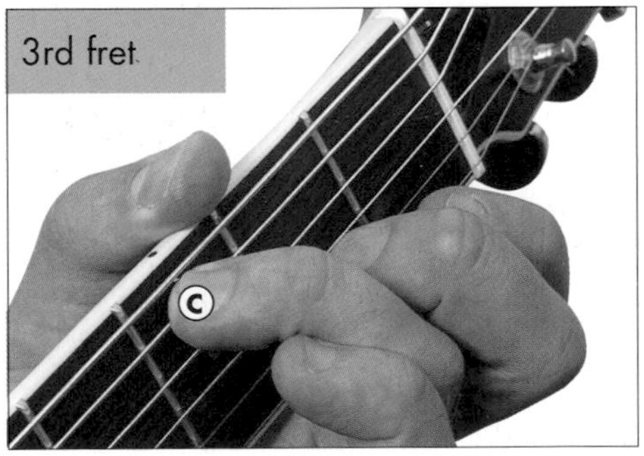

3rd fret — C

NOTES ON 4TH (D) STRING

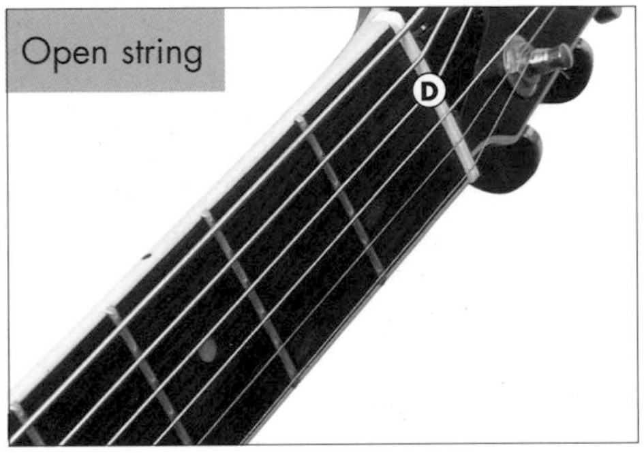

Open string — D

2nd fret — E

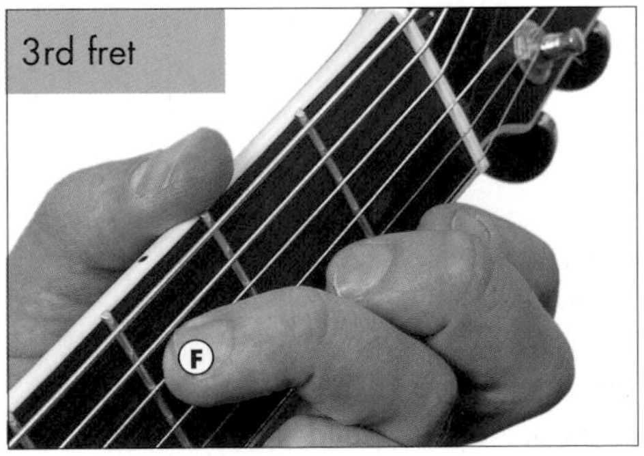

3rd fret — F

LOW

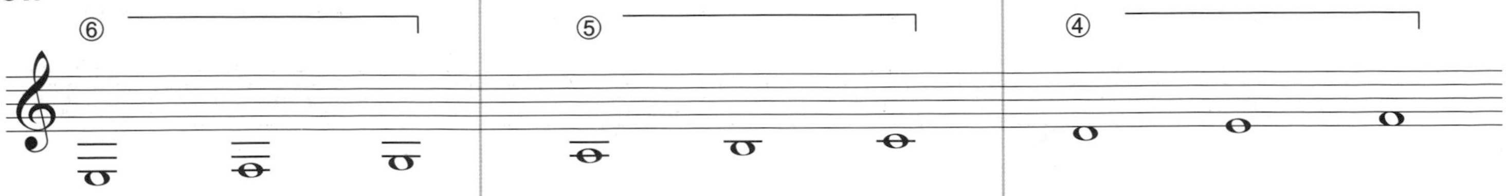

⑥   ⑤   ④

Note	E	F	G	A	B	C	D	E	F
Fret/Finger	0	1	3	0	2	3	0	2	3

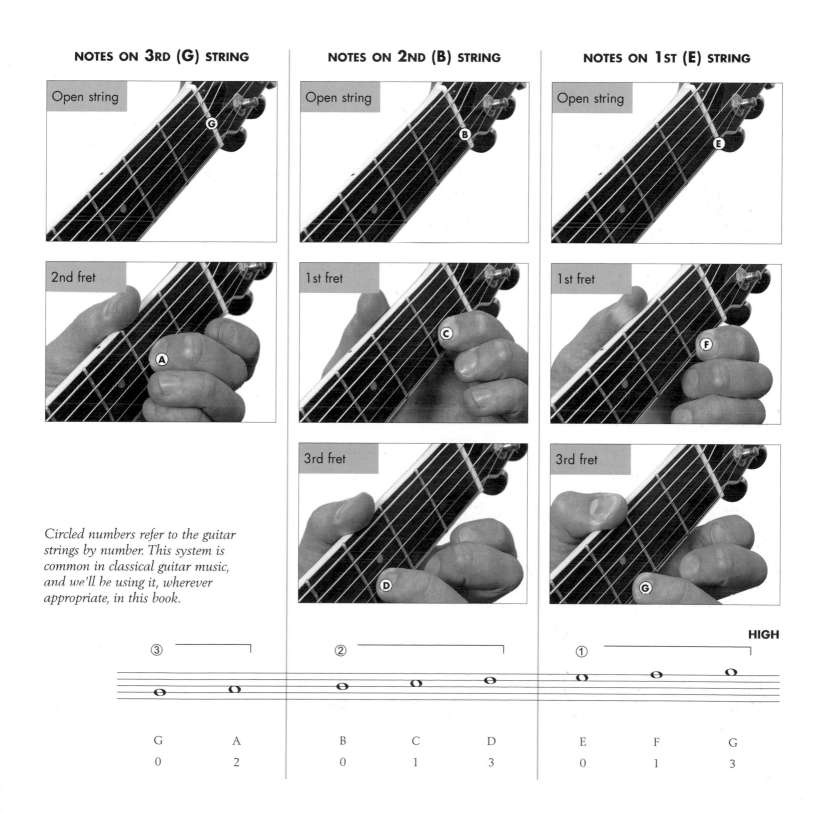

NOTES ON 3RD (G) STRING

Open string

2nd fret

NOTES ON 2ND (B) STRING

Open string

1st fret

3rd fret

NOTES ON 1ST (E) STRING

Open string

1st fret

3rd fret

Circled numbers refer to the guitar strings by number. This system is common in classical guitar music, and we'll be using it, wherever appropriate, in this book.

HIGH

③   ②   ①

G	A	B	C	D	E	F	G
0	2	0	1	3	0	1	3

Lesson 4.3: Easy Tunes to Practice

These two pages contain some simple tunes for you to try out your lead guitar skills. All tunes use only notes and durations (whole, half, quarter) that we've covered so far.

"MICHAEL ROW THE BOAT ASHORE"

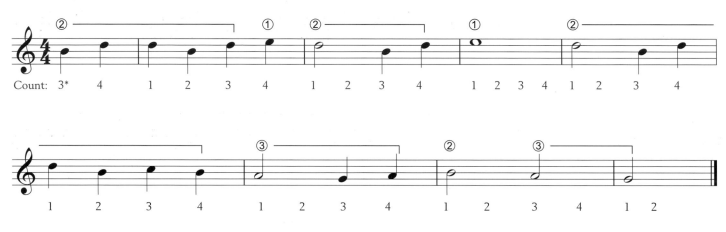

Note: This song has 4 beats per bar, but starts on beat 3, so the first bar has only 2 beats. The last bar also has 2 beats, so that if you want to repeat the tune, you can go straight from beat 2 to beat 3.

EXPERT'S TIP: Keeping time
Metronomes measure time in beats per minute (or "bpm").
Try setting a metronome to a slow tempo, such as 60 bpm, and play the tune along with the metronome's click. Concentrate on hitting each note, with the pick, exactly in time with the metronome. Each note should happen at exactly the same time as the click of the metronome.

"JINGLE BELLS"

"TWINKLE, TWINKLE, LITTLE STAR"

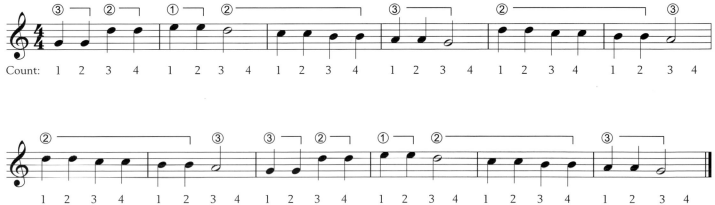

David Gilmour

1946—
GUITAR: FENDER STRATOCASTER

Recommended Listening:

The Dark Side of the Moon

Wish You Were Here

The Wall

The Final Cut

There has never been another band in the same league as Pink Floyd, whose unassuming members managed to build a career on their art alone.

David Gilmour joined Pink Floyd in the late 1960s, near the end of its first phase, led then by the brilliant but unstable Syd Barrett. The early Pink Floyd epitomized British psychedelia; epic instrumentals shared album space with vignettes about bicycles and mice.

Barrett's departure coincided with the gradual emergence of a new Pink Floyd under the joint leadership of Gilmour and bassist Roger Waters. The breakthrough 1973 album *The Dark Side of the Moon*, which sold more than 20 million copies and stayed on the charts for around 25 years, is one of the few successful "concept" albums.

The album is sonically stunning, even by today's standards, with its use of rhythmic sound-effect loops ("Money"), synthesizers, Gilmour's Stratocaster, and, surprisingly, pedal steel. This instrument, more usually associated with country music than progressive rock, adds a lushness to the texture, sitting perfectly between guitars and synthesizers.

Wish You Were Here (1975), another huge seller, is dominated by "Shine On You Crazy Diamond," a nine-part musical tribute to the band's founder, Syd Barrett.

The Wall (1979), in many ways the most ambitious album of the band's career, is also the last "proper" Pink Floyd album. Keyboard player Rick Wright was edged out of the band soon afterward by Roger Waters,

whose dominance of the band's songwriting and musical direction would ultimately result in one of rock's most acrimonious breakups. His recipe worked superbly for *The Wall*, however. Waters wrote and sang most of the album, which amounts to a rock opera (later filmed and staged), and Gilmour generally got on with the business of playing the guitar. "Another Brick in the Wall," the album's theme, was a huge hit single across the world— Gilmour's solo is one of the most memorable, "singable" guitar solos ever recorded.

The final Pink Floyd album of the Waters–Gilmour partnership, appropriately entitled *The Final Cut* (1983), stands up musically with any of the band's albums and is regarded by some as their finest, but it is essentially a Roger Waters album with Gilmour relegated to the role of session guitarist.

Gilmour re-formed Pink Floyd after Waters's departure, continuing to record and tour, though for many fans Pink Floyd was simply not Pink Floyd without both halves of its central partnership. After years of bitter legal disputes, and Waters's insistence that he would never again work with Gilmour, the two reunited with Wright and Mason in June 2005 to perform at Bob Geldof's Live8 concert.

Lesson 4.4: Scales Practice 1

Many people who have learned to play an instrument will tell you that learning scales is the most tedious part. We'll keep scale playing to a minimum in this course.

Scales are important, however, both in helping with the geography of the instrument (knowing which notes are where) and in helping you to develop an even playing tone and good timing. We'll further explore these ideas in a later chapter. For now, let's look at a couple of simple scales to get started. Both of the scales here are in first position—only the first three frets (and open strings) are used.

Scales in C

Frets 1–3 are played by fingers 1–3, respectively. The scale of C major is relatively straightforward.

C MAJOR

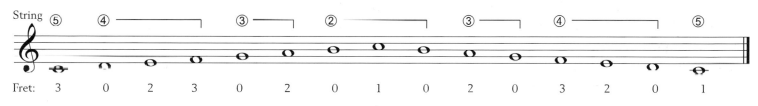

Lesson 4.5: Scales Practice 2

Scales can also be played in other keys.

Scales in F

The scale of F major (below) introduces B♭. (Flats are explained in detail on page 58.)

Indicating a flat note

In music notation, B♭ (B flat) is indicated by placing a flat symbol (♭) just before the note B:

B flat

Finding B flat on your fretboard

B♭ is located on the third fret of the 3rd (G) string.

B♭

F MAJOR

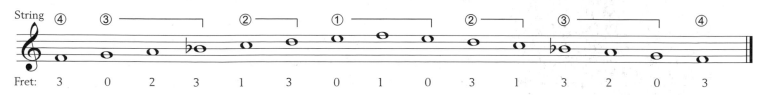

Lesson 4.6: Filling the Gaps with Sharps and Flats

You may have noticed that the notes we have learned so far have left some frets in the first position unused. The notes used so far (with the exception of B♭) have all corresponded to the white notes on the piano.

"Black" and "white" notes

A quick glance at a piano or other keyboard instrument will reveal that for every seven white notes, there are five black notes. These are named after the adjacent white notes. For example, the note between C and D is higher (*sharper*) than C but lower (*flatter*) than D, and can therefore be named either C sharp (C#) or D flat (D♭). The B♭ in the F major scale could, in another context, be called A#.

Sharps and flats on the staff

These sharps and flats are shown on the staff by placing a sharp or flat symbol directly before the note in question (see below).

This naming system is exactly the same on the guitar. For example, the 2nd fret on the B string, as it lies between the notes C and D, is called either C# or D♭. The interval, or distance, between two adjacent frets, or between two adjacent keyboard notes whether black or white, is called a half step. This is the smallest interval in general use in Western music. A half step, as its name implies, is half of a whole step, which is the interval between most pairs of white notes.

All the notes in first position

The complete set of notes available in first position is shown below. Remember, F# and G♭ are physically the same note and, therefore, appear at the same fret—this applies to all "black" notes. Also note that there is no "black" note between E and F or between B and C on the piano; therefore, there are no sharps or flats between these notes.

Take your time to learn all of these notes—you can use this chart for reference.

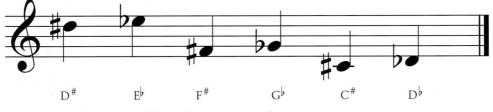

An example of sharps and flats shown on a staff.

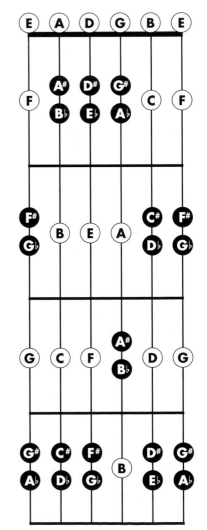

Including the open strings, there are 30 notes in the first position.

EXPERT'S TIP: Playing scales

Playing scales can help with many aspects of your playing—not only will you learn the fretboard thoroughly, you will also be equipped with the knowledge to improvize. (We'll cover this later.) Scales make a great warm-up and can also help you learn to play in time. Once you are familiar with any of the three scales encountered so far in this book, try playing with a metronome or drum machine.

Jon Buckland

1977—

GUITARS: FENDER JAGUAR, JAZZMASTER, THINLINE TELECASTER

Recommended Listening:

Parachutes

A Rush of Blood to the Head

As lead guitarist of highly successful post–Brit pop sensation Coldplay, Jon Buckland has provided haunting melodies and stadium-filling atmospherics to match lead singer Chris Martin's introspective lyrics and intense vocals. Born in London and raised in North Wales, Buckland was encouraged into the music scene by his brother. He began playing guitar when he was 11, initially inspired by the Manchester band the Stone Roses, and he met the other members of Coldplay while studying astronomy and mathematics at University College London.

The band soon achieved widespread popularity with their debut album *Parachutes* (2000), featuring such anthemic tracks as "Trouble" and "Yellow." The band's early material combined a variety of influences, at moments reminiscent of Radiohead, U2, and REM. *A Rush of Blood to the Head* (2002) brought new influences from the likes of Johnny Cash and Kraftwerk, as well as Indian-inspired slide guitar on "Daylight." A third album, *X & Y* (2005), picked up where *A Rush of Blood to the Head* left off.

Inspiring influences

Jon Buckland's playing is like a collage of some of the best guitarists in history. With spooky E-bow droning, soothing acoustic strumming, and atmospheric pulsing tremolo, Jon's playing brings together jangle and twang (influenced by Johnny Marr of the Smiths) with the echo-fueled dronings of U2, and even luscious slide guitar in the vein of Pink Floyd's *The Dark Side of the Moon*. Never flashy, always atmospheric, Jon Buckland could teach most guitarists a thing or two about crafting inspiring and emotionally involving music.

Lesson 4.7: More on Rhythm

A good understanding of rhythm is essential to developing as a musician. These concepts are applicable to players of all instruments.

Eighth notes

So far, we have looked at three note values: whole, half, and quarter notes. As you might expect, quarter notes can be divided in two, resulting in eighth notes.

Eighth notes look like this on their own…

…and like this in pairs:

The thick line joining the two notes is called a *beam*. More than two notes can also be beamed together:

In 4/4 and 3/4 (or any time signature where the lower number is 4) the beat is represented by quarter notes; therefore, eighth notes last half a beat. A whole measure of eighth notes is therefore counted: "1 and 2 and 3 and 4 and…"

Rests

Though the main purpose of written music is to give the player notes to play, most pieces of music also contain "gaps" between notes. These gaps can be very short (one beat or less) or several measures long. At the most extreme, some orchestral musicians, such as percussionists, often have only a few notes to play during a piece. However, their parts have to contain more than those notes alone. It is most important to know when to play the notes.

In written music, these gaps are called rests. There are corresponding rests for all note values (whole, half, quarter, and eighth notes, and so on). In this way, each measure can contain the correct total number of beats, even if some or all of those beats are rests.

The rests corresponding to the note values we have seen so far look like this:

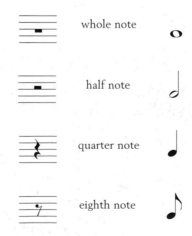

Rests in use

Look at the following measure:

This example is a measure of 4/4 containing two quarter notes and two quarter-note rests. The notes are played on beats 1 and 3; beats 2 and 4 are silent.

Try the following exercises, which combine notes and rests:

George Harrison

1943–2003

GUITARS: GRETSCH, FENDER, RICKENBACKER

"It doesn't matter if you're the greatest guitar player in the world. If you're not enlightened, forget it."

—George Harrison

Recommended Listening:

A Hard Day's Night
Revolver
Sgt. Pepper's Lonely Hearts Club Band
Abbey Road
All Things Must Pass (solo)
Cloud Nine (solo)

The Beatles may have been "just a band," in John Lennon's words, but they were undoubtedly the most influential band in history, and it is hard to see how that influence could ever be matched.

John, Paul, and George were all accomplished players, but while Lennon and McCartney wrote the lion's share of the songs and fronted the band from its very earliest days, George was content to sit back and be "the quiet one." From the Beatles' formative years belting out rock 'n' roll to drunken audiences in Hamburg's red-light district, George concentrated on one thing—playing the guitar.

Early records show us the strong influence of one of rock 'n' roll's early pioneers, Carl Perkins. Like Elvis, Perkins fused country music with the blues. His song "Blue Suede Shoes," covered by Elvis, was a staple of the early Beatles' live sets, as was "Honey Don't" (later covered on record and sung by Ringo).

Though George's early lead-guitar sound was characterized by Perkins's playing style and twangy Gretsch tone, many later developments in the group's sound (and, invariably, the sound of current pop on both sides of the Atlantic) took them in very different directions and were often driven by George. Slide guitar (in evidence as early as 1965) on "Drive My Car" and later a Harrison trademark, sitar ("Norwegian Wood," "Within You Without You"), and twelve-string guitar ("A Hard Day's Night") are the most obvious examples.

By the time the Beatles had split in 1970, Harrison had perfected the slide-guitar style that would characterize most of his solo work, from the massive triple album *All Things Must Pass* (including the hit "My Sweet Lord") to such 1980s hits as "Got My Mind Set on You," "When We Was Fab," and his work with Bob Dylan, Tom Petty, Roy Orbison, and Jeff Lynne in the Traveling Wilburys.

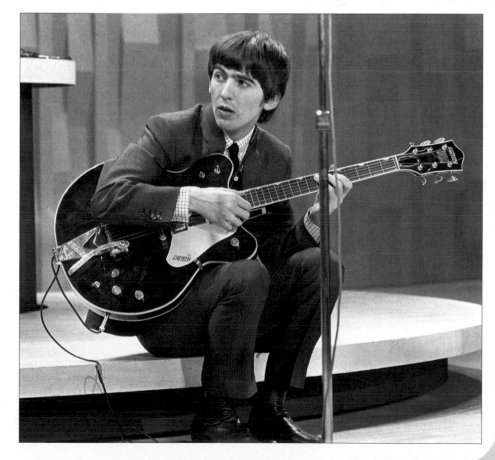

"Edelweiss"

Words and Music by **Rodgers and Hammerstein**

Here's a longer tune for practicing your lead guitar skills. Although all of the notes can be found on the top E string, a slight stretch is needed to play the note A, which is found on the top E string, 5th fret:

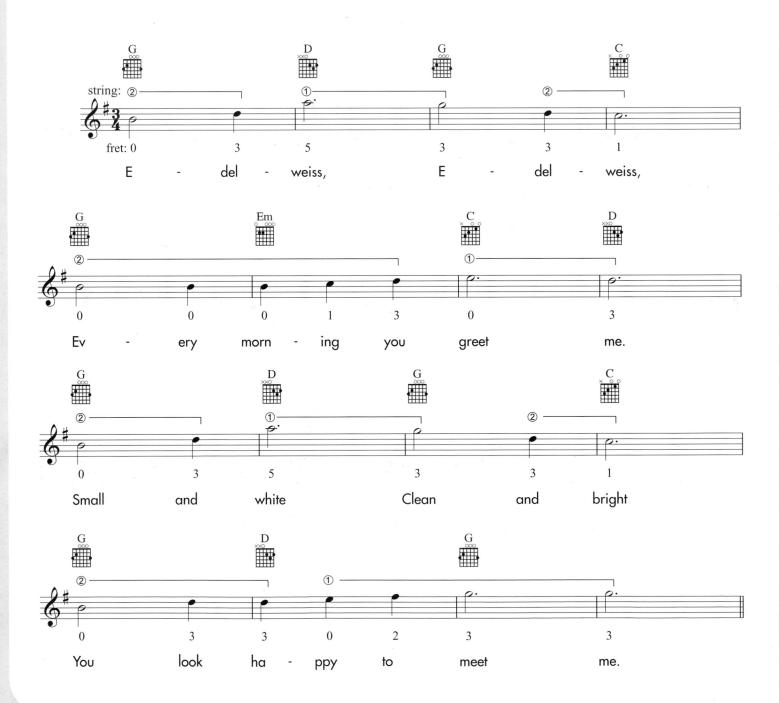

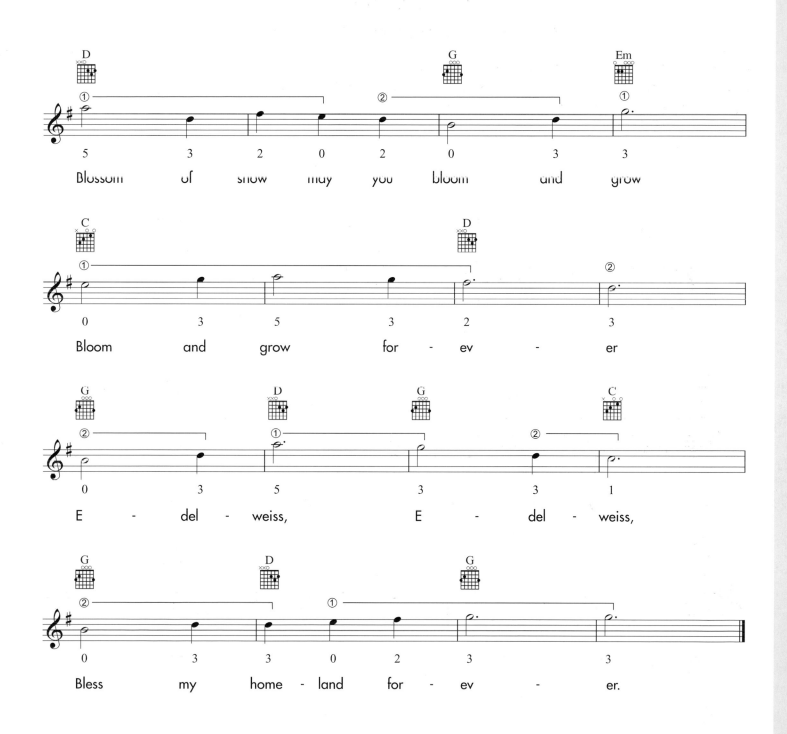

More Lead
Playing

Adding Upstrokes

Introducing Tablature

Upstrokes and Downstrokes

More Scales

Beyond a certain level, fluency cannot be achieved without the use of upstrokes, so it's a good idea to start using them now. In this lesson we'll also look at different ways of writing guitar music and introduce you to the minor scales.

Lesson 5.1: Adding Upstrokes

Though there are other approaches, lead playing usually involves playing downstrokes on the beat, and upstrokes on the offbeat. The symbols are:

⊓ downstroke

∨ upstroke

Combining upstrokes and downstrokes

The following example would generally be played using alternating downstrokes and upstrokes:

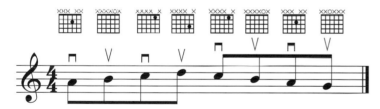

Playing quarter notes and eighth notes

When combining quarter notes and eighth notes, take care to follow the rule: Down on the beat, up on the offbeat.

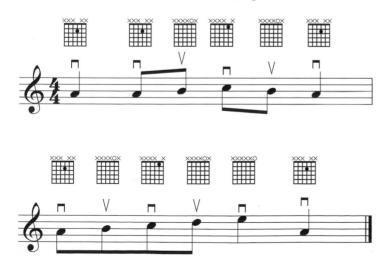

Resist the temptation simply to alternate between downstrokes and upstrokes. This will not lead to rhythmic fluency.

Economy of movement

Right-hand movement should generally be as economical as possible. Ideally, when playing a downstroke, the pick should not move far enough to touch the next string.

Upstrokes are generally even smaller, since the stress in most music is on the downbeat.

It's important that your right hand is positioned comfortably and is supported by the body of your guitar. Your wrist should be relaxed when playing upstrokes and downstrokes to ensure rhythmic fluency.

Lesson 5.2: Introducing Tablature (TAB)

Guitar music can be written in a number of different ways. So far, we have mostly used standard musical notation and chord symbols.

Limits of standard notation

The great advantage of standard notation is that the same basic system is used for all instruments. This makes it relatively easy for a guitarist who can read music to read from a part written for another instrument.

This advantage can also be a drawback. As you will discover as your guitar playing advances, most notes can be played in more than one place on the guitar; some can be found in four or five places. This can make sight-reading hard for beginners. Even a simple scale can be played in many different shapes, but which is best? Which shape will end up with your fingers in the right position for whatever comes next? Of course, guitar fingerings can be added, such as those used earlier in this book, but the page can soon become too overcrowded.

The TAB system

One system in common use gets around the problem by using an additional staff to specify exact fingerings. This system is called tablature (often abbreviated as TAB) and dates back to the Middle Ages.

The tablature staff uses six strings: one for each guitar string.

These are used to show exactly where each note is played. The bottom line represents the bottom E string, the next line up is the A string, and so on.

Numbers placed on the horizontal lines indicate the frets to be played. For example, the note C on the B string is shown with a "1" on the second line down:

The ascending part of the C major scale in first position (see page 51) is shown like this:

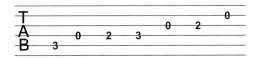

And the chord of A (see page 30) is shown like this:

Limits of TAB

Notating music using TAB on its own has one major disadvantage—there is no indication of rhythm.

TAB with standard notation

There are various possible solutions to this, and the best one is also the most common. The TAB staff is simply placed underneath a conventional staff, and the same notes are written in corresponding position on both staffs. Whereas the upper staff contains rhythm information but no indication where the note should be played, the TAB staff does exactly

the opposite. The C major scale left would now look like the one below.

This combination offers the best of both worlds. Experienced readers can follow the upper staff (though they may still find it useful to consult the TAB staff). Less experienced players can draw extensively from the TAB staff. The upper staff is still essential, however, for there is no music without rhythm. That is one of the reasons why we introduced standard notation first in this book.

Use both methods

Many players—and their teachers—fall into the trap of relying only on TAB. We will use TAB where appropriate during this course, but remember that the upper staff is needed to complete the picture.

The Birth of the Electric Guitar

The name Rickenbacker, while associated today with a particularly distinctive brand of electric guitar, is also crucial to the development of the electric guitar itself. Indeed, many historians see Adolph Rickenbacker and George Beauchamp as the true inventors of the instrument.

The first electric guitars

Adolph Rickenbacker and guitarist George Beauchamp began the manufacture of metal-bodied resonator guitars in the early 1920s, but a dispute with The National Company, for whom Rickenbacker was already involved in manufacturing guitar bodies, coupled with a general dissatisfaction with the volume of these instruments, led Beauchamp to experiment with electric alternatives.

Adolph Rickenbacker with the original "frying pan" electric Hawaiian guitar.

Electrical microphones and loudspeakers were still very new inventions in the 1920s, and they existed only in very crude forms by today's standards. A microphone essentially uses a sensitive diaphragm and an electromagnet to pick up airborne vibrations. The diaphragm is usually made of a very thin metal, and when it moves, a current is induced in the magnet. Because the diaphragm moves back and forth rapidly, an alternating current is produced. A loudspeaker reverses this process, translating electrical impulses into the movement of a speaker cone (diaphragm).

After experimenting, Beauchamp realized that he did not need a microphone diaphragm to amplify the guitar. If steel strings were used, the string vibration itself could be used to generate an electrical signal in an adjacent horseshoe magnet.

Mass production

The first Rickenbacker electric guitars were steel-bodied Hawaiian steel guitars. Even at this early date, Rickenbacker had the foresight to realize that the large body needed to

Wooden-bodied Rickenbacker guitars remain immensely popular today. This is a modern replica of one of John Lennon's first guitars, which he purchased in Hamburg in 1960.

produce a reasonable acoustic volume was no longer required, resulting in a model nicknamed the "frying pan."

By the mid-1930s, Rickenbacker and Beauchamp had given up trying to protect their design via patent law as other guitar makers were rushing to cash in on the possibilities. The "soap-bar" pickup common on guitars of this type had evolved from the original Beauchamp design. Individual poles for each string, which were first used by Leo Fender, were not introduced until the 1950s.

Gibson added soap-bar pickups to its existing arch-top guitar designs, such as the L-series, popular with jazz and swing players of the day. Rickenbacker also ventured into the production of wooden-bodied guitars at this time (see above). Charlie Christian (Benny Goodman's guitarist and one of the most influential players of the time) spotted the potential. With his electrified Gibson ES-150, he fulfilled his ambition to promote the guitar to an equal status within the jazz combo, playing his guitar "like a horn" and placing the electric guitar firmly on the map.

Lesson 5.3: Upstrokes and Downstrokes

To get used to adding the upstrokes introduced on page 65, play the tunes on this page, observing the downstroke/upstroke rule strictly.

PRACTICE 1

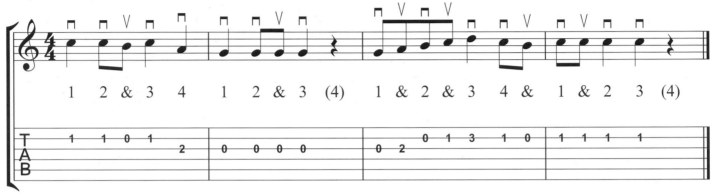

PRACTICE 2

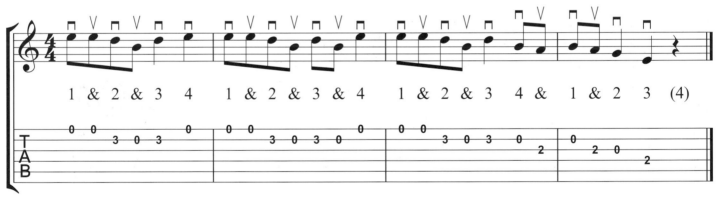

PRACTICE 3

Buddy Holly

1936–1959

GUITARS: FENDER STRATOCASTER, GIBSON J-45

Buddy Holly was one of the pioneers of rock 'n' roll. Preceded by the likes of Bill Haley and Elvis Presley, Holly brought a new sophistication to the emerging style. His innovations range from oddities such as using a celesta on "Everyday" to experimenting with double-tracked vocals—a technique later embraced by bands such as the Beatles and the Kinks. Holly could write boy-meets-girl love songs to match any other artist of the time, but at his best, his songs exhibited more complex harmonies and melodies, combined with thoughtful lyrics, that put him very much ahead of his time.

Holly was born into a musical family and learned piano, violin, and guitar early on. By the age of 13, he and his friend Bob Montgomery were playing country music and Western Bop in local clubs. It seemed that Holly's big break had come when Buddy and Bob, as they were known, were chosen to open for Bill Haley and the Comets at a local concert, where Buddy was spotted by a scout from Decca Records. However, after an attempted recording session with the label, Buddy was dropped and encouraged to keep developing his music.

Following Decca's advice, Holly formed the Crickets with some of his friends, and he soon caught the label's attention again with the lively "That'll Be the Day." The group was signed to one of Decca's subsidiaries, Brunswick Records, and subsequent recordings, such as "Oh Boy!" and "Peggy Sue," soon became popular with teenagers. Success abroad followed when The Crickets toured Britain in 1958, becoming more popular there than in the United States. In the audience of one of their UK concerts were a pair of teenagers named John Lennon and Paul McCartney, who would later name their band the Beatles in homage to the Crickets.

Short Career

Tragedy struck, however, during a 1959 tour with Ritchie Valens and the Big Bopper. The tour bus had been unreliable throughout the tour, so Holly finally decided to charter a plane to the next town. The plane crashed en route, killing Buddy Holly and everyone on board.

Buddy Holly and the Crickets achieved success and popularity during their short career, but the scale of their influence was not realized until long after Holly's death. Not only were Holly's songwriting and recording techniques ahead of his time, but the idea of a rock 'n' roll star writing his own songs was previously unknown. At the time, songwriting and performing were considered to be separate arts, with bands performing "standards" or songs written for them by professional songwriters. This was not noticed by the public at the time, but it was noted by, among others, the young Lennon and McCartney. Indeed, partly because the lanky, bespectacled Holly looked like an ordinary person rather than a "star," he succeeded in inspiring a generation to try for rock'n'roll stardom.

Lesson 5.4: More Scales

The scales we have looked at so far have all been major scales. This is a very familiar and important sound in Western music, but it's far from the only one.

The minor scale

On this page, we'll introduce a few others and expand on them later in the book. For now, try to get these simple versions under your fingers by playing through them every time during your music practice.

The minor scales are often described as "sad," "Spanish," or "Arabic." The A minor scale is actually based on the major scale, but it starts on a different step.

Various versions of the minor scale make alterations to certain notes.

The harmonic minor scale

In this A minor scale, every note is also found in C major except for the raised seventh step (G#). This results in a scale called the *harmonic minor scale*.

THE A MINOR SCALE

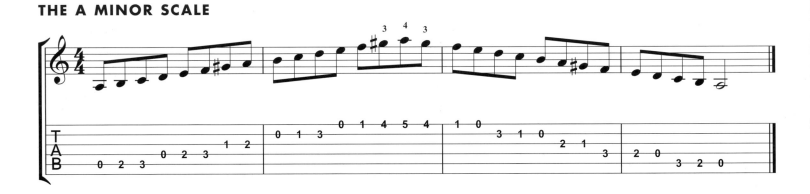

THE BLUES SCALE

We'll be looking at this scale in depth later in the book, too. Here it is in first position in the key of E.

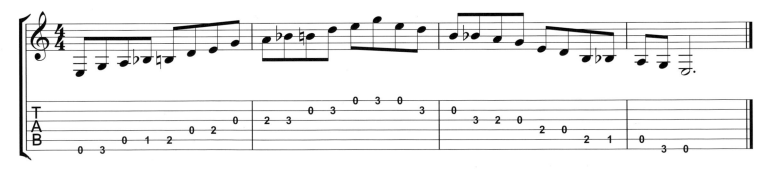

The natural symbol

The natural symbol (♮) cancels out the effect of a sharp or flat symbol, which otherwise lasts for the rest of the bar. So the fifth note of this scale is a B, or a B natural, if you want to distinguish it from B♭.

Jimmy Buffett

1946—

GUITAR: PAUL REED SMITH

Recommended Listening:

A White Sport Coat and a Pink Crustacean

Changes in Latitudes, Changes in Attitudes

Jimmy Buffett is a man of many talents. Co-owner of the Margaritaville and Cheeseburger in Paradise restaurants, he has also written three best-selling books, made a cameo appearance in the movie *Cobb*, and still finds time to play a part in the work of the Save the Manatee Foundation. Also an enthusiastic pilot, Buffett was shot at by Jamaican police in 1996, an incident that is related in the song "Jamaica Mistaica." But the majority of Parrotheads (Buffet fans) are attracted by his sense of humor, his laid-back "beach-bum" attitude, and, most important, his music.

Beach-bum success

Buffett began his official music career in Nashville in the 1960s, but it became clear that he could not be straitjacketed by Nashville's orthodox music establishment. When his first album *Down to Earth* sold poorly and Barnaby Records "lost" his second album (miraculously rediscovered after his breakthrough), Buffet moved to Key West and began to establish the easygoing beach bum persona for which he is known. In 1974, he formed the Coral Reefer Band, an idea that had been in his mind for some time. Long before he had a single sideman, let alone his Coral Reefer Band, Buffett would pause in the midst of a number and say, "Take it, Coral Reefers."

"He'd stop and tap his foot, and there'd be no damn band there," recalls former Coral Reefer, Greg "Fingers" Taylor, with a laugh.

The 1970s saw a plethora of album releases, including the critically acclaimed *A White Sport Coat and a Pink Crustacean* (1973). Buffett revealed his more thoughtful side in *Living and Dying in 3/4 Time* (1974), with its song of marital separation, "Come Monday," which became his first hit single. *Changes in Latitudes, Changes in Attitudes* (1977) featured the hit song "Margaritaville." In the 1980s, Buffett made most of his money touring and writing best-selling fiction. Over the next 20 years, he released a series of albums mostly for devoted fans, including a collection of Christmas songs.

More Chords

Introducing More Chords

Building Chord Knowledge

Seventh and Minor Chords

Using a Capo

Keys and Key Signatures

In this chapter, we'll be learning some more new chords, as well as a new variety called sevenths. We've also included some songs and exercises to help master them. We'll be looking at using the capo, too, a useful piece from your guitar kit that will help you if you want to sing along while you play.

Lesson 6.1: Introducing More Chords

Let's start with a new minor chord—Dm (D minor), then two more chords which we'll need for the next song—Am and F major.

You may have noticed already that major chords (such as F) sound bright and happy, while minor chords tend to have a more melancholy feel.

D MINOR	A MINOR	F

DM

AM

F

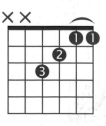

"Killing Me Softly"

Words and Music by **Charles Fox and Norman Gimbel**

This song is a bit of a workout, using some of the chords learned so far in this chapter, with a couple of new ones: Em7 ("E minor seventh") and Am7 ("A minor seventh").

EM7 CHORD 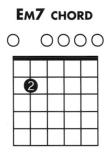 **AM7 CHORD**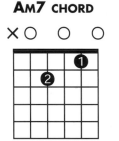

These shapes are actually very simple to play. The easiest way to learn them is simply to play either an Em or Am chord, which should be getting familiar by now, and remove the third finger in each case, letting the open string sound instead.

"Top line and chords"

This song is presented in a format found in many songbooks, called "top line" or "top line and chords." This means that the vocal line is written in standard notation, with chord symbols or boxes for guitar. The strumming/picking pattern is up to the individual player. For this song, try using either of the patterns below, or alternate between them.

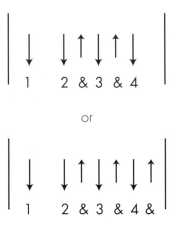

Working in "blocks"

Only the first verse is given in the notation itself; the second and third verses are written in a "block" at the end. This prevents the music itself from looking too cramped and is very common in songbooks.

"Killing Me Softly" was a huge hit in 1973 for Roberta Flack.

CHORUS

(continued)

VERSE 1

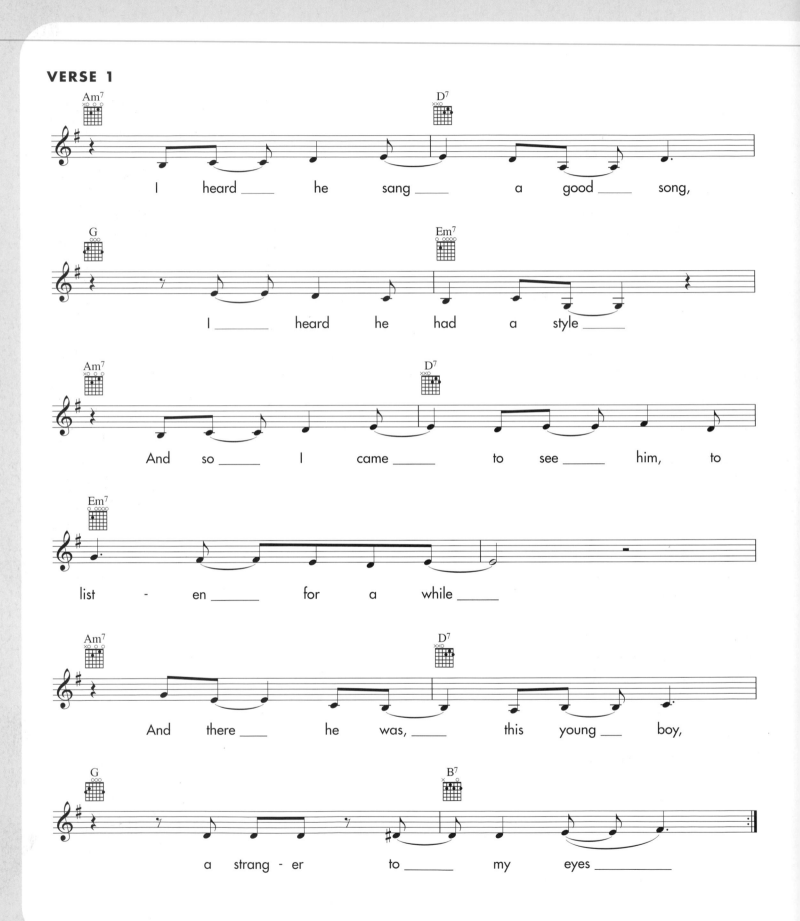

CHORUS

Strumming my pain with his fingers
Singing my life with his words
Killing me softly with his song
Killing me softly with his song
Telling my whole life with his words
Killing me softly with his song

VERSE 2

I felt all flushed with fever, embarrassed by the crowd
I felt he'd found my letters and read each one out loud
I prayed that he would finish, but he just kept right on

CHORUS

Strumming my pain with his fingers
Singing my life with his words
Killing me softly with his song
Killing me softly with his song
Telling my whole life with his words
Killing me softly

VERSE 3

He sang as if he knew me in all my dark despair
And then he looked right through me as if I wasn't there
But he was there, this stranger, singing clear and loud

CHORUS

Strumming my pain with his fingers
Singing my life with his words
Killing me softly with his song
Killing me softly with his song
Telling my whole life with his words
Killing me softly with his song

"Killing Me Softly" was given a new lease of life when a new version was recorded in 1996 by the Fugees, fronted by Lauryn Hill.

Lesson 6.2: Building Chord Knowledge

Let's delve further into the world of chords and add some "seventh" chords to your knowledge.

Sevenths

Seventh chords have a richer sound than the chords covered so far and can also allow a direction to other chords. Any major chord can be turned into a seventh chord by adding an extra note, which is a whole step lower than the root of the chord. For example, C7 is formed by adding the note B♭ to a C major chord:

C7 CHORD

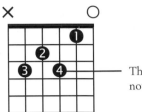

The "seventh" note

C7 CHORD

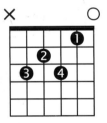

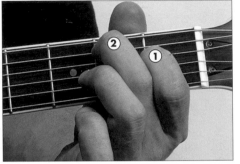

E7 CHORD

A7 CHORD

D7 CHORD

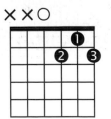

G7 CHORD

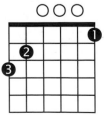

B7 CHORD

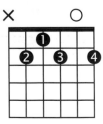

Lesson 6.3: Seventh and Minor Chords

Try these practice sequences to get used to the new chords. These exercises are written using "rhythm slashes" on a standard staff. The "slash" noteheads tell you to play the chords indicated, in a given rhythm. The "slash" noteheads look slightly different from regular "pitched" note heads:

Repeat: play the preceding four measures again before playing the final measure.

Neil Young

1945—
GUITARS: GIBSON LES PAUL, MARTIN

Recommended Listening:

CSN&Y: *Déjà Vu*

After the Gold Rush

Harvest

One of the most influential guitarists and songwriters of his generation, Neil Young has also been one of the most musically promiscuous. Often characterized by his high-pitched nasal voice and thoughtful, personal lyrics, Young's early work mostly consisted of the country-tinged folk rock evident on the 1972 number one single, "Heart of Gold."

In the 1960s and early 1970s, Young worked with the briefly successful Buffalo Springfield (of which he was a founding member), formed his long term backup band, Crazy Horse, and played Woodstock as part of the supergroup Crosby, Stills, Nash & Young, reaching his commercial peak in 1972 with the Stray Gators and the album *Harvest*. Highlights of this period include Buffalo Springfield's eponymous debut, CSN&Y's *Deja Vu* (1970), and Young's solo classic *After the Gold Rush*.

Country roots
Following the death of Crazy Horse guitarist Danny Whitten in 1972, Young formed the Santa Monica Flyers and took a new direction with *Tonight's the Night,* a darker effort now seen by many critics as a precursor to punk rock. Re-forming Crazy Horse in 1975 for the hard rock album *Zuma,* Young returned briefly to his country roots for 1977's *American Stars 'n' Bars,* before embarking on the *Rust Never Sleeps* tour. A direct response to punk rock, each concert featured an acoustic set and a hard-rocking electric set with Crazy Horse.

Young has also dabbled in more experimental areas of music with 1982's *Trans,* which was recorded almost exclusively using synthesizers, leaving fans utterly baffled.

Raw-edged
Though musically inconsistent, Young's influence is not to be underestimated. Pioneering a rawer form of heavy rock, he has been dubbed the "godfather of grunge." Kurt Cobain was outspoken about Young's influence, and Young would later come to regret the line "It's better to burn out than to fade away" from his song "My My, Hey Hey."

Eclectic
Young's musical eclecticism has given him one of the broadest appeals of any artists—part of the reason he continues to influence musicians to this day.

Lesson 6.4: Using a Capo

If you sing and you've tried to play and sing some of the songs in this book or other songbooks, it's quite possible that you've hit upon a familiar problem. Since people have different vocal ranges, sometimes a song's original key won't suit your range. But don't give up…

Transposition

Many instrumentalists in this situation (pianists, for example) would have to spend some time working out how to play a song in a different key, writing it all out again if necessary. This process is called transposition. While this is actually not as hard as it sounds once you have grasped a few essential points of music theory, there is an even easier option available to guitarists—the capo.

Raising the pitch

This handy device is available in a variety of designs but all versions clamp around the neck of the guitar, raising the pitch of all six strings at once. This has the same effect as retuning the guitar at a higher pitch, without risking string breakage.

Attaching the capo

The capo is placed just behind the desired fret and tightened or snapped into place. This fret can then be treated as though it were the nut of the guitar. Frets behind the capo are not used.

For example, placing the capo at the second fret raises the pitch of the guitar by a whole step. If you play a regular A major chord here, the sounding chord is actually B major, a whole step higher. Any song or chord sequence can be transposed simply, and the best thing about the capo is that you don't have to work anything out—just move it around until the key suits your voice!

Changing the sound

The capo can be used creatively, too—the higher up the neck it is placed, the more the guitar begins to sound like a completely different instrument. Perhaps the most famous example of this is the Beatles' song "Here Comes the Sun," in which George Harrison plays the main acoustic guitar part with a capo at the seventh fret. The song is written around the D chord; this capo position transposes this to the key of A, but more important, the guitar sounds almost like a mandolin.

Multiple guitars

Many songs have been recorded using two or more guitars (with and without capo) layered together. This can produce a very rich sound. If the capo is placed at the twelfth fret, the same shapes can be used for each part and the result sounds similar to a twelve-string guitar—each note of the chord sounds at its regular pitch and also an octave above.

The word capo is short for capotasto *which is Italian for "head note." In practice, it is a clamp that is attached to the fretboard to raise the pitch of the strings. Here it is seen on the second fret, transposing the C chord to a D chord—a whole tone higher.*

"That'll Be the Day"

Words and Music by **Jerry Allison, Buddy Holly, and Norman Petty**

Here's a great early rock 'n' roll number. The song uses seventh chords throughout, except for the last chord of the chorus, which sounds better as a straight major chord.

The basic strumming pattern uses downstrokes on the beat and upstrokes on the off-beat:

Swing

Notice that the upstrokes are placed close to the next downstroke. This means that they should be played later than halfway between the beats. This is called *swing*.

The chorus

The verse and chorus chord sequences are almost the same.

Here's the chorus pattern:

Verse pattern

Only the last two bars are different in the verse pattern:

D7

CHORUS Well that'll be the day When you say good-bye,

A7

Yes that'll be the day When you make me cry.

D7

You say you're gonna leave - You know it's a lie,

A7   **E7**   **A**

'Cause that'll be the day - ay - ay When I die.

D7

VERSE 1 Well you give me all your lovin' And your turtle dovin',

A7   **D7**

All your hugs and kisses and your money too. Well you know you love me baby,

E7

Still you tell me maybe, That someday well I'll be blue.

Repeat Chorus

D7

VERSE 2 Well oh when cupid shot his dart, He shot it at your heart,

A7   **D7**

So if we ever part then I'll leave you. You sit and hold me and you,

E7   **E7**

Tell me boldly, That someday well I'll be blue.

Repeat Chorus

Lesson 6.5: Keys and Key Signatures

You will often hear phrases such as "key of C," "key of G minor," and you may have wondered exactly what they mean. In simple terms, the key of a piece of music refers to a family or group of notes that define that piece—all or most of the notes in the piece will belong to that family of notes.

Keys

For example, if a piece is said to be in the key of C major, all or most of its notes will belong to the scale of C major.

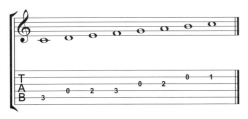

This is the easiest scale to remember, as it contains only "white" notes; that is, no sharps or flats.

To most of us, the major scale is a very familiar sound. If you try playing a major scale using "white" notes only, but starting on the key of G, you will notice that one note sounds wrong: The note F is too low, and needs to be raised by a half step to F♯. This is necessary in order to preserve the relationships between the steps of the scale—the seventh note is always a half step below the octave.

In the key of C, these notes are B and C, which have no "black" note in between, but in the scale of G, the seventh step must be F♯, in order to maintain the same relationship—F♯–G is a half step. Similarly, the scale of F,

which we have already encountered, requires a B♭ for the fourth step.

Key signatures

While it is possible to write music in any key using sharps or flats as and when they are required, the result can look very messy on the page. For example, the key/scale of F♯ major has six sharps. That is, six of the seven notes of the scale are sharps, or "black" notes.

This looks rather messy. The key signature system solves the problem by placing a number of sharps or flats (never both together) at the beginning of each line of music. Here are some examples:

The key signature acts like a global instruction, indicating that all the notes specified are to be played sharp or flat throughout the piece unless specifically canceled by a "natural" symbol (♮).

For example, this is the key signature of G major:

Here, the sharp sign is on the top line—F. Therefore, all written F notes in this piece are to be played as F♯, unless canceled. A natural sign, like sharps and flats, affects the rest of the measure in which it appears.

The other useful function of the key signature is that it tells you the key of the piece instantly; otherwise you would have to go through counting sharps or flats in order to work this out.

For now, try to remember these four common keys:

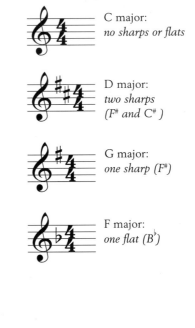

C major:
no sharps or flats

D major:
two sharps (F♯ and C♯)

G major:
one sharp (F♯)

F major:
one flat (B♭)

The Fender Telecaster

Leo Fender stumbled almost by accident upon an idea that would change the guitar forever. Fender's original research into pickup design was intended to apply to hollow-bodied instruments.

Solid body

In the 1940s, Fender owned a shop called Fender's Radio Service, where he repaired and built electromagnetic pickups and amplifiers. Fender and his partner, Doc Kauffman, built a crude guitar from a single block of wood as a testing rig for pickups. They found that a guitar with a solid body produced a brighter sound and greater sustain than the electric semi-acoustics that had been available since the 1920s, and sensing that he was on to a good thing, Fender set about designing a playable prototype.

The single-pickup Fender Esquire was launched in 1950, soon to be joined by the Broadcaster, a two-pickup version; the Broadcaster was renamed the Telecaster in 1951 when Gretsch claimed a conflict with their "Broadkaster" drum kits. With a modular design consisting of a neck and fingerboard made of a single piece of maple bolted, rather than glued, to the ash body, the Telecaster was ideally suited to mass production. The electronics could be easily accessed from behind the bakelite pickguard, and a pair of single coil pickups gave the guitar a bright,

cutting tone that made it an instant hit on the country and rock 'n' roll scenes. With futuristic stylings and characterful tone, the Telecaster set a trend, and major manufacturers such as Gibson soon reacted with their own solid bodied models, most notably the Les Paul.

The bridge pickup was mounted on a steel tray holding Fender's own-designed bridge saddles, adjustable for intonation and string height; the strings are passed through the body and anchored at the back, eliminating the strain on the bridge common in guitars of the day. The bridge assembly originally came with a detachable chrome bridge cover; this was never popular with players, because it prevented palm muting, and was dropped from the design in later years.

Classic design

The Telecaster has changed very little since 1951. Current models often feature 22 frets rather than the original 21, and a rosewood fingerboard has been added as an option, but players have largely been more than happy with the original design. From the blues wailings of Albert Collins to the rap-rock of Rage Against the Machine, the Telecaster has held its own for more than 50 years, and it looks set for another 50.

Power Chords and Overdrive

Cranking Up the Gain

Power Chords in Action

Movable Power Chords

Finding Root Notes

Power Chord Exercises

More Power Chord Exercises

So far, you have probably been playing a basic clean guitar sound. If you have an electric guitar, there are many other possible sounds to be made using an amp and various other pieces of equipment. In this chapter we'll be showing you how you can utilize overdrive with just the basic controls found on most amplifiers.

Lesson 7.1: Cranking Up the Gain

Some confusion surrounds the words *overdrive* and *distortion*. Are they the same, or are they different? As with many musical questions, the answer really depends on whom you ask, but it's true to say that, in general terms, overdrive and distortion are the same.

If you listen to just about any heavy rock song, most of the guitar sounds used will probably be very different from the sound of an acoustic guitar, or an electric guitar played through an amp using a "clean" setting. The term "fuzz" was coined in the 1960s to describe this sort of sound, and that nomenclature aptly describes it.

Volume and gain

Many guitar amps have at least two controls: *gain* and *volume* (sometimes called master volume). The gain control is actually the heart of the amplification circuitry. Turning it up not only results in higher volume but it also causes the sound to begin to "break up," or distort. In most equipment —for example, hi-fi systems—this would be undesirable, but distortion has become integral to the sounds available on the electric guitar.

Try playing a note or chord repeatedly as you crank up the gain control. Once you get about halfway on the dial (usually five out of ten), the effect generally begins to be very noticeable. The sound will also be getting louder. Here's where the master volume control comes in— simply reduce the master volume to compensate. By the time you get to maximum gain, the sound will have changed completely, and the guitar hardly sounds like the same instrument.

Clean and overdrive channels

Using these two controls alone to change quickly between a clean sound and overdrive, while maintaining the same overall level, is quite difficult especially if you're in the middle of a song. For this reason, many amps have two independent *channels*, allowing two different sounds to be set up independently, and a foot switch is often used to switch instantly between the two. A dedicated overdrive pedal can do the same job. This is considered in greater depth in Lesson 18.

In this chapter, we're going to learn how to use overdrive/distortion. If your amp hasn't got the necessary controls, or you're playing acoustic guitar, this chapter is still worth studying from a musical standpoint.

Try playing a full chord in first position, such as A or C, using heavy distortion. Although you can sometimes get away with it, chances are it's a pretty horrible sound. There are just too many notes, and the sound is too complex to sound good using distortion.

Now try playing just the two lowest notes of the A chord:

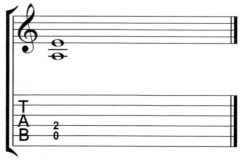

This sounds a lot better. There's a simplicity to the chord that really suits this sound. It works fine using a clean sound, too, but it can sound a little bare.

Power chords

This type of chord, which contains only two different notes, has come to be known as a "power" chord. Because the notes in question are the root and the note a fifth above, these chords are often notated using the symbol "5"; the third (which usually determines whether a chord is major or minor) is missing altogether.

As power chords are neither major nor minor, they can be used even if other instruments—for example, keyboards—are playing major or minor chords. This is very common in many rock styles.

Try the easy power chords on this page.

"Thicker" power chords

Notice that the second shape for each of these chords contains an extra note, but they are still power chords because the extra note is the root note, just an octave higher. These three-note power chords still sound simple and uncluttered when played with overdrive, but they are a bit "thicker" sounding.

A5 CHORD

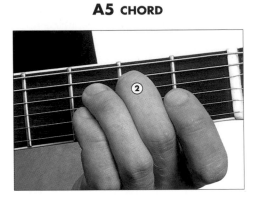

A5

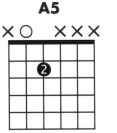

or

A5 CHORD

A5

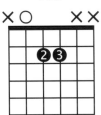

E5 CHORD

E5

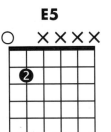

or

E5 CHORD

E5

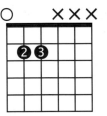

Lesson 7.2: Power Chords in Action

Try this simple pattern using any of these chords. The pattern is usually played using downstrokes only and is sometimes called a chugging pattern.

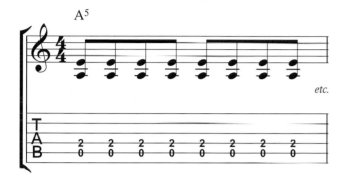

Power chord practice

Practice a chugging pattern using the pattern below. Keep the rhythm going while you change chords.

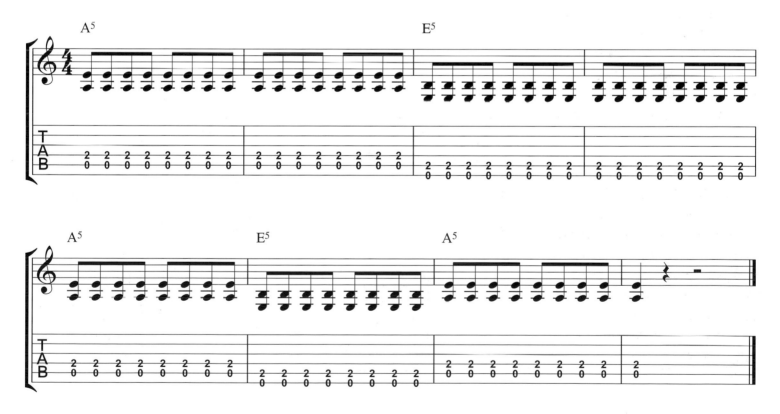

Lesson 7.3: Movable Power Chords

A great many songs use movable power chords. Getting familiar with the shapes and principles shown here will open up many styles of music for exploration.

Try the power-chord shape, F5, taking care to play only the fretted notes. This power-chord shape can be moved along your fretboard.

MOVING POWER CHORDS

1 The F5 shape is not a great deal harder to play than the A5 and E5 shapes, but it has the great advantage of being movable. Try moving all of the fingers one fret up the neck.

2 Again, make sure that you are only playing the fretted notes, not the open strings.
   Now move the shape up again.

3 As long as it contains no open strings, any chord can be moved in this way. This is an enormous advantage.

F5 CHORD

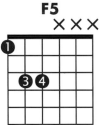

F#5 CHORD

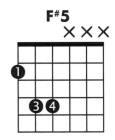

G5 CHORD

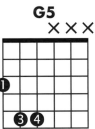

F5

F#5

G5

Now try moving the same chord shape with the root on the A-string.

B♭5 CHORD

B5 CHORD

C5 CHORD

B♭5

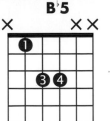

B5

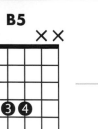

C5

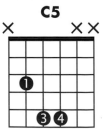

Lesson 7.4: Finding Root Notes

The root note

The lowest note within each of these shapes (played by the index finger) is the *root*, or the note that gives the chord its name. So to find any power chord, with the root on either the E- or A-string, simply refer to the root-finder chart below. Place the index finger at the appropriate fret, and the other finger(s) in relation to it. Note that for these two shapes, the highest note is optional, being an octave above the root note.

For example, you will see that the A-string, tenth fret, is the note G. Therefore, this is a G5 chord.

G5 CHORD

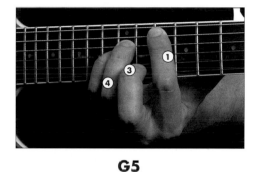

G5

10TH FRET

Finding the right chord

In order to familiarize yourself with these chords, try finding the following shapes on both the A-string and E-string:

C5 G5 D5 E5 F5 A5
B♭5 E♭5 A♭5 F#5

Note: E5 and A5 can be found in three positions, including the open shapes.

ROOT FINDER

This chart will help you find any power chord with the root (first finger) on either the 6th or 5th string.

LOW

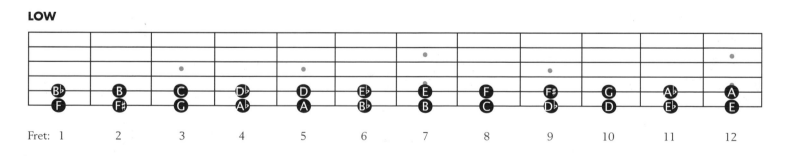

Fret: 1   2   3   4   5   6   7   8   9   10   11   12

Lesson 7.5: Power Chord Exercises

These exercises are designed to improve your fluency in playing power chords all over the neck. You may need to play them slowly at first, since it's important to try to stay in time. You could use a metronome to help you with this, starting at around 80 bpm (beats per minute), then getting gradually faster until you are proficient at around 120 bpm.

RAW POWER

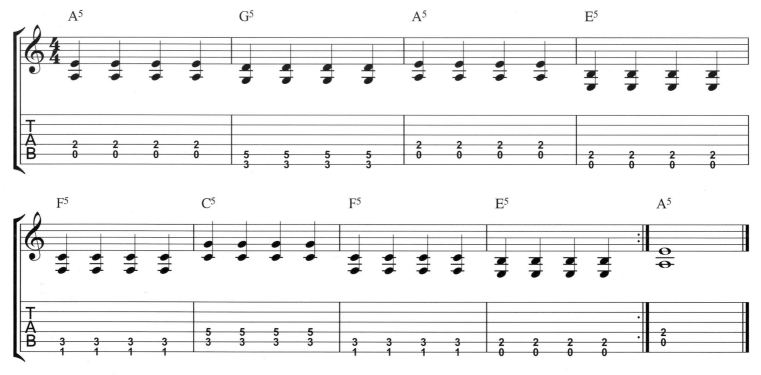

MOLTEN LEAD

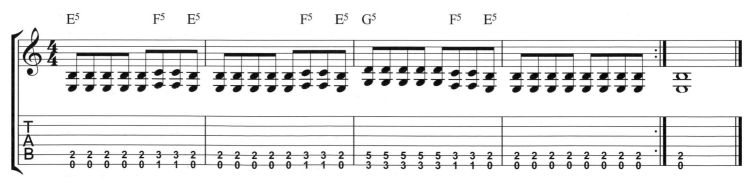

The Fender Stratocaster

The Stratocaster, or "Strat," is without doubt the most iconic electric guitar of all time, one of the revolutionary designs of the mid-twentieth century—arguably as distinctive and influential as any piece of contemporary design or art. Leo Fender was arguably the first to really grasp the possibilities of electric guitar design by realizing that since the instrument did not need to produce any acoustic volume, he could jettison any remaining links to conventional guitar-making that did not suit his purpose.

While most players of the dance bands of the 1930s and 1940s had been content to play sitting down, eclipsed by the rest of the band, country music, rockabilly, blues, and the emerging new rock 'n' roll all placed the guitar at the forefront. The power of amplification now enabled guitar players to be heard properly. Not surprisingly they also wished to be seen.

Most electrified hollow-bodied guitars of the time were poorly equipped for the demands of this new role. Many guitars of the period did not have a strap button, so the strap had to be fastened to the headstock, resulting in poor balance and neck strain—the instrument jutted out visibly in front of the player and the right-angled back edge dug into his rib cage. Gibson and Fender's innovations (the Les Paul and the Telecaster) had each gone some way to addressing these problems.

Many innovations

In 1954 the Stratocaster ushered in a new age in guitar design. Leo Fender aimed to create an instrument that was comfortable to play, and perfectly balanced, whether played sitting or standing. The new shape tipped its hat to the hollow body but was in fact radically different. A double cutaway greatly improved access to the higher frets across all the strings. The back of the body was sculpted to fit snugly against the player's chest, and the lower front was carved to accommodate the right arm comfortably without a sharp edge.

Many other innovations that we now take for granted were born with the Stratocaster. Perhaps the most important of these is the least obvious—the idea that a single instrument could be versatile enough for a wide range of players in a wide range of styles. The Strat's three pickups provide three very different types of tone. These were initially linked to a three-way selector switch, but a happy accident of Leo Fender's design enabled the switch to be "jammed" halfway between two positions, giving five settings in all. This was later made deliberately with the introduction of a five-way switch.

The tremolo arm was not an entirely new invention, but existing models suffered from poor tuning and stability. Fender's design eliminated the friction responsible for this instability by balancing the tension in the strings against the tension of springs in the guitar's body.

Modern copies

The Stratocaster has been copied, more or less slavishly, by virtually every major manufacturer since a legal test case in the 1980s effectively destroyed the Fender company's ability to protect every aspect of the design. Since then, many companies (including Fender) have introduced "Superstrats," catering specifically for the heavier end of the rock spectrum, featuring one or more humbucking pickups and floating tremolo designs.

The Strat's success has been so great that a roll call of its famous players could fill a book of its own. Perhaps the most famous of all, Jimi Hendrix, who was left-handed, played a right-handed Strat upside down.

"Born on the Bayou"

Words and Music by **John Fogerty**

Killer riff

You don't get very far into the world of guitar playing without hearing the word riff many times. What's a riff? Simply put, it's any repeated instrumental figure. Riffs are typically between one and four measures long and form the basis of many great blues, rock, and pop songs. The riff itself is often the starting point for writing a rock song and is in many cases the most memorable feature.

Try to call to mind any of the following songs, and the chances are that the first thing to pop into your head will be not the words or vocal melody but the guitar riff:

"Day Tripper"—the Beatles
"Rebel Rebel"—David Bowie
"Not Fade Away"—Buddy Holly/the Rolling Stones
"All Right Now"—Free
"Enter Sandman"—Metallica
"Desire"—U2
"Play That Funky Music, White Boy"—Wild Cherry

In all of these songs the riff just keeps on repeating throughout the verse. Sometimes it moves up or down as the chords change (as in "Day Tripper") but more often a great riff-based song will stay one chord anyway. Sometimes the riff changes for the chorus, but again sometimes it just keeps going!

Two simple riffs

Our next song, the Creedence Clearwater Revival classic "Born on the Bayou," features a killer two-measure riff that just keeps going and going all the way through each verse. This then changes to a three-chord riff in the chorus. Learn both riffs, and you know the song. Simple!

Let's start with the intro/verse riff. It's really very simple: just hold down an E7 chord and play the notes indicated in the given rhythm. The last beat of the second measure involves lifting the first finger to play the open G string, then replacing it for the last note.

This is known as a syncopated rhythm as many of the notes fall on the offbeat (the "and"). This can be hard to count. The best way to learn a riff like this is to listen to the record.

VERSE RIFF

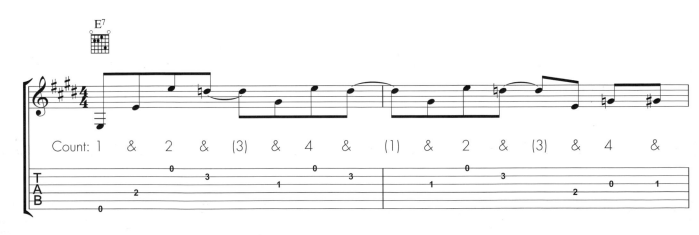

CHORUS RIFF

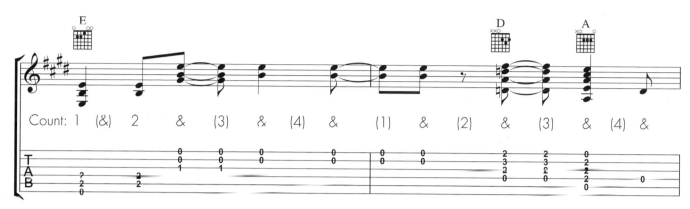

INTRO

VERSE 1

(continued)

pop-pa said, Son, don't let _ the man get you,   Do __ what he done to me._   'Cause he'll get

__ you, now.   Yes he'll get __ you now, now.

VERSE 2/3

2. I can re-mem-ber the fourth __of july,__   Run-nin' through the back-wood, bare. __   And
3. Wish I was back on the bay - ou._   Rollin'   with some ca-jun queen. _____

Song: "Born On the Bayou"

97

Lesson 7.6: More Power Chord Exercises

HEY PUNK

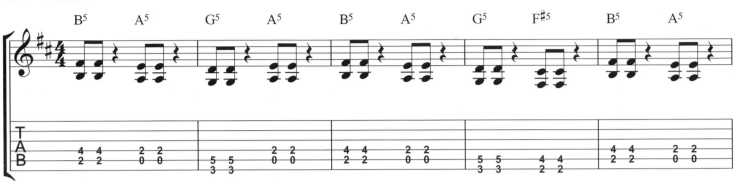

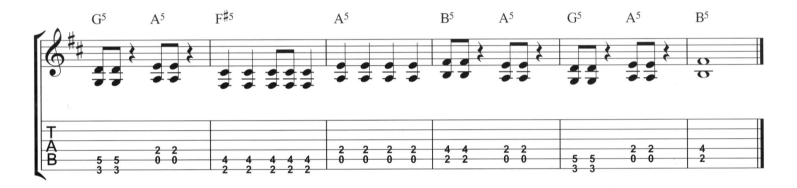

ONWARD AND UPWARD

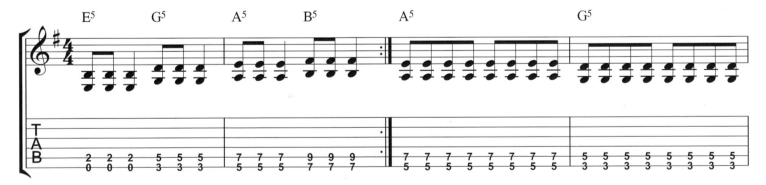

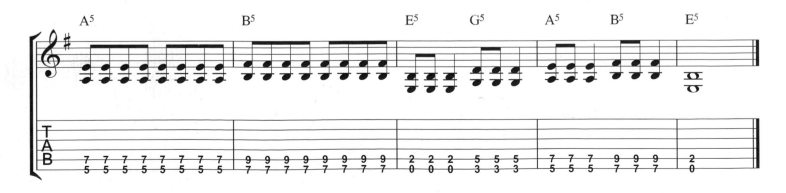

Slash

1965—

GUITARS: GIBSON LES PAUL, BC RICH HUMMINGBIRD

Recommended Listening:

Appetite for Destruction

G N' R Lies

As lead guitarist in the explosive Guns N' Roses, Saul Hudson, better known as Slash, combined the in-your-face attitude of the Rolling Stones with the bluesy lead playing of Jimmy Page. With his mane of shaggy black hair, top hat, and a cigarette hanging from his mouth, Slash has become one of the great rock icons.

One-string guitar

Born in Britain of an African-American mother and a British-Jewish father, Slash moved to the United States with his family at the age of 11. At age 15, his grandmother gave him a one-string guitar, which he soon learned to play, and he began to devote at least 12 hours each day to guitar practice, skipping school when necessary, until he finally dropped out in the eleventh grade.

Appetite for destruction

Free from the burden of school work, Slash became involved in the LA band scene, where he met drummer Steve Adler and formed Road Crew. The two met future Guns N' Roses rhythm guitarist Izzy Stradlin at a gig, where he played for the duo a demo tape of Axl Rose singing. When Rose advertised for a drummer and guitarist, Adler and Slash leaped at the opportunity, joining what would soon become the world-conquering Guns N' Roses. The band's 1987 debut album *Appetite for Destruction* gained the band worldwide notoriety, as did their second major effort, the simultaneously released *Use Your Illusion I* and *Use Your Illusion II*.

However, the clash of inflated rock-star egos, famously excessive lifestyles, and artistic differences led Slash to leave the band in 1996 to concentrate on his own group, Slash's Snakepit, recording the platinum-selling *It's Five O'Clock Somewhere* and touring, but the group disbanded in 2001. Slash went on to form Velvet Revolver with former Guns N' Roses musicians Duff McKagan, Matt Sorum, and former Stone Temple Pilots frontman Scott Weiland in 2003. Guns N' Roses have continued with Axl Rose as the only remaining original member, but many fans feel that the band just isn't Guns N' Roses without Slash.

Blues influence

Slash has always been a guitarist who wears his influences on his sleeve. The love of rock giants such as Led Zeppelin and Aerosmith, the blues-infused soul of Jimi Hendrix and Eric Clapton, and the pomp rock excesses of Queen are implicit in Slash's music. But then Slash has never egotistically tried to "revolutionize" music—he has always been about loud, raw, raucous rock n' roll.

Rock 'n' Roll

Doing the Shuffle

Twelve-Bar Blues

Rock 'n' Roll in Any Key

"Rock 'n'" in G

Adding Spice

Some More Theory

In this chapter, you will learn what is possibly the most played guitar riff ever. Known by many names, including the *Chuck Berry Boogie*, the *Sixth Shuffle*, and simply *The Rock 'n' Roll Pattern*, this pattern has appeared on so many records, in various guises, that you will recognize and feel instantly at home with it as soon as you start to play it.

Lesson 8.1: Doing the Shuffle

The rock 'n' roll pattern is played in many different keys, but many of them involve big finger stretches, so we're going to start in the key of A, which reduces the stretch by using open strings.

The basic pattern involves "rocking" back and forth between a root-and-fifth power chord...and a "power sixth," where the fifth is raised by a tone to a sixth above the root.

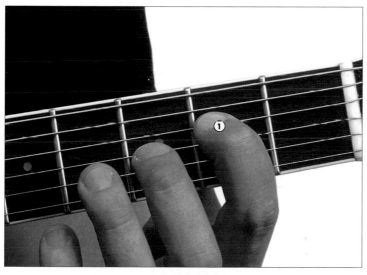

A5 CHORD

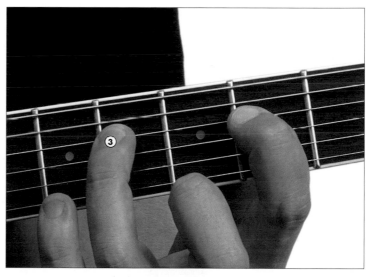

A6 CHORD

Note: A sixth chord is normally considered to be a major chord with an added sixth. This chord, like the fifth power chords, has no third.

Rock 'n' roll pattern

Playing these chords twice each results in this pattern:

If you've listened to the radio at all in the last 50 years, this should sound very familiar! The granddaddy of all songs based on this pattern is Chuck Berry's "Johnny B. Goode" (at a fast rock 'n' roll tempo), but it works equally well at other tempos, as a shuffle (see page 107 for more on this) or a slow blues.

Extending your repertoire

Let's call this (A5/A6) the "A" pattern. To play songs in the key of A using this pattern, you will also need to learn a "D" pattern (D5/D6) and an "E" pattern (E5/E6). These can be found by simply shifting up or down by one string.

Playing the "D" pattern

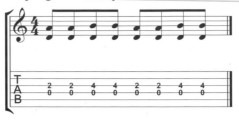

Playing the "E" pattern

Gene Vincent's "Be-Bop-A-Lula" is considered to be one of the greatest rock 'n' roll records of all time.

Lesson 8.2: Twelve-Bar Blues

Almost all of the songs that you might want to play using this pattern use a chord sequence based on the Twelve-Bar Blues, a strong sequence found in many related styles, from rock 'n' roll to soul and jazz. It's worth trying to really get this sequence under your belt because it forms the basis of songs in many styles and keys, and you can pull it around until it sounds very different.

Classic examples

To get an idea of the importance of the Twelve-Bar Blues in popular music, listen to the Beatles' "Revolution" or the Led Zeppelin classic "Rock 'n' Roll," or, of course, any number of Chuck Berry songs including "Johnny B. Goode" and "No Particular Place to Go." Here's a basic twelve-bar using the Chuck Berry/Rock 'n' Roll Riff.

Note: Many rock 'n' roll songs vary this pattern by going to E in the last bar, rather than staying on A.

Lesson 8.3: Rock 'n' Roll in Any Key

Playing the rock-'n'-roll pattern in other keys is a little harder, as there are some finger stretches involved. (The "A," "D," and "E" patterns were easier because the root notes can be found on open strings.) Other 5/6 patterns involve playing a power chord with the first and third fingers, and adding the sixth with the pinky. Try this pattern in G. The G5 and G6 shapes you need are shown below:

Higher frets
Although power chords can be found with the root on the 6th or 5th string, many players simply slide this pattern up and down the 6th string. This gives the left hand a rest from stretching quite so far, since the higher frets are closer together!

Blues keys
Since you are able to find power chords and boogie patterns on any root note, you can now play a twelve-bar sequence in any key. This can be useful for playing along with a great many songs. The easiest way to work out which chords you need is to think of the three chords as being steps I, IV, and V (one, four, and five) of the given key.

For example, in the key of A, chord I is A, chord IV is D, and chord V is E. In the key of G (opposite page), all of these are transposed down by a tone, giving chords G, C, and D.

Finding the chords
To make this even easier, refer to the chart on page 105. This gives the chord name and the fret on the 6th string for each chord. Simply move the power chord/boogie shape up and down as previously discussed.

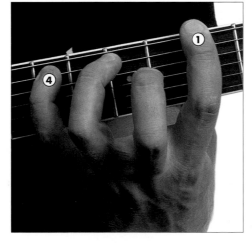

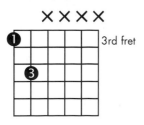

G5 CHORD

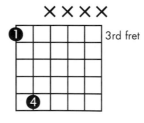

G6 CHORD

Lesson 8.4: "Rock 'n" in G

Here's the twelve-bar rock'n'roll pattern in the key of G,
moving the same shape (root on the 6th string) up the neck.

TWELVE-BAR BLUES CHORD FINDER

Key	Chord I	(fret)	Chord IV	(fret)	ChordV	(fret)
C	C	(8)	F	(1)	G	(3)
D	D	(10)	G	(3)	A	(5)
E	E	(open)	A	(5)	B	(7)
F	F	(1)	B♭	(6)	C	(8)
G	G	(3)	C	(8)	D	(10)
A	A	(5)	D	(10)	E	(12/open)
B	B	(7)	E	(open)	F#	(2)

Keith Richards

1943—
GUITARS: FENDER TELECASTER, GIBSON LES PAUL TV

Though best known for his excessive lifestyle and apparent indestructibility, Keith Richards is acknowledged as one of the great rock-'n'-roll rhythm guitarists. His gutsy rhythm and wailing lead guitar work with the Rolling Stones has infected millions with his childlike love of raw, dirty rock 'n' roll.

A founding member of the Stones, Keith Richards was influenced by his hero, Chuck Berry, as well as his grandfather, a talented big-band musician, who encouraged him to take up guitar. The Stones began their career as a covers band playing popular blues and rock-'n'-roll songs such as the Buddy Holly classic "Not Fade Away," but as the Beatles began to popularize the idea of bands writing their own songs, the Stones started to pen their own tracks. "The Last Time" was the first song Jagger and Richards took to the band, and it was followed by classics such as "(I Can't Get No) Satisfaction," which made them superstars in the United States as well as the UK.

Delta blues

Richards's style and technique have always been unusual. Not much interested in lead guitar, his use of open tunings harks back to the Delta Blues guitarists of the early twentieth century, such as Charlie Patton and Blind Willie McTell. Richards usually tunes the top five strings to open G tuning (GDGBD) and removes the bottom E string.

Master of styles

While in the early 1960s he usually played Chuck Berry–inspired rhythm guitar, Richards is a master of many styles, from the country twang of "The Worst" to the reggae feel of "You Don't Have to Mean It." Indeed, after Ron Wood replaced Mick Taylor as the Stones's second guitarist in 1974, Richards developed his own style of combining lead and rhythm, which he calls "the ancient art of weaving."

For many years, Keith Richards was happy within the confines of the band, but eventually his growing exasperation with the Stones's extrovert front man, Mick Jagger, led him to seek seek solo success. In the late 1980s he formed the band Organized Crime and released the critically acclaimed *Talk Is Cheap*, which was followed by

a brief but memorable tour of the United States. This success rekindled the dying embers of the Rolling Stones, and a world tour followed.

While often upstaged by the prancing Mick Jagger, Keith Richards's contribution to the success and sound of the Rolling Stones should not be underestimated. With his raunchy, muscular guitar sound and instinctive sense of guitar cool, Keith Richards is the living embodiment of rock 'n' roll.

Lesson 8.5: Adding Spice

The boogie pattern can be spiced up by the addition of an extra note. So far, we've used the fifth and sixth against the root note of each chord. Taking the sixth up half a step to the seventh adds a bluesy quality.

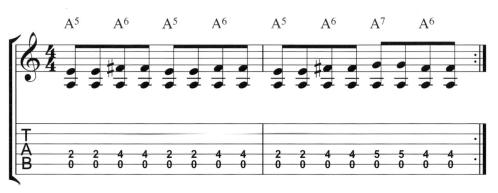

Adding the seventh

Applying this to the movable shapes involves either a huge stretch or a barre chord, which we'll explore in greater depth later. For now, let's apply it to the open A pattern.

The "seventh" in the second measure is played with the little finger. This works with the open "D" and "E" patterns, too.

Lesson 8.6: The Swing/Shuffle Feel

The boogie pattern can be played in many different ways, with many variations, but there are essentially two main types of rhythm —this applies across many styles of jazz, blues, and rock. The rhythm in any of these styles is either straight or swing. "Straight" means that all eighth notes have the same length—that the offbeat occurs exactly halfway between beats:

1 & 2 & 3 & 4 & 1...

This is sometimes referred to as straight eights.

The swing feel involves playing the offbeats later, closer to the next beat than the previous beat:

1　　& 2　　& 3　　& 4　　& 1...

Getting into swing

This rhythm is generally called swing when applied to jazz, and shuffle when applied to blues or rock.

The concept is quite hard to get across on the printed page. It may help to think of (or listen to) the famous songs listed below to make the distinction clear.

Straight	Swing/Shuffle
"Get Back"	"Sweet Home Chicago"
"Satisfaction"	"A Horse with No Name"
"Beat It!"	"Build Me Up Buttercup"
"Yesterday"	"Heartbreak Hotel"

Chuck Berry

1926—

GUITARS: GIBSON ES-335

Recommended Listening:

Greatest Hits

In the words of John Lennon, "If you were going to give rock 'n' roll another name, you might call it 'Chuck Berry.'" Perhaps the greatest pioneer of rock 'n' roll, Berry created many of the clichés we now take for granted: the standard "Berry" guitar intro (as heard on "Johnny B. Goode" and "Roll Over Beethoven") or the timeless blues/boogie shuffle (see page 107) found on countless records. With his inventive lyrics and energetic stage show, Berry took rock 'n' roll to new heights, establishing it as a lasting musical style, rather than a passing fad, influencing many would-be rockers in the process.

Child star

As a child, Berry cultivated a love of poetry and the blues from early on. Influenced by his heroes Nat King Cole and Muddy Waters, Berry began playing and singing the blues in his teens and won a school talent contest singing Jay McShann's "Confessin' the Blues." After a brief apprenticeship playing with a local band, Berry went to Chicago to follow his heroes. There he met Muddy Waters, who encouraged him to take his demo tape to Chess Records, who signed him immediately.

Berry's first single, "Maybellene," combined blues and country music in a way that no one had before, with teenage lyrics about girls and cars that would become the standard for rock 'n' roll. It was a hit, reaching number five in the Billboard charts, and was soon followed by other classics like "Roll Over Beethoven." In 1957 Berry went on tour with the Everly Brothers, Buddy Holly, and other stars of the day. However, trouble with the law followed, leading to a conviction, and he didn't return to the music scene until his release in 1963. But rather than retiring to the "has-been" circuit, he emerged from prison to find British bands such as the Beatles and the Rolling Stones playing his songs, and was soon touring Britain with his disciples. With his place in rock 'n' roll history secured, Berry has continued to tour, often on his own with his trusty Gibson, secure in the knowledge that in any town, he can find a backup band familiar with his music, leading to accidental collaborations with artists such as Bruce Springsteen and Steve Miller.

Rock 'n' roll legend

Merging musical styles like never before, Berry undoubtedly changed the course of musical history. Keith Richards famously claimed to have "lifted every lick he played," and the Beatles faced a lawsuit for basing "Come Together" on Berry's "You Can't Catch Me." Many all-time classics are secret Berry covers, including the Beach Boys' "Surfin' USA," based on Berry's "Sweet Little Sixteen."

Lesson 8.7: Some More Theory

This page covers a few more concepts that you will need to understand in order to come to grips with the music later in this book and elsewhere.

Triplets

So far, we have looked at note values and time signatures where the beat is divided into equal halves. There are other ways of dividing the beat. The most common alternative is to divide it into threes.

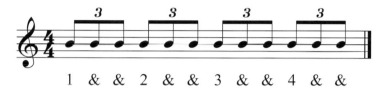

1 & & 2 & & 3 & & 4 & &

These are called triplets. In this case, these are eighth-note triplets. There are three of them per beat, and they should all be the same length. If ordinary eighth notes and triplets are combined in the same piece, the resulting change of "feel" can sometimes be quite hard to achieve.

Compound time

If the triplet feel persists throughout a piece, it can be easier to use a time signature that divides each beat into three by default. The most common of these is 6/8.

1   2   3   4   5   6

This means that there are six eighth-note beats per measure. By convention, these are grouped into threes, with beats one and four being felt as strong beats, so the measure is also divided into two; hence the term compound time.

The other compound-time signature used in popular music, particularly the blues, is 12/8. At fast tempos, the first of each group of three is felt so strongly that it is usually counted as 4/4 with a triplet feel.

1 & & 2 & & 3 & & 4 & &

Dots

You will often see notes with dots after them.

These dots lengthen the note in question. Specifically, they add half the note's original value. So in 4/4, a dotted half note (above) is worth three beats (2+1). A dotted quarter note is worth one and a half beats (1+fi).

Dotted quarter notes are often combined with eighth notes, as shown below.

1   (2)   &   3   (4)   &

This is called a dotted rhythm. If you're having trouble counting it, listen to the opening bass line on Andy Williams's "Can't Take My Eyes Off You."

Ties

A tie is a curved line joining two notes and is a simple device to add their durations together.

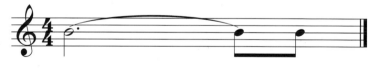

In this example, the dotted half note already lasts for three beats (see above) but is tied to an eighth note, extending the note by a further half beat. This note now lasts for three and a half beats.

Les Paul

1915—

Recommended listening:

Les Paul & Mary Ford: The Best Of The
Capitol Masters

By any standards, Les Paul (born Lester William Polfuss in Waukesha, Wisconsin) is a remarkable man. To guitarists today, his name is synonymous with the guitar that was central to the 1960s blues boom and to heavy rock from its inception to the present day.

Jazz roots

It is easy to forget that he was also a star of the prewar jazz scene, a million-selling recording artist in his own right in the 1950s, and casually invented multitrack tape recording.

Les toyed with harmonica and piano as a child and, after a brief attempt at mastering the banjo, took up the guitar relatively late in his youth. At 17 he left school to play with the local radio band. By the mid-1930s, he was in Chicago, working under his own name playing jazz in the style of Django Reinhardt, while also doing a radio spot as a hillbilly by the name of Rhubarb Red. His career as a sideman blossomed; by 1945 he was playing with the likes of Nat "King" Cole, Bing Crosby (with whom he had a number one hit) and the Andrews Sisters.

Innovator

Les Paul had been playing electric guitars since their invention. In the 1930s, the instrument was essentially still an arch-top acoustic guitar with a single crude pickup. In the early 1940s, Les Paul experimented with solid-bodied designs, some of which he persuaded the Gibson Guitar Corporation to make for him, though they insisted on leaving their name off the product.

At this time, Les also began his experiments with the process that would become known as multitrack recording. Les would record a guitar part straight to a disk-cutting lathe in his garage studio. He would then play this disk on a regular turntable while adding a second guitar part, cutting the mixed result to a new disk on the lathe. This process would be repeated until there were six or more parts recorded, but any mistakes carried a high price in both time and money: A shellac disk could only be cut once and so would have to be discarded. Furthermore, too many attempts to perfect a part would result in wearing out the disk containing the previously recorded parts, and the whole process would have to begin again. There were often hundreds of

Les Paul playing one of his many customized Gibsons.

spoiled disks piled up outside the garage.

The results were worth the effort, however. In the late 1940s, Les Paul had several million-selling instrumental hits featuring no other musicians. "Lover (When You're Near Me)" was the first multitrack recording ever commercially released. (The process still involved Les with his cutting lathe—even tape itself was still in its infancy.) In the early 1950s, he began to add the voice of his wife, Mary Ford, into the mix. The duo scored many hits, including million-sellers "How High the Moon" and "Mockin' Bird Hill."

Eight track

In 1948 Les commissioned the tape recorder manufacturer Ampex to make a tape deck capable of recording and playing back parallel tracks simultaneously. The resulting eight-track machine was put into service in the creation of hits for the duo, from Les's garage, long before commercial studios took up the idea. Some 15 years later, the Beatles's first records were made using two-track machines—even the Beatles's *Sgt. Pepper's Lonely Hearts Club Band* was made using only four-track machines. But Les Paul was always a man far ahead of his time.

The Gibson Les Paul

In the early 1950s, some 10 years after Les Paul had originally tried to interest them in the idea, the Gibson Guitar Corporation decided that the time had come for commercially produced solid-bodied guitars. This

was no great feat of prediction: Leo Fender was stealing the market share from them with his outlandish solid-bodied designs. Fender, having no background in instrument making, started with a "clean sheet" and designed radically new instruments, since it was inevitable that Gibson would take a more conservative approach, marrying years of tradition to new technology.

The Les Paul Model, as it was originally called, had a sculpted arch-top body and a traditional shape, though a cutaway provided easy access to the upper frets. The neck was glued to the body in the traditional manner, but the thin body meant that the usual "heel" at the base of the neck was much less prominent, further improving access to the upper frets.

Like the Stratocaster and Telecaster, the basic Les Paul design has changed very little since it first hit the stores in 1952. The only important alteration was the adoption of Gibson's "PAF" (Patent-Applied-For) humbucking pickups, which replaced P-90 single coils in 1958. This is an essential ingredient of the guitar's enduring success. Though originally designed

mainly to eliminate the hum caused by interference from lighting circuits and electrical goods, humbucking pickups also have a noticeably higher output than single coils. This not only gave the obvious advantage of being heard more clearly through small amplifiers—serious power didn't arrive until the 1960s—but made it much easier to produce the creamy overdriven sound favored by blues-rock players and heavy rock pioneers alike before the development of amplifiers specifically designed to produce such sounds.

Vintage

The list of players associated with this instrument could fill a book on its own. The fact that it ranges from Les Paul himself to Peter Green, Eric Clapton, Jimmy Page, Pete Townshend, Gary Moore, Slash, and many of today's Nu-Metal brigade is a testament to the timelessness and versatility of a classic design.

Many players and collectors have found something so special in certain Les Paul "vintages" (the 1958 sunburst model, for example) that some of them now change hands for truly ludicrous prices.

lesson 9

Barre Chords

Movable Chord Shapes

Barre Chords in Use

Rhythm Guitar Techniques

In the last chapter, we saw how power chords that contained no open strings could easily be moved up and down the neck. This is very handy, but what about the chords with open strings? Here we introduce barre chords, in which all six strings are fretted. Mastering the technique of playing barre chords—which can hurt at first—will enable you to play a wide range of well-known songs.

Lesson 9.1: Movable Chord Shapes

If you try playing an E chord and moving it up the neck, you'll notice that the basic sound or quality of the chord changes. This is because the fretted notes are moving but the open strings are not. To make the E chord movable, some way of moving the open strings is necessary. Other than using a capo, which can't be moved rapidly between chords in a song, this is done using a barre (pronounced "bar").

Barre chords

Try this exercise. Lay the left-hand index finger across all six strings behind the first fret, as shown in the photograph below left.

Press the finger down firmly and evenly, so that all six strings sound when strummed. This should sound exactly like the open strings of the guitar except higher.

EXPERT'S TIP:
Ouch! These barre chords hurt
Barre chords tend to hurt until you get used to them, and they will probably sound muffled and "buzzy" until you develop the necessary finger strength. The answer, as usual, is practice. But there's no need to play only barre chords for days on end—instead, throw them in every now and then. It's generally easier to hold a barre chord down with sufficient pressure, despite a bit of pain, if you know you can relax again for the next chord.

Barre chord shapes

The remaining three left-hand fingers are now free to play any chord shape. Most basic open chords can be turned into barre chords—some are easier than others.

Adding an E shape to a barre at the first fret gives this chord:

F BARRE CHORD

Other than the E shape, the most common are probably A- and C-shaped barre chords. For example, playing an A shape at the second fret gives a B chord.

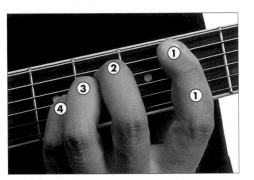

B BARRE CHORD

And a C shape with a barre at the second fret gives an alternative D shape.

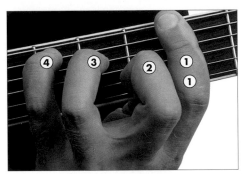

D BARRE CHORD

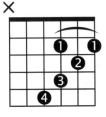

Increase your barre knowledge

Barre chords, once you can manage to keep them held down, provide a means of knowing that you can play just about any song from a songbook. For example, you may never have played a G minor chord before, but if you recognize that it is a minor chord, you will also know that you have two basic minor shapes at your disposal: Em and Am. All you have to do is work out where each shape would give you a G minor chord and

play whichever makes more sense. For example, the note G is three frets above the note E, so taking the E-minor shape up three frets (by barring at the third fret) will give you a Gm chord.

Try to find G minor using both the E-minor and A-minor shapes. As the root of the E-minor chord is the open low E string, simply find the note G on this string (you will see from the chart that it occurs at the third fret) and barre here. Similarly,

finding G minor with the A minor shape involves finding a G note on the A string—this occurs at the tenth fret.

In practice, the first six frets are enough to give you access to the roots of any chord. For added simplicity, the table opposite shows a variety of chords (including some new shapes) barred at the first fret, with the resulting chord names when these shapes are moved.

1st Fret/ Chord Shape	2nd Fret	3rd Fret	4th Fret	5th Fret	6th Fret
F	F#/Gb	G	G#/Ab	A	Bb/A#
Bb	B	C	Db/C#	D	Eb/D#
Fm	F#m/Gbm	Gm	G#m/Abm	Am	Bbm/A#m
Bbm	Bm	Cm	Dbm/C#m	Dm	Ebm/D#m
F7	F#7/Gb7	G7	G#7/Ab7	A7	Bb7/A#7
Bb7	B7	C7	Db7/C#7	D7	Eb7/D#7
FM7	F#m7/Gbm7	Gm7	G#m7/Abm7	Am7	Bbm7/A#m7
Bbm7	Bm7	Cm7	Dbm7/C#m7	Dm7	Ebm7/D#m7
Db	D	Eb/D#	E	F	F#/Gb

Lesson 9.2: Barre Chords in Use

This exercise takes the E shape and moves it around the neck using a barre—a very common musical device found in classic songs by such bands as the Troggs, the Kinks, and just about the entire punk movement.

SOMETHING WILD

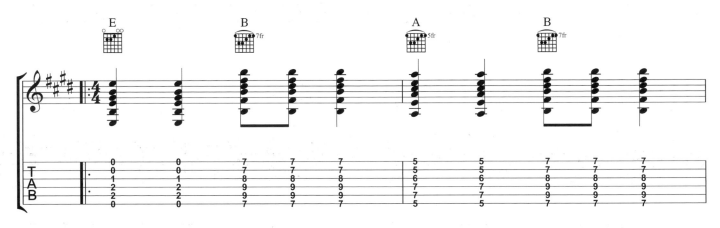

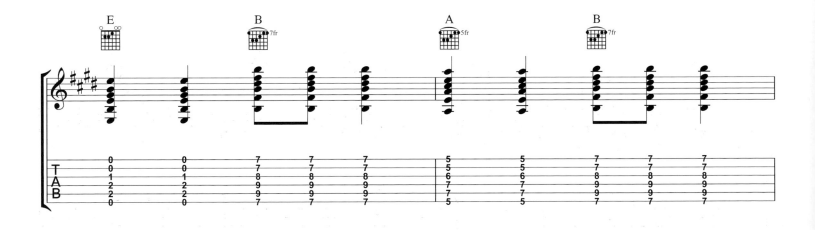

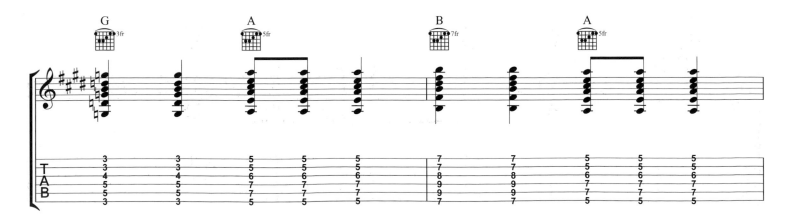

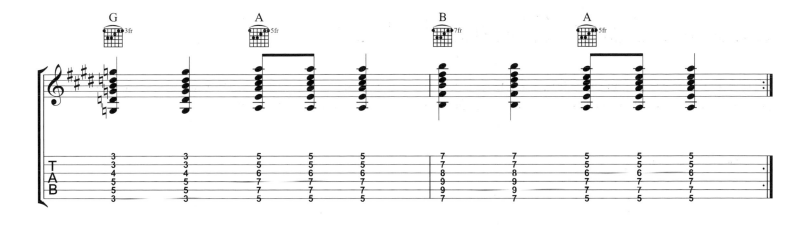

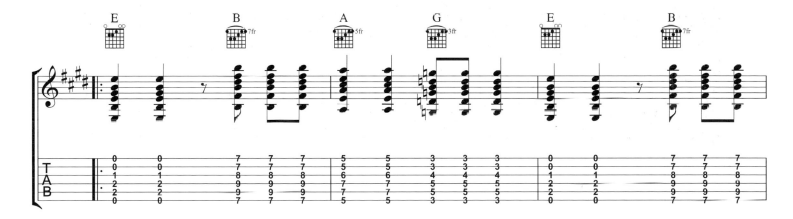

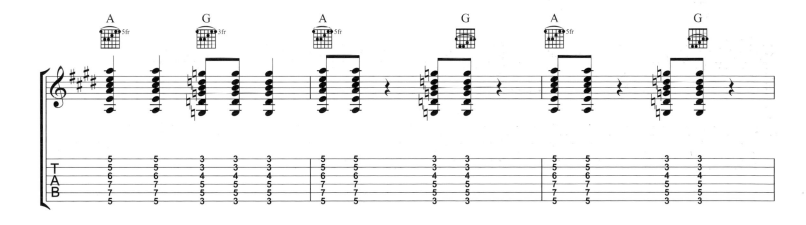

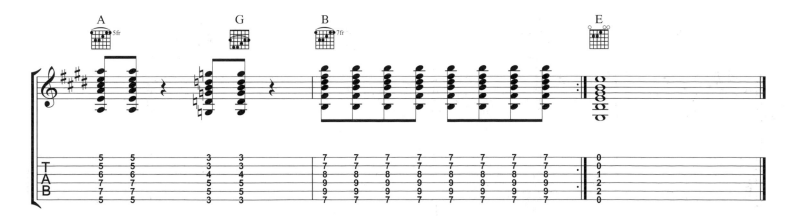

Pete Townshend

1945–
GUITARS: RICKENBACKER, FENDER, GIBSON

Along with the Beatles and the Rolling Stones, the Holy Trinity of British rock bands that conquered the world in the 1960s is completed by The Who. As much as either the Beatles or the Stones, The Who underwent a series of transformations, reinventing themselves and pushing the boundaries of rock each time.

Rebel with a guitar
Born as World War II ended, Pete Townshend came to typify the rebelliousness of the British baby boom. Early Who singles, such as "My Generation" and "I Can't Explain," managed to seem part of the emerging "British Invasion" sound but were actually far grittier. While the Beatles were still writing songs such as "I Want to Hold Your Hand" and "Can't Buy Me Love," and the Stones, for all their rebellious image, were still regurgitating American rhythm and blues, Townshend was sneering at his elders with lines such as the famous "I hope I die before I get old."

Townshend shared the influences of most British players emerging in the 1960s, particularly early American rockers such as Duane Eddy and Eddie Cochran.

Louder and heavier
The Who quickly became the loudest, brashest band around. Townshend's boast to Paul McCartney that he had just recorded the heaviest, dirtiest thing ever written led directly to McCartney creating "Helter Skelter," arguably the first heavy rock track, by today's standards.

Carnival of destruction
By the late 1960s, The Who were possibly the biggest live act around, though their profitability was seriously undermined by their habit of smashing their equipment at the end of each gig. Dozens, maybe hundreds, of Les Pauls, Strats, and Rickenbackers were smashed on the stage or thrust through the speaker cones of Marshall stacks. This destructive streak can be seen as directly responsible for the later stage antics of heavy metal acts such as Kiss and Alice Cooper. Apparently, the whole thing started as an accident but, like Jimi Hendrix's guitar-burning, was encouraged by fans in the audience, who came to expect this carnival of destruction as an integral part of the show.

Rock opera
In the 1970s Townshend created the phenomenon of rock opera with the films *Tommy* and *Quadrophenia*, while The Who pioneered stadium rock, playing to huge audiences and taking advantage of powerful sound systems not available in the 1960s. This inevitably took its toll on Townshend's hearing, as did the famous incident involving an impromptu firework display (which had been organized by drummer Keith Moon), which exploded within inches of Townshend's head.

Lesson 9.3: Rhythm Guitar Techniques

So far, we've concentrated on just playing the chords, without worrying too much about how they are played. It's time to try a couple of simple techniques that will add musicality and interest to your sound.

Palm muting

This involves using the flesh of the right-hand palm to change the sound, and can be applied equally well to rhythm and lead playing. The edge of the hand is placed across the bridge in order to absorb some of the sound.

Right-hand picking/chord playing carries on as normal except that the hand remains "anchored" to the bridge. Position and pressure are both critical—a few millimeters can make the difference between no muting and too much. The notes should sound slightly muffled but should still have some audible pitch.

Experiment with the technique until you find a position that sounds good.

Palm muting can be particularly effective with rock 'n' roll patterns and power chords, with or without overdrive. The contrast between muted and ringing chords can also work very well, and all that is needed is a very slight shift in right-hand position.

The symbol "P.M." is often seen in Tab books to indicate palm muting:

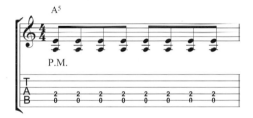

Left-hand damping

Total control over the duration of any fretted note or chord is very easy.

As soon as you release the pressure of the left hand even slightly, the note or chord stops ringing. This is much easier than stopping the sound any other way and can be used to play very short, detached notes. A very short note is known as a staccato note, and this is usually shown by a dot above or below the note (not to be confused with the lengthening dot, which goes *after* the note, see page 109).

Try this example, making the staccato notes as short as possible while still retaining some sense of pitch.

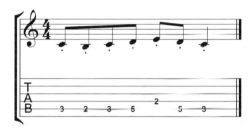

Palm muting: The flesh of the side of the hand covers the bridge, deadening the sound slightly.

Leo Fender

1909—1991

See also

Fender Stratocaster (see pages 93, 207)
Fender Telecaster (see page 208)
Fender Amps (see page 220)

Few nonmusicians have had anything like Leo Fender's influence on the course of music history—and very few musicians either, for that matter.

Two of the most popular and iconic guitars of all time originated on Leo Fender's drawing board. He also pioneered a new instrument.

Bass guitar

Interestingly, Fender was long thought to have invented the bass guitar; he certainly believed this to be the case, but an earlier instrument has recently come to light that Leo Fender may or may not have been aware of. Either

way, Fender's bass guitars certainly got the ball rolling; for many years, the term "Fender bass" was synonymous with "bass guitar." Leo Fender was the first major figure to pick up on the fact that bass players (which until that time meant double bass players) wanted a more portable instrument that was capable of a louder, punchier sound. Without the bass guitar, pop and rock music, as we know them today, simply would not exist—it's hard to imagine many styles, including heavy rock, funk, and reggae, using the double bass. The new instrument also gave guitarists an easier route into the role

of bass player. The bass guitar is tuned the same way as the double bass, which happens to be an octave below the bottom four strings of the guitar. Many great bass players (of whom Paul McCartney is the most famous) started on guitar but moved on to the bass because someone in the band had to.

Pioneering days

While running a radio repair business in Fullerton, California, in the 1940s, Fender began to experiment with making amplified Hawaiian guitars that were similar to Rickenbacker and Beauchamp's "frying pan" (see page 67). After a split with his business partner, Fender decided that the real market lay in perfecting a solid-bodied "Spanish" (as opposed to Hawaiian) electric guitar. This was some years before Les Paul persuaded the Gibson company to take his designs seriously. Most of the required hardware either didn't exist or existed only in a form that Fender thought could be greatly improved.

Birth of the Telecaster

In 1948 Fender Electric Instrument Manufacturing began development of the guitar we have come to know as the Telecaster. Later innovations included the Precision Bass in 1953 and the Stratocaster in 1954. These instruments shared many common

Leo Fender's name has become synonymous with the electric guitar.

features, including Fender's patent pickup designs and bolt-on necks. The reputation of these classic instruments is so strong that they have managed to survive strong competition and still remain little affected by the many close copies of Fender designs produced cheaply in the Far East. Landmark legal rulings in the 1980s reduced Fender's ability to protect its designs, but this actually seems to have worked in its favor: many other companies have effectively been doing Fender's marketing for free since then, constantly reaffirming the iconic status of Fender's designs. Sooner or later, most players starting out with a copy, no matter how good, are going to want to own the real thing.

Fender amps

Along with guitars and basses, some of the best-loved amplifiers of all time have been Fender designs, with the Bassman and the Twin Reverb the most obvious examples. The creator of Marshall amps, Jim Marshall, also admits that his original design was essentially a version of the Fender Bassman design.

Research

Leo Fender's achievements are all the more remarkable in light of the fact that he never learned to play guitar himself. Perhaps this gave him the necessary distance to see what guitarists really needed. The early Fender research process involved making a prototype, taking it to a local musician on a gig, and begging him to try it.

Electric piano

The other iconic instrument associated with the Fender name is, of course, the Fender Rhodes electric piano, beloved of funk, soul, and jazz keyboard players from the '60s to the present, including Herbie Hancock and Stevie Wonder. Though not directly involved in the instrument's design, Leo Fender had the vision to acquire the Rhodes company in 1959 and took the decision to put Fender's market muscle behind it.

Big business

Leo Fender sold his business to CBS in 1965, mainly because of ill health, but he continued to be involved in making instruments after his recovery until his death, designing guitars and basses for Music Man in the 1970s (the latter, in particular, gaining a loyal base of users) and making refined versions of his most famous guitar designs— not without a certain amount of legal saber-rattling from the Fender Company, under the "G&L" name. The Fender name itself has gone from strength to strength, particularly after the company's management was able to buy it back from CBS in 1985.

Leo Fender is credited as the inventor of the first mass-produced electric bass guitar.

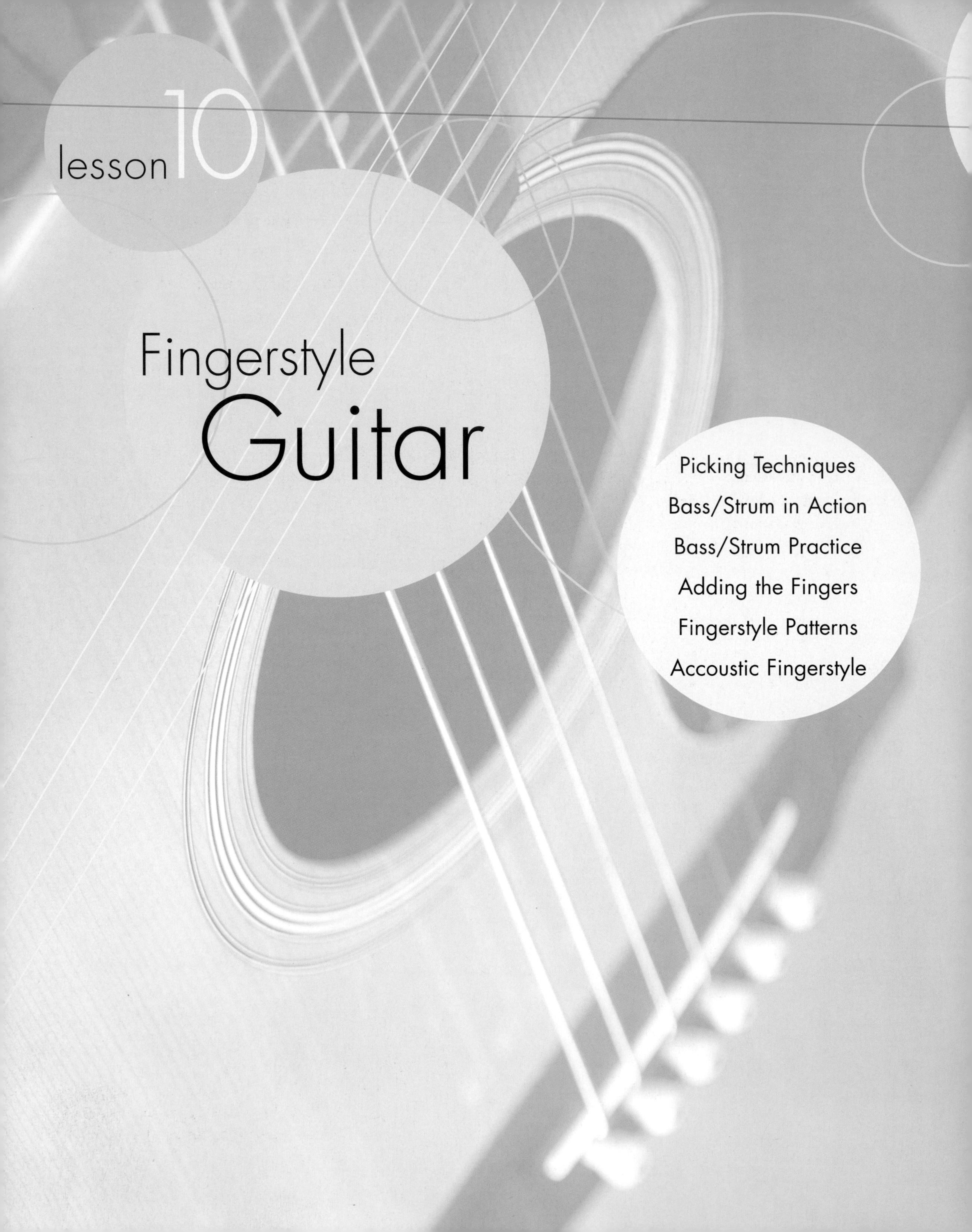

Fingerstyle Guitar

Picking Techniques

Bass/Strum in Action

Bass/Strum Practice

Adding the Fingers

Fingerstyle Patterns

Accoustic Fingerstyle

There are many ways to play the guitar—almost as many as there are guitarists. Rock and pop playing tends to focus on playing with the pick. In this chapter, we're going to look at playing fingerstyle guitar. While this is found mainly in folk-based acoustic-guitar styles, it can also be applied to the electric guitar and other styles such as jazz.

Lesson 10.1: Picking Techniques

Picks and fingers

There are many ways to use the fingers of the right hand. Rock players tend to use a pick as shown below...

...while acoustic players often use the thumb and first three fingers as shown below. This is similar to classical right-hand technique (see Lesson 11 for more detail).

Thumb and finger picks

Some folk and country players use individual thumb and finger picks instead of growing their  nails. The thumb and fingers are then used as in normal playing except that the thumb employs more of a "sideways" approach, as shown below.

EXPERT'S TIP: Arpeggios

The musical term for playing the notes of a chord one at a time, either with a pick or with fingers, is an arpeggio. In an arpeggio, the notes should be played in rapid succession. Arpeggio means "broken chord."

Jazz style

Some jazz players use a standard pick between the thumb and first finger while picking with the remaining fingers, including the pinkie.

The choice is yours. Have a go at all of these techniques and find one that suits you. We'll look at them all in a bit more detail as we progress. What all of these styles have in common is that they tend to separate the bass (lower three) and treble (upper three) strings. The thumb (or pick) plays the bass strings while the fingers pick or strum the treble strings.

We're going to focus initially on picking with the thumb while strumming with the fingers to develop some independence. This is sometimes called the "bass/strum style."

Playing a chord

To get started with this style, play an ordinary D chord. First pick the D (fourth) string with your thumb.

Then strum the treble strings with your fingernails.

Now pick the A string with your thumb, and strum again.

This can be notated in a few ways; we're going to use the following system. The measure you have just played looks like this:

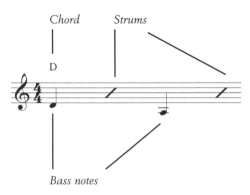

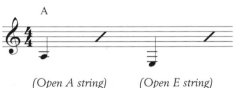

(Open A string)   (Open E string)

Lesson 10.2: Bass/Strum in Action

It's possible to provide varied and interesting accompaniments using the bass/strum style.

Variations

There are many possible patterns involving different bass notes and up/down strums. For instance, in addition to the pattern we just looked at, you can play a bass note on beat 1 only, strumming for the rest of the measure.

Or you can vary the strumming with eighth notes.

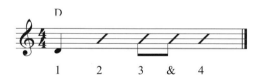

Either way, it's useful to know which bass strings to play.

Roots and fifths

You may have noticed that the D and A patterns on the previous page had a country-ish flavor. This is because they use a "root and fifth" bass-note pattern, which means that the first bass note is the root of the chord; the second is the fifth. If in doubt, just stick to the root. This should be easy to find—it's the lowest note in the chord with the same letter-name as the chord itself.

This chart shows you which strings to use in order to play the root-and-fifth pattern with some of the first position chords we have learned so far.

Going back to your roots

The root is found on the A string, as normal (3rd fret). The fifth is the low G on the E string (3rd fret).

Alternatively, you can simply play the standard C shape and move the third finger across to the E string to play the lower bass note.

Example patterns

The patterns on the next two pages consist of familiar shapes, alternating between the root and fifth of each chord, with a few additional points of interest.

NC = no chord. In these patterns, simply play the written bass notes instead. These are known as bass runs, and they serve to join the chords together and create a more interesting bass line. By all means, experiment with some bass runs of your own.

C7/E: Play the C7 chord, but with the open low-E string in the bass. This is actually the third of the chord (rather than the root or fifth) and works well as a means of joining up the C chord and the F chord.

CHORD ROOTS AND FIFTHS FINDER

Chords	Root is on	Fifth is on
A, A7, Am	A string, open	E string, open
E, E7, Em	E string, open	A string, 2nd fret
D, D7, Dm	D string, open	A string, open
G, G7	E string, 3rd fret	D string, open
C	A string, 3rd fret	G string, open*

*Although the open G string found within a standard C chord does give you the fifth of the chord, it's a bit high to work as a bass note. This alternative shape works much better in the bass/strum style.

Lesson 10.3: Bass/Strum Practice

COUNTRY WALTZ

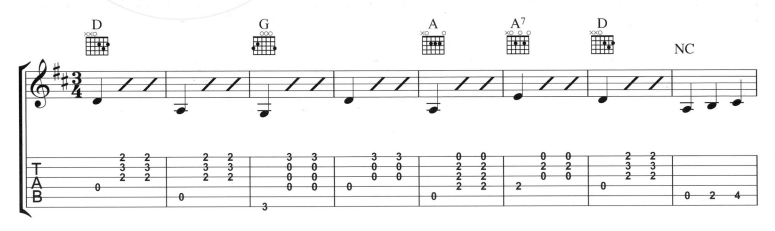

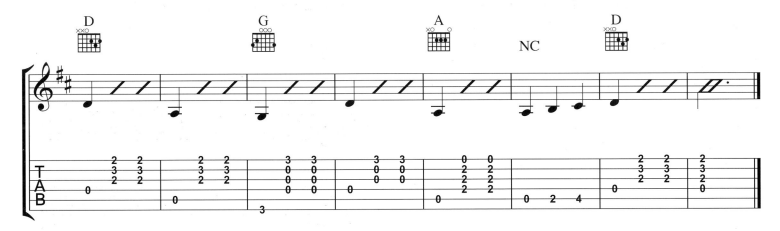

BOUNCY

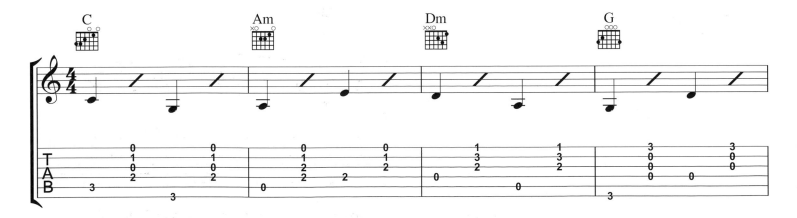

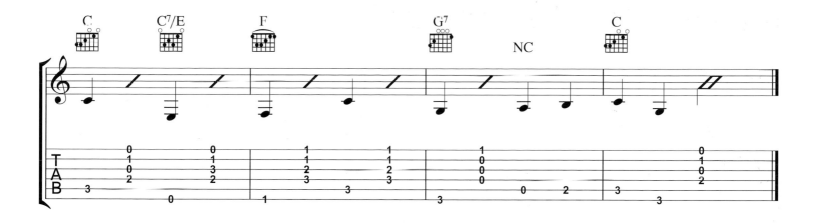

Lesson 10.4: Adding the Fingers

It's time to start using your fingers more creatively. Most of the time in fingerstyle patterns, the thumb will play the bass strings and the first three fingers will play the top three strings.

This also forms the basis for a lot of classical playing (see Lesson 11), though classical players often use the fingers to play bass strings, too.

For the rest of this chapter, we'll use the following abbreviations where appropriate, though you should feel free to apply other techniques to these patterns and songs.

P = thumb

i = index finger
(first finger)

m = middle finger
(second finger)

a = ring finger
(third finger)

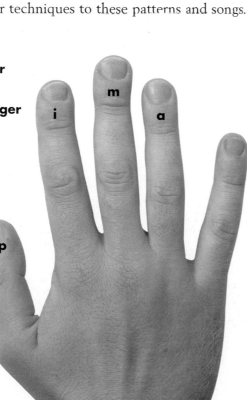

Try picking a few chords; for example, C:

Or E:

If you're trying this with the "pick and fingers" technique, "P" represents the pick (between the thumb and first finger) and "m,""i," and "a" represent the remaining fingers.

James Taylor

1948—

GUITARS: MARTIN, OLSON

Recommended Listening:

Sweet Baby James

Mud Slide Slim and the Blue Horizon

New Moon Shine

Hourglass

October Road

James Taylor, along with Joni Mitchell, brought a new sophistication to the singer/songwriter genre in the early 1970s. To many, James Taylor is "the" singer/songwriter, and though he's rightly famous as such, he's also one of the most accomplished fingerstyle guitarists around.

Born in 1948 to a well-off Boston family, Taylor played in local bands in his teens, notably the Flying Machine, with guitarist and long-term collaborator Danny Kortchmar. Somehow finding himself in London in 1968 turned out to be one of Taylor's lucky breaks: The Beatles were launching their Apple record label and advertizing for talent. They were soon deluged with thousands of demo tapes, most of which were never heard, but through a lucky association with Peter Asher (half of the duo Peter and Gordon but, more importantly, a man with the ear of Paul McCartney, who was engaged to Peter's sister Jane Asher), James Taylor managed to get heard. Signing with Apple, his first, eponymously titled album was recorded in London with guest appearances from many British stars of the time, including Paul McCartney on bass. The album is a period piece, combining a glimpse of things to come in Taylor's career with a large dose of 1960s kitsch.

The Apple album was not a success at the time, however—largely due to the chaos within the Beatles' empire toward the end of their career—and Taylor returned to America.

Renaissance

Eighteen months later, after some health problems and a horrific motorcycle accident, he again teamed up with Peter Asher, who was by this time embarking on a career as a West Coast record producer. Asher managed to get Taylor a contract with Warner Brothers and the breakthrough album *Sweet Baby James* garnered huge sales and instant international fame. The follow-up, *Mud Slide Slim and the Blue Horizon,* included a massive hit single—Taylor's cover of Carole King's "You've Got a Friend"—and that album outsold its predecessor.

Though the quality of James Taylor's work has varied in the last 30 years, with 15 albums to his name, he has earned his place as one of the foremost exponents of guitar-based songwriting. His later work includes some big hit singles, a platinum-selling duet with his then wife, Carly Simon, consistent album sales, and regular tours. His *Greatest Hits* (released in 1976 by Warner Brothers after Taylor had been lured to the Columbia label) has sold more than 11 million copies to date.

James Taylor uses a simple thumb-and-fingers fingerpicking style and generally sticks to a folk-influenced chord repertoire, though there is also a noticeable country influence, along with abundant jazzy moments—particularly in his later work.

Lesson 10.5: Fingerstyle Patterns

Here's a practice piece using many different fingerstyle patterns.

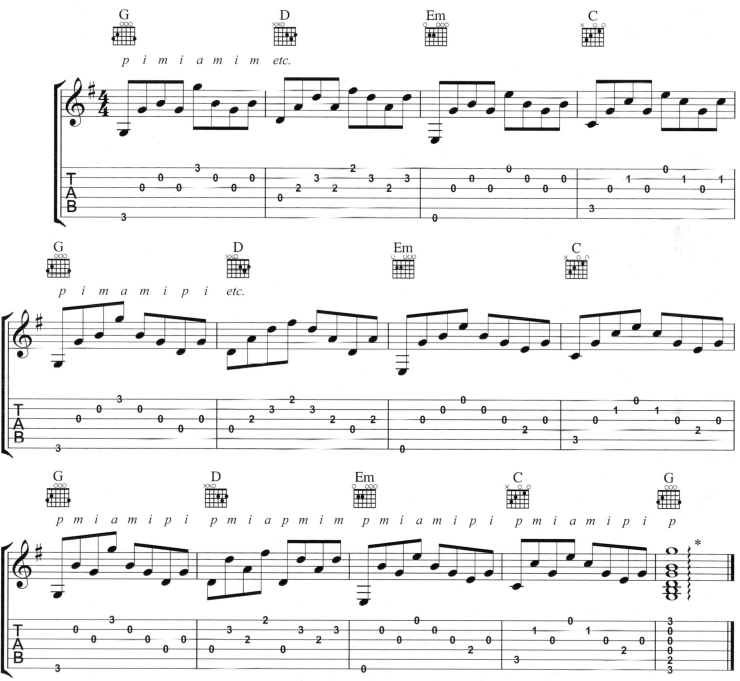

* Strum downward (with the thumb)

EXPERT'S TIP: Bass notes

As with the bass/strum style, the same picking patterns
apply to bass notes, but you can be a little more relaxed
because the bass notes do not stand out quite as much. Steel strings
generally sound better if played with the nails than with the flesh, but worse
if the nails are ragged. For a good fingerstyle sound, the nail should be long
enough to catch the string and filed to a smooth curve.

"Greensleeves"

Words and Music **Traditional**

An old English folk song, "Greensleeves" is a familiar tune and has been arranged here for fingerstyle guitar. Though often played on the Spanish (classical) guitar, "Greensleeves" has long been a favorite of fingerstyle acoustic players, too—check out the bluesy version on James Taylor's eponymous debut album.

In general, all notes/chords in this piece should be made to ring for as long as possible, usually until the next chord change. We could have used separate voices for this (see page 141), but it is just as common to see the instruction let ring; this helps keep the notation neat.

This piece introduces a new chord shape: G/B ("G over B"). This is a G chord, but with the note B in the bass. Just two notes are needed to play this chord as

seen here in the diagram over the second measure of the second section. Most players use fingers 1 and 3, but 1 and 4 work fine, too.

Generally, the fingers and thumb of the right hand should be used as shown on page 124; that is, the thumb covers the bass strings while the fingers cover the treble strings. You will occasionally need to bring the index finger over to the D string (and move the other fingers relatively) to play chords—for example in the "G/B" measure.

The time signature here is 6/8. This means that there are six eighth-note beats per measure; beats 1 and 4 should be stressed more heavily than the others: count 1 2 3 **4** 5 6, **1** 2 3 **4** 5 6…

Joni Mitchell

1943 —
GUITARS: MARTIN

Recommended Listening:

Ladies of the Canyon
Blue
The Hissing of Summer Lawns
Mingus

Roberta Joan Anderson, who has been known throughout her career as Joni Mitchell, may well prove to be the most influential female recording artist of the twentieth century. For the last 35 years, she has been relentless in her exploration of new sounds, from the conception of her songs through any one of dozens of guitar tunings of her own invention, to recording and production.

Unusual tunings

Joni claims that her original tunings originated simply because she had never learned standard tuning. Most of her great guitar-based songs use unique tunings, with each tuning creating a sound-world specific to one song. Changing tunings with every song can make performing live difficult, so it is not surprising that Joni tours infrequently.

As a studio-based artist, Mitchell has been uncompromising in her search for her own artistic path. Though her early work owes much to her experience playing the folk clubs of Toronto, Detroit, and New York, her mature work is impossible to classify. Jazz influences are strong, though she avoids conventional jazz song forms; her collaborators have included Jaco Pastorius, Pat Metheny, and the omnipresent Michael Brecker. *Mingus*, an album of songs based on the late jazz bassist Charles Mingus's compositions, met with suspicion from the jazz community—partly because of Joni's good fortune in securing Mingus's collaboration in the months preceding his death, and possibly because her songs defied the "jazz police" by not conforming to any particular "official" jazz style.

Few of Joni's consecutive albums are recognizably similar. Like Miles Davis, she seems driven to forge ahead at every opportunity—to repeat a formula would be boring and predictable. *Blue*, *For the Roses*, *Court and Spark*, *The Hissing of Summer Lawns*, and *Hejira* were released at roughly annual intervals during her 1970s peak but, except for the unifying strand of her glorious voice, could easily be by five different artists. Her pioneering achievements are too many to list; only time will tell which will be her legacy.

Lesson 10.6: Acoustic Fingerstyle

Here's a traditional folk classic, arranged in the style of James Taylor. Though it's hard to show in simple notation, the main point in playing this tune is to achieve a good balance between melody notes (on the top strings) and the underlying arpeggios. All notes should be allowed to ring for as long as possible.

This piece may be played either by using the "strict" fingerstyle technique, where the bass strings are played by the thumb and the fingers play only the treble strings (see page 127), using hybrid pick-and-fingers technique, including the pinkie, or by using the pick alone.

THE WATER IS WIDE (TRADITIONAL)

The Twelve-String Guitar

This book focuses on the six-string guitar, which has been the central instrument in much of the popular music of the last century.

Octave pairs

The twelve-string guitar is a close relative and, unlike other stringed instruments such as the mandolin, banjo, and lute, can easily be played by a six-string guitarist.

The reason for this is simple. Instead of six single strings, the twelve string has six pairs of strings. The lower four pairs are generally tuned in octaves, while the top two are tuned in unison (the same note). This means that the twelve-string is played like a standard guitar. The strings in each pair are close enough that they generally sound together but with a rich, ringing sound and greater volume.

The quest for steel strings

The instrument seems to have originated in the late-nineteenth century, during a period when luthiers were looking for ways to increase the guitar's volume—a quest beginning with the introduction of steel strings and culminating in the evolution of the electric guitar. Renaissance guitars had originally had four or five pairs ("courses") of strings, as do European instruments of the mandolin family.

Blues and folk tradition

The acoustic twelve-string gained popularity with blues and folk players such as Blind Lemon Jefferson, Leadbelly, and Jesse Fuller, suiting their requirement for a louder acoustic instrument for vocal accompaniment.

Headstock design

Accommodating twelve machine-heads on a conventional acoustic-style headstock inevitably results in a somewhat unbalanced-looking instrument. Rickenbacker solved this problem neatly with its twelve-string electric headstock design, which is a cross between steel-strung and classical headstock designs. One string from each pair feeds onto an acoustic-style machine head, the other to a classical-style roller within one of two slots in the headstock.

The strings of a twelve-string guitar are arranged in six pairs. Each string can be tuned separately.

135

Classical Guitar

Sitting Position

Classical Guitar Exercises

Your First Classical Piece

Although there are many different guitar styles and types, guitar players seem to fall into two broad camps: classical players on the one side and on the other side, just about everyone else.

Lesson 11.1: Sitting Position

Although advanced classical guitar playing is in some ways well beyond the scope of this book, we're dipping a toe into the water in this chapter. If classical guitar strikes your fancy, you may want to explore it further on your own or with a teacher. We recommend the latter approach, since classical techniques are very specific and it's easy to fall into bad habits.

Learning from tradition

To get the most out of this chapter you will need a classical (nylon strung) guitar, but failing that, you can still get an idea of what it's all about by using an electric or steel-strung acoustic guitar.

We're going to approach classical playing from the point of view of the rock/pop guitarist; although we've looked at some fingerpicking styles, let's start from scratch with classical technique to make sure everything is clear.

Posture

Rock/pop guitarists (and teachers) are generally fairly relaxed about posture. The classical tradition is very precise about the sitting position, however; although there are classical players who break the rules, it's a good idea to know what they are.

The first thing you will need is a footstool. If you do not have a footstool, you can use a stack of books, but the footstool is preferable—it's a question of angle as well as height.

Sit on an armless chair with the left foot on the footstool. The guitar will then rest comfortably on the left leg, and will tend to "point" upward.

The guitar neck should make an angle of about 45 degrees to the horizontal. The best test of classical posture is to remove the left hand from the neck; the guitar should not move. The point of this is that the left hand's strength is used purely for playing, not for supporting the guitar.

World-famous guitarist Julian Bream in the classical sitting position. This pose not only provides a balance for the guitar but also instills a sense of personal discipline in your playing.

Left Hand

Classical technique is very strict. The thumb generally should not move away from an imaginary line along the back of the neck.

The "thumb over the top" position, favored by many rock players, is considered incorrect by classical teachers.

Right Hand

Classical technique is very specific here, too. The thumb and first three fingers are used; these are referred to by letters rather than numbers:

p = thumb (Spanish: pulgar)
i = index (indice)
m = middle (medio)
a = ring (anular)

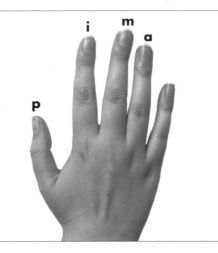

Nails

For the correct tone, the strings must be played with the nails rather than the fingertips. Serious classical players spend a lot of time on nail care! For now, if you want to get a feel for this style, try growing your nails and filing them to a reasonably rounded shape.

Fingers

For many classical pieces, the right hand thumb plays the bass strings (6,5,4), while the fingers play the treble strings (3,2,1).

Rest the thumb on the bottom E string; place the index, middle, and ring fingers on strings 3, 2, and 1, respectively. This is a good "at rest" position for classical guitar.

Motor skills

To be an excellent classical guitarist, your fingers need to be coordinated and supple. Some guitarists practice the same piece of music over and over again. The aim is to be able to train your fingers to move quickly and accurately without thinking about them too much!

EXPERT'S TIP: Classical Guitar Notation

Tablature is not used in classical guitar notation; instead, roman numerals (I, II, etc.) indicate the position (lowest fret used in a given section/phrase), numbers (1,2,3,4) indicate left-hand fingerings (zero represents an open string), and P, i, m, and a indicate right-hand fingerings. This information is not always given in published music—you often have to improvize. Note also that the chord boxes in this lesson show only the left-hand fingers used. Classical players tend not to think in terms of "shapes" as much as rock/pop players; in fact, chord boxes, like TAB, are seldom used.

Lesson 11.2: Classical Guitar Exercises

Let's put these techniques into practice with a few simple exercises.

Playing arpeggios
Try this exercise:

This involves playing the strings in the "at rest" position in the order shown, resulting in an E minor arpeggio (the notes of the E minor chord played one after the other). Play this repeatedly until it feels fluent.

Now try arpeggiating some fretted chords:

This is a C major arpeggio. The roman numeral "I" indicates first position. You may instinctively play the full C major chord in first position, but in fact, classical players generally fret only the notes that are written. In this case, fret the note C on the first fret of the 2nd string with the first finger; the third finger plays the bass note C (5th string). The G and E are open strings; the other left-hand fingers are not used but should hover just above the fretboard, ready for use.

Lesson 11.3: Bass Line Exercises for Classical Guitar

MOVING BASS LINE

This is a simple bassline moving against an open-string arpeggio. Note the key signature: one sharp. In this case, this signifies E minor, a very common classical guitar key. The second bass note of the first bar is therefore an F#.

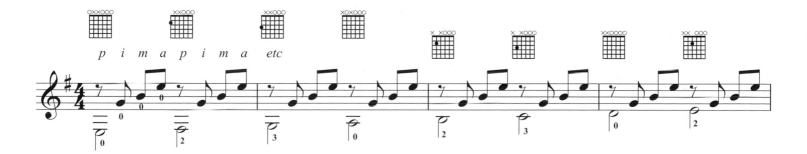

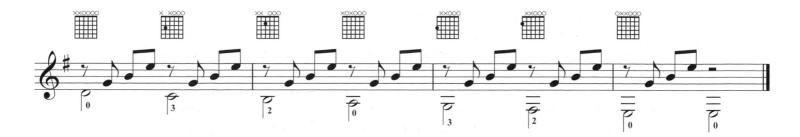

STATIC BASS, MOVING CHORDS

In the practice piece below, the first eighth note of each bar is a "pinch." The thumb plays the bass note, while the third finger plays the top string. The final chord is played by all the fingers and thumb simultaneously (all open strings)—if you like, you can "spread" this chord slightly by playing *P i m a* in very quick succession but not quite together.

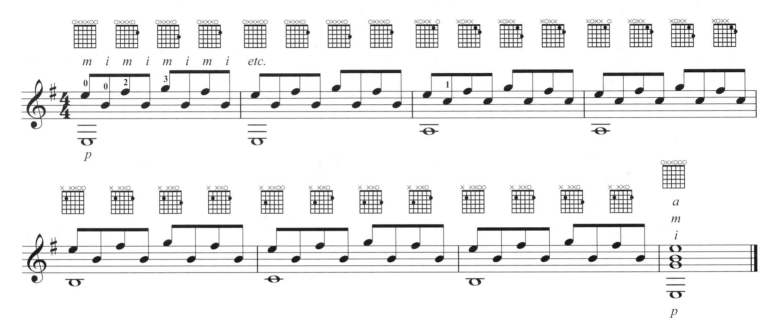

BASS/CHORD ACCOMPANIMENT

This is an example of an effective accompaniment in the classical style, using a very common chord sequence that is found in many baroque and classical pieces, such as Pachelbel's Canon. It's also useful as a folky fingerstyle accompaniment; the chords here are C G Am Em F C F G. (Chord symbols are not usually shown in classical music.)

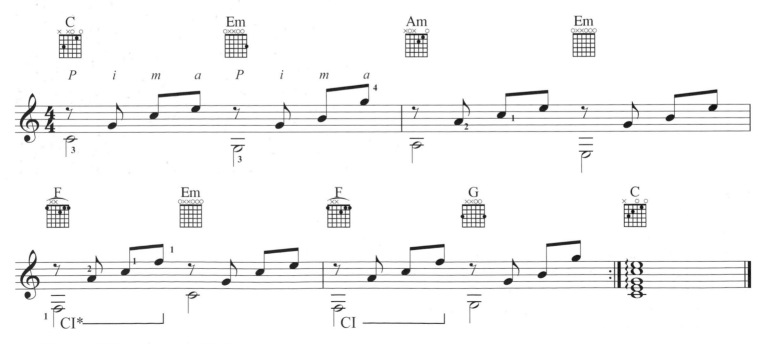

Note: "C" = barre; "CI" means barre at the first fret.

THE PINCH

This is another very common classical style. Make sure the
pinched notes sound simultaneously.

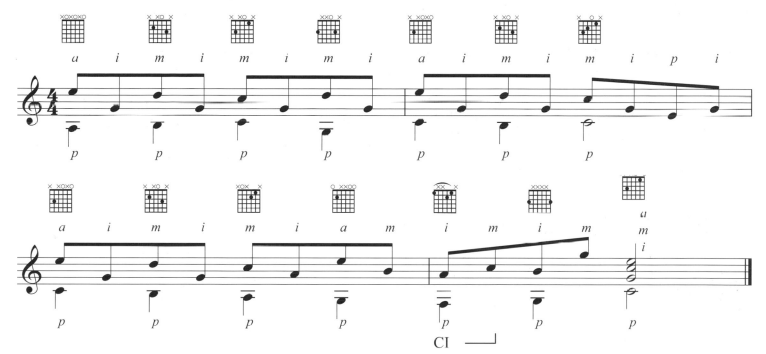

*John Williams, performer and
prolific songwriter, playing a
rapid arpeggio in E, using the
C barre chord.*

EXPERT'S TIP: Voices

You may have noticed that the exercises on this page use notes with tails pointing
downward for the bass notes and tails pointing upward for the treble strings. This is a
common device in classical guitar music and is used as a way of showing that the bass
notes should ring on while the other notes are played, so there are actually two musical
lines going on at once; these are known as independent *voices*. Classical guitar music
sometimes contains even more than two voices; the arpeggiated notes in these exercises
should ring on for as long as possible, too, but it is not always possible to reflect this
accurately in the notation; three or more voices can be rather hard to read.

Andrés Segovia

1893–1987

GUITARS: RAMIREZ, HAUSER

Recommended Listening:

The Legendary Segovia

Andrés Segovia is considered by many to be the father of modern classical guitar. Indeed, many feel that without his tireless work to promote his instrument, the guitar would still be known as a "peasant's instrument," suitable for the café-bar but never the concert hall.

Segovia's imaginary guitar

The son of a prosperous lawyer, Segovia was born in the Andalusian city of Linares, Spain. Segovia's interest in music was sparked early on, when, at the age of four, he would sit and watch his uncle sing songs to him while strumming an imaginary guitar. Tutored in both piano and violin, Segovia lacked enthusiasm for either and, enchanted by the color and richness of the guitar's sonority, took up the instrument.

International stature

Segovia set himself a goal that would take him and his guitar across the globe: to bring guitar studies to every university in the world and to have the guitar played on every major stage.

Segovia gave his first concert at the age of sixteen but made his professional debut in Madrid at the age of twenty, playing his own transcriptions of Bach and Tárrega. Many "serious" musicians believed that Segovia would be laughed off the stage—the guitar could not play

classical music! In fact, Segovia astounded the audience. This was followed by concerts in Barcelona, London, Paris, and South America. He made his New York debut in 1928, and his phenomenal success led to more appearances in the United States and Europe, as well as a trip to the Far East in 1929. Segovia and the classical guitar had truly arrived on the international stage.

Legacy

Andrés Segovia died in 1987 after a long and distinguished career, having fulfilled his ambition. The guitar is now seen as a "proper" classical instrument, taken seriously by both musicians and audiences.

New generation

While Segovia had to rely on renaissance and baroque pieces for lute, we now have an ever widening classical repertoire for guitar, thanks to Segovia's pioneering work. But perhaps Segovia's most important achievement has been to pass his passion and dedication for his instrument on to a whole new generation, both through his inspirational recordings and his tireless teaching efforts at music schools around the world.

Lesson 11.4: Your First Classical Piece

This practice piece should whet your appetite for classical guitar. There's nothing too challenging here; everything is in first position so there is generally only one possible fingering. The goal is to pay attention to detail, working through the piece slowly and carefully.

Recognizing the key

This piece is in A major, indicated by the three sharps in the key signature. In this piece, all written Fs, Cs, and Gs are actually F#, C#, and G#, respectively. These are easy to find: Simply play one fret higher than the natural note. If you are in doubt about finding any of them, check the fingering diagram/chromatic scale on page 58.

Time signature

Waltz in A, composed by Ferdinando Carulli, is written in the unusual time signature of 3/8. This means that there are three beats per measure, and each beat is represented by an eighth note. The dotted quarter notes last three beats, or a full measure, as the dot has the effect of extending the duration of a note by half its usual value; in this case, a quarter plus an eighth equals three eighths.

WALTZ IN A

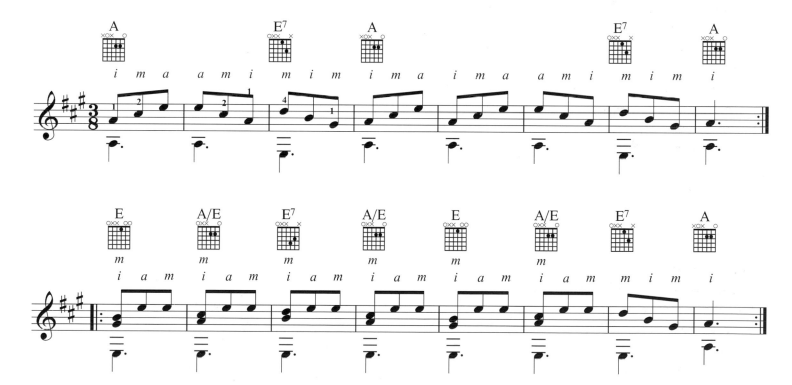

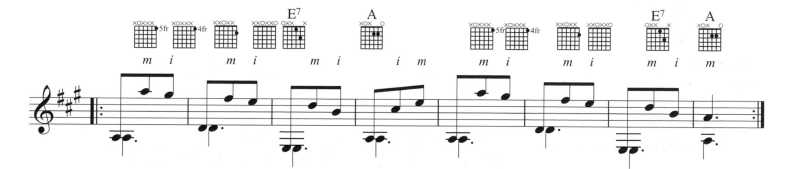

The
Blues

Blue Notes

Blues Practice Tunes

"Wade in the Water"

Blues Improvisation 1

Blues Improvisation 2

Earlier in the course we looked at the twelve-bar blues structure as it applied to rock 'n' roll. Here, we are going to delve right back into blues. One of the important features of most blues songs, tunes, and solos is the use of so-called "blue" notes. These are notes that are not present in the major scale of a given key center and, therefore, create a dissonant sound against the chord structure.

Lesson 12.1: Blue Notes

Flattened thirds and sevenths

The two blue notes present in the blues from the beginning were the flattened third and flattened seventh—"flattened" means one semitone lower than the degree of the major scale in question. For example, the third and seventh steps of C major are E and B; the blue notes in this key are E♭ and B♭.

The minor pentatonic scale

Combining these notes with the root, fourth, and fifth of the major scale gives us a useful scale for blues tunes and improvisation.

This is called the minor pentatonic scale. As well as being central to the blues, it is no accident that pentatonic scales are commonly found in the folk music of many countries throughout Africa, Europe, and Asia.

C MAJOR SCALE

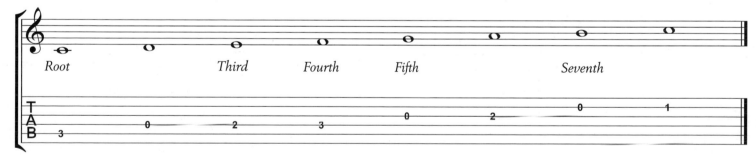

C MINOR PENTATONIC SCALE

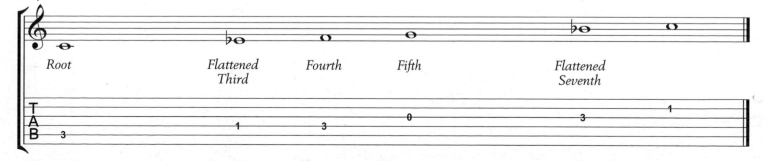

Movable minor pentatonic scale

Let's have a look at the most common shape for the minor pentatonic scale. This is a movable scale shape; the key (or root note) is shown by the symbol ⓡ.

Find the root...find the key

This shape can be played anywhere on the neck; the key is determined by the position. As the root of the scale is played by the index finger on the bottom string, the power-chord root finder on page 91 can be used to find the scale in any given key. For example, the third fret gives the note G; the key of A, shown in the scale below, can be found by starting at the fifth fret.

This is an important scale shape to master, so we'll look at several tunes and solos in this chapter to help you learn it fluently.

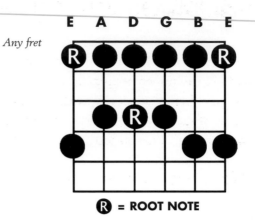

E A D G B E

Any fret

ⓡ = ROOT NOTE

This scale "shape" can be moved anywhere on the neck. The key is determined by the lowest fret used. In the example below, the lowest fret is the fifth fret. As the fifth fret of the E string is an A, this results in a minor pentatonic in the key of A.

THE MINOR PENTATONIC: KEY OF A

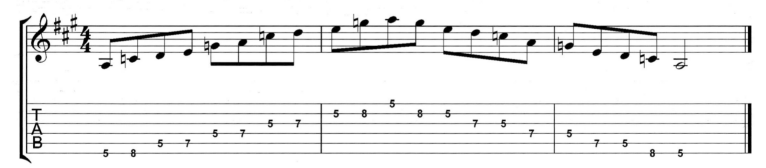

EXPERT'S TIP: Know your roots

One of the great things about the blues is that it can be played in any key. Once you have a "start chord," you will know "where to go next." Blues, therefore, is especially useful for jamming and improvising with other musicians because you will all know what to play next. If you know your roots, you will know the blues.

Lesson 12.2: Blues Practice Tunes

The practice tunes on the next few pages all follow the twelve-bar blues sequence in A and use the minor pentatonic scale, with the root at the fifth fret. By all means, play them very slowly, with a metronome, at first. To really appreciate the effect of the blue notes, have a friend play the chords or record them yourself and play the tunes on top.

BLUES PRACTICE: MOOCHIN'

* LH fingering

BLUES PRACTICE: SHUFFLIN'

Endings

Play the piece from the beginning.

After the first two measures of the last line, play the "1st time" ending, as shown by the bracket:

1.

Observe the repeat marking at the end of this measure, and play the piece once more from the beginning.

This time, after playing the first two measures of the last line, omit the 1st time measure and play the 2nd time ending instead:

2.

Though these endings are only one measure long in this piece, they can often be longer—in that case, the bracket simply extends over more measures as required.

148

Lesson 12.3: "Wade in the Water"

Here's a traditional spiritual tune that makes a great practice vehicle for learning the minor pentatonic scale. During the period of slavery in the United States, black slaves would sing spirituals such as these in the fields as they worked. It is believed that "Wade in the Water" was in part an exhortation to fellow slaves to escape across the Ohio or Mississippi rivers to freedom.

Eric Clapton

1945—
GUITARS: FENDER STRATOCASTER, GIBSON LES PAUL

Recommended Listening:
John Mayall: *Bluesbreakers with Eric Clapton*
Cream: *Disraeli Gears; Wheels of Fire*
Derek and the Dominos: *Layla And Other Assorted Love Songs*
Eric Clapton: *461 Ocean Boulevard; Slowhand; Journeyman; Unplugged; Me And Mr. Johnson*

Ask the man in the street to name five guitarists, and you'll almost certainly hear the name Eric Clapton among those put forward. Since the early 1960s, "Clapton" has been almost synonymous with "guitarist" in the public perception—and for good reason.

The illegitimate son of a Canadian pilot who returned to Canada after World War II, Eric Clapton was raised near London by his grandparents. The discovery of his family's secret at age nine had a strong emotional effect, and Clapton gravitated toward the blues—particularly the music of Robert Johnson—from an early age.

Pop goes the blues

Clapton's first major professional experience was with the Yardbirds—a blues-influenced pop group—in the early 1960s. The group scored several hits, and made an album with blues legend Sonny Boy Williamson. Clapton left the band in 1965, disillusioned with its musical direction. (He refused to play on the hit "For Your Love," which owed little to the blues that Clapton held so dear.)

Bluesbreakers

After some months of manual work and intensive practice, Clapton joined John Mayall's Bluesbreakers. Both the Bluesbreakers and the Yardbirds were important spawning grounds for some of the most influential musicians of the following decade, including Clapton himself, Jack Bruce, Jimmy Page, Peter Green of Fleetwood Mac, and Jeff Beck. Clapton played on the Bluesbreakers' influential and acclaimed first album—probably the single most important moment in the establishment of the blues as a mainstream musical style—but he left the band (to be replaced by Peter Green) in mid-1966. Around this time, the slogan "Clapton is God" started appearing as graffiti in London—a status that, although not sought by Clapton, nevertheless ensured him a permanent place in rock aristocracy.

150

High voltage

Eric Clapton's next band, Cream, matched or exceeded the long-term influence of the Bluesbreakers. Cream is now seen as both the first ever supergroup (a group made up of musicians who have already been successful either on their own or in other groups) and the first power trio: a band consisting of just guitar, bass, and drums, compensating for this with high amplification, virtuoso playing, and sonic experimentation. Bassist Jack Bruce (also from the Bluesbreakers) and drummer Ginger Baker—both adventurous players—together provided the perfect foil for Clapton's increasingly fiery, virtuoso guitar style.

Cream sold 15 million records and played to huge crowds throughout Europe and America during a career lasting just three years. The albums *Disraeli Gears* and *Wheels of Fire*, in particular, were hugely influential and contained some of Cream's most enduring hits: "White Room," "Badge," (written by Clapton and George Harrison), and "Sunshine of Your Love."

Around this time, Clapton also supplied the lead guitar for George Harrison's "While My Guitar Gently Weeps" on the Beatles' *White Album*. Clapton's presence helped to calm the increasingly tense atmosphere that had developed within the Beatles, and—against considerable odds—the two guitarists remained friends for the rest of Harrison's life.

"Layla"

Cream split up in 1969, mainly as a result of arguments between Bruce and Baker. The next few years were a roller-coaster ride for Clapton: battles with addiction, another supergroup (the short-lived Blind Faith), a stint as a sideman with the American group Delaney and Bonnie and Friends, as well as one of the most widely acclaimed albums of Clapton's career: *Layla and Other Assorted Love Songs*, credited to Derek and the Dominos. "Layla," one of Clapton's biggest hits and a staple of his live repertoire to this day, was a love song for George Harrison's wife, Patti Boyd—as, in fact, was most of the album. Clapton eventually lured Patti away from her Beatle husband, yet still retained his friendship with Harrison.

Solo years

Clapton's first solo albums— *Eric Clapton* and *461 Ocean Boulevard*—launched his career as a singer and songwriter, as well as a guitarist, that endures to this day. Clapton's 1970s albums, including *Slowhand* (one of many nicknames) and *There's One in Every Crowd* (abbreviated from the original, self-mocking title—*The World's Greatest Guitarist: There's One in Every Crowd*) contained jukebox classics such as "Wonderful Tonight" and "Lay Down Sally," as well as covers of Bob Marley's "I Shot the Sheriff"

and Bob Dylan's "Knocking on Heaven's Door."

Influential

Eric Clapton has, perhaps unwittingly, been a major influence on the prevalent tastes among guitar players and makers throughout his career. During the 1960s, Clapton's use of a late-1950s Les Paul probably brought the model back from obscurity, while the ES–335 and SG also benefited enormously. From the early 1970s, Clapton has been most closely associated with the Fender Stratocaster —probably a result of the ubiquitous influence of Jimi Hendrix. Clapton's most famous guitar, known as "Blackie," was, in fact, built from the best parts of six late-1950s Strats purchased for $100 each!

Unplugged

Despite a low point in his career in the 1980s, Clapton has maintained his position as the preeminent guitarist of his generation, thus reestablishing himself in the top echelon of blues guitarists, as well as presiding over a resurgence in the popularity of the acoustic guitar. His *Unplugged* album is by far the best-selling album to come from the MTV TV show of that name. It contains the definitive version of "Tears in Heaven," Clapton's heartfelt homage to his four-year-old son Conor, who tragically died after falling from a 53rd-story window.

Lesson 12.4: Blues Improvisation 1

The blues makes a great vehicle for learning to improvise. Most blues-influenced recordings feature at least one instrumental solo (of 12 measures) or more.

Licks

The great blues guitarists such as B. B. King and Eric Clapton often seem to be *speaking* as directly with their guitars as with their vocals—if not more so.

The best way to learn blues improvisation is to treat it like a language and learn some vocabulary. Guitarists often talk about "licks," and while it's important not to get stuck in the rut of wheeling out the same old licks all the time, most players seem to have a cache of those they like best, which they can pull out if they get stuck. You can expand your vocabulary of licks by listening to the great players. After a while, you'll probably find that you can absorb the essence of a given blues player's style without working out his solos note for note—the key is to keep listening.

The flattened fifth

The licks on the following pages are all in the key of A for the sake of simplicity and comparison. Most of them use the blues scale. This is derived from the minor pentatonic (see page 146) with the addition of one extra note: the flattened fifth. Try the scale first, in fifth position for the key of A (the index finger at the fifth fret).

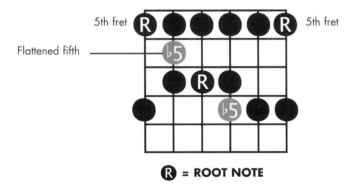

BLUES SCALE (IN THE KEY OF A)

The blues originated in the southern United States—the often gloomy quality of the music being informed by the tough lives of the black rural poor. The blues tradition continues today in many forms and has universal appeal.

Robert Johnson

ca.1909–1938
GUITARS: UNKNOWN

Recommended Listening:

The Complete Recordings

Robert Johnson is a truly mythical figure. Perhaps the most famous Delta blues singer and guitarist, legend has it that as a young man in Mississippi, ho was consumed with a burning desire to become a great blues musician.

The man who sold his soul

The story says that he was instructed to go down to the local crossroads at midnight, where a large man appeared. He took Johnson's guitar from him, tuned it, and handed it back to him—Johnson had sold his soul to the devil in return for his astounding musical talent. His death is also shrouded in mystery. He is said to have died after drinking poisoned whiskey, given to him by the jealous husband of a lover. Those who claimed to have been there swore he was last seen alive foaming at the mouth, crawling around on all fours, hissing and snapping at onlookers like a mad dog. His last words, written on a scrap of paper, were "I pray that my redeemer will come and take me from my grave."

Chicago style

While the reality may be less glamorous than the legend, Johnson is without a doubt the most influential blues musician of the twentieth century. He played with the young Howlin' Wolf and

mentored Elmore James. And it was Johnson who persuaded Muddy Waters to take up the blues. These crucial figures created the Chicago rhythm 'n' blues sound—essentially Robert Johnson electrified. In this way, Johnson directly influenced the rock 'n' roll music that was to come.

Delta blues

However, claims of Johnson's originality may be exaggerated. He was very much a man of his time, influenced by his peers. He was certainly influenced by Son House, a musician who, more than anyone else, invented Delta blues, and would have listened to blues singers of the day such as Leroy Carr. Several of

Johnson's songs are based on those of Kokomo Arnold, who was the source for the famous "Sweet Home Chicago."

Blues combination

Johnson's importance lies in the fact that he combined these influences to create something greater than the sum of its parts, adapting piano boogie bass for guitar, blending the jazzy inventiveness of Lonnie Johnson with the wailing vocals of Skip James.

Prized recordings

Robert Johnson recorded only 29 songs during his lifetime, which have been in continual circulation ever since through various compilations and bootlegs. Notable tracks include "Walking Blues" and "Crossroads."

Long-lasting legacy

Many have become blues standards, covered by players as diverse as Eric Clapton, Steve Miller, and Led Zeppelin. Through his influence on the electric blues players of the mid-twentieth century, Johnson was instrumental in shaping such rock 'n' roll bands as the Rolling Stones and the Beatles and, through them, most popular music since. In the words of modern bluesman Keb' Mo', "It all seem to revolve around Robert Johnson."

Lesson 12.5: Blues Improvisation 2

The following licks can be used anywhere in the twelve-bar sequence. Try them with a friend (or a recording of yourself), playing the chords in A, or just use them to play along with any blues record in A. All of these should be played with a shuffle feel.

BLUES LICKS

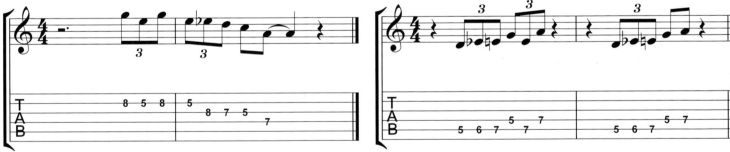

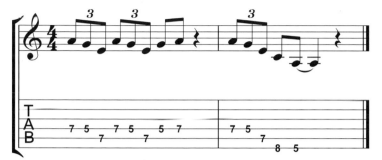

Blues end phrases

The phrases on this page are particularly useful as endings. First, the classic blues ending. This actually moves out of the blues scale shape but is really quite easy. The first measure should be played with the second finger on the G string and the third finger on the top E string, at the same fret, moving downward together, one fret at a time:

Here's a common variation:

Here's another great ending phrase, popularized by Duke Ellington. Shift down to the second position (index finger at the second fret) to play it.

EXPERT'S TIP: Learn the licks
Learn the licks in this chapter, and try to play them in different keys. Commit to memory the minor pentatonic shape. Having these skills will improve and enhance your playing and give you a good "rock foundation." Remember that the blues musical structure forms the basis for hundreds, if not thousands, of popular songs.

Lead
Techniques

String Bending

Blues Party Piece

The Hendrix Chord

Lead Techniques Exercises

Let's take a look at a few techniques that make the difference between just playing notes and getting more expressive power out of them. These techniques are used by guitarists all the time. You should aim to make them so much a part of your vocabulary that you don't even think about them.

Lesson 13.1: String Bending

Almost every rock guitar solo ever recorded has made use of this technique. While string bending is possible on acoustic or classical guitars, the extra tension in the strings can make it rather difficult, so it's usually considered in terms of electric guitar technique.

Bend the string—raise the pitch
"String bending" describes the technique perfectly. The left hand bends the string being played, stretching the string and thereby raising its pitch. If this is done as the note sounds, you will actually hear the note bending.

Let's take a look at string bending in action. The string is pulled, or pushed, away from its naturally straight course. Either way, the pitch of the string is raised. In practice, the choice is dictated by the string being bent. The outer strings are generally bent toward the center of the neck, to avoid pulling them off the fretboard; the D and G strings can be bent in either direction.

Notice that the fingers behind the fretting finger are on the string, too. This adds strength. Most players bend only notes played by the third or fourth finger. It's perfectly possible to bend with the first finger. Obviously, it is impossible to use any other fingers to add strength.

Bend outer strings toward the center of the fretboard. The D and G strings can be bent in either direction.

Using other fingers can give you the necessary added strength to bend the strings.

There are several types of string bend in common use—all can be mastered with a little practice.

Simple bend

The easiest bend to execute, this generally involves bending the note played by either a whole or half step. The following bend involves playing a D on the G (3rd) string and bending it by a whole step to reach the note E. Try it with the third finger, using the first and second fingers for support. Check this against the note E—the open top E string is the easiest to find—to make sure the bend is reaching its target.

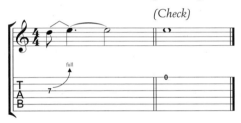

Now try bending the note by only a half step to reach the note E♭.

Bend and release

This involves bending a note, by either a half or whole step, and then releasing the bend so that the note returns to its original pitch.

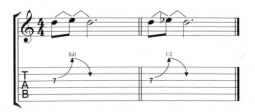

Prebend and release

Here, the note is bent *before* being played, and then it is released. In this way, it's possible to achieve the sound of bending downward. This takes some time and experience to perfect.

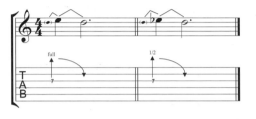

Hammer-on

Hammer-on involves picking a note and then fretting a higher note on the same string, *without* picking the second note. Some force is required when placing the second finger on the string, so that the second note sounds at around the same volume as the first, hence the term "hammer-on."

Pull-off

The opposite of a hammer-on: two fingers are placed on the string, and the higher note is played first. The higher fretting finger is pulled off the string, revealing the lower note, which then sounds. This technique is tricky to perfect—don't be put off if you find it hard to get much sound out of the lower note at first. Ultimately, the finger playing the higher note should not simply be

removed, but it should, to some extent, "pick" the string.

Slide

A fairly easy technique, the slide simply involves sliding the fretting finger up or down the neck as the note sounds. The sound can die away if sufficient pressure is not applied, but this should not be tried if you are an absolute beginner, since there is a risk of cutting the skin if you haven't been playing long enough to have formed calluses on your fingertips.

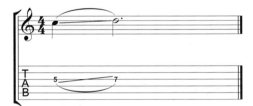

B. B. King

1925–

GUITARS: GIBSON LUCILLE SIGNATURE

Recommended Listening:

The Ultimate Collection

A vegetarian, nonsmoking teetotaler, B. B. King hardly epitomises the rock 'n' roll lifestyle. A formidable improviser, every modern blues master, from Eric Clapton to Stevie Ray Vaughan, has learned from King's heartfelt vocals, rock-solid rhythm, and—most of all—his childlike enthusiasm for his music.

Gospel and blues

King grew up as part of a sharecropping family in Mississippi, and from an early age, he came to love the music of T-Bone Walker, Lonnie Johnson, and Django Reinhardt. During the week, he would pick cotton, and on Sundays, he would sing in a gospel choir in his hometown, where he first discovered his musical talent. King soon picked up the guitar, and in 1946, he moved to Memphis, where his cousin, country blues guitarist Bukka White, helped him perfect his blues technique.

Calling himself Pepticon Boy (and later Beale Street Blues Boy, which would first be shortened to Blues Boy, and then just B. B.), King appeared on the Memphis radio station WDIA. This led to a recording contract with Los Angeles's RPM Records, and in the 1950s, King recorded many enduring R&B classics such as "Woke Up This Morning" and "Every Day I Have the Blues."

It was during this era that B. B. King first named his guitar Lucille, a name that he would subsequently give to all of his guitars for the following reason. In a dance hall in Twist, Arkansas, two men began fighting over a woman. They knocked over the burning barrel of kerosene that had been lit to heat the place. The hall was evacuated, but once outside, King realized that he had left his guitar onstage, and he rushed into the burning building to retrieve his Gibson acoustic. The next day, King found out that the woman the two men had been fighting over was named Lucille. He has called every guitar he has had since after that woman as a reminder "never to do a thing like that again."

Bottleneck blues

B. B. King has continued to tour, although since the 1980s, he has recorded less and less. From 1951 through 1985, King appeared on *Billboard* magazine's R'n'B charts an impressive 74 times. King has lived an adventurous life, and his instantly recognizable bottleneck-inspired guitar style has influenced just about every blues guitarist. It seems that despite the onslaught of many younger pretenders to the crown, the Blues Boy remains the undisputed king of the blues.

Lesson 13.2: Blues Party Piece

Mastering this blues piece will provide a lot of enjoyment for you and your audience. The techniques required should be within your capabilities at this point in the course. First, the classic "Chuck Berry Boogie" pattern (see lesson 8) is varied by using a "rocking" rhythm. Here, rather than playing all the notes of each chord together, the pattern alternates between the two strings used. The strings should ring on, although palm muting may be used for an alternative effect.

The unison triplet

The other very common blues device is the unison triplet, as in the first measure. This is heard in the playing of many blues players, from Robert Johnson to John Lee Hooker. "Unison" simply means two notes of the same pitch sounding at the same time. In this piece, this is achieved by playing the note E (B string, fifth fret) at the same time as the open top E string, which gives the same note.

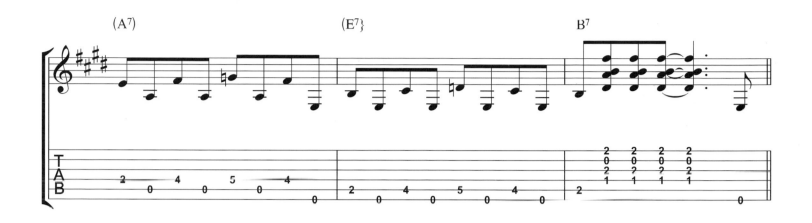

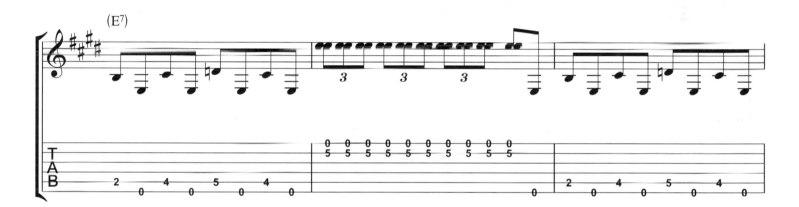

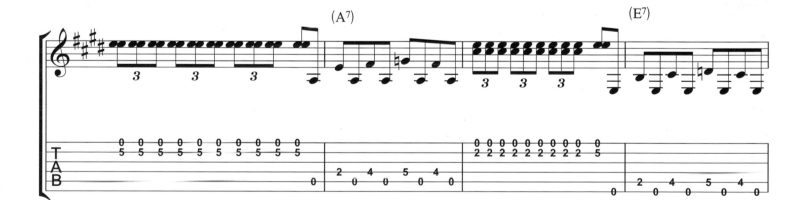

(continued)

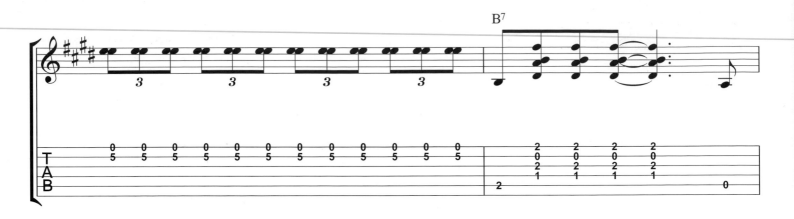

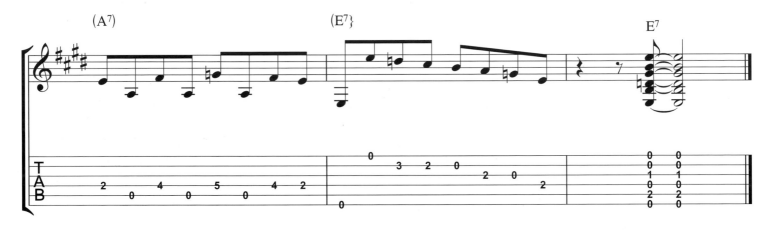

Lesson 13.3: The Hendrix Chord

There is one chord that is featured in many styles of music, from blues to jazz, but is particularly identified with Jimi Hendrix. Try it yourself—if you've ever listened to "Purple Haze" or "Voodoo Chile," you'll recognize it instantly. This chord is movable, but in the key of E, as shown below, either of the open E strings can be played as well.

The classic Hendrix riff (right) uses the E7(#9) chord against the open low E string. Try combining this chord with a G and an A chord too.

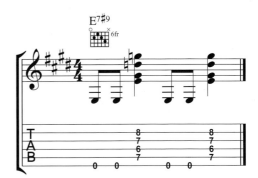

CHORD E7(#9)

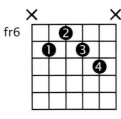

EXPERT'S TIP: Distortion

If there is one pioneering exponent of sonic distortion, that person is Jimi Hendrix. Try the Hendrix chord using different volumes, adjusting your gain controls on your amp to see if you can develop your own version of the Hendrix sound.

Jimi Hendrix

1942–1971

GUITARS: FENDER STRATOCASTER

Recommended Listening:

Are You Experienced?

Axis: Bold As Love

Electric Ladyland

When Jimi Hendrix assaulted the London music scene in 1966, it must have seemed as if he had appeared from out of nowhere. This previously unknown figure revolutionized rock music in the four brief years before his death, pushing back the boundaries of sonic decency with his effects-laden, feedback-soaked rock 'n' roll and wild stage shows. But in fact, this legendary and influential guitarist had served a lengthy musical apprenticeship that began the day his father bought him his first guitar for $5 from a junk shop.

Born in Seattle, Washington, Hendrix was completely self-taught and learned by imitating his heroes. These included such blues greats as Muddy Waters and Albert King, soul musicians such as Curtis Mayfield, and saxophonist Rahsaan Roland Kirk, most famous for playing two saxes at once.

Obsessive perfectionist

After a brief spell in the army, Hendrix moved to Nashville to play in its various blues clubs with his army companion Billy Cox. He soon found more lucrative work as a stand-in guitarist for bands such as the Isley Brothers and that of Little Richard. However, these stars did not always appreciate Hendrix's show-stealing antics, and in 1966 he moved to London to form the Jimi Hendrix Experience, with bassist Noel Redding and drummer Mitch Mitchell. The trio's first single "Hey Joe," was an instant hit, and with the release of his debut album, *Are You Experienced?*, Hendrix was catapulted to fame. In 1967 Hendrix returned to the United States, where he was still relatively unknown, to play the Monterey Pop Festival on the recommendation of Paul McCartney, and Hendrix's electrifying performance won him international recognition.

A perfectionist, Hendrix suffered from bouts of insecurity and had an incessant desire to break new musical boundaries. Toward the end of his life, Hendrix spent most of his time improvising in his Electric Ladyland studio with anyone who happened to be around. He disbanded the Experience, forming Band of Gypsies with Buddy Miles and his old friend Billy Cox, but the results, while at times brilliant, were never as consistent as his earlier efforts.

The Hendrix legacy

In 1970 Hendrix died of a sleeping pill overdose. He left behind more than 300 unreleased recordings besides the five LPs and various singles he recorded in his lifetime. An adventurous sonic explorer, he pioneered the use of distortion, feedback, and effects units such as the wah-wah pedal. Famous for his showmanship during his life, after his death the true importance of his music has become apparent. Hendrix blended funk, rock, and blues effortlessly, creating some of the most passionate and soulful rock guitar ever recorded.

Hendrix's legacy continues to this day. His influence is immediately obvious in the music of many well-known musicians, including Prince, Lenny Kravitz, Hawksley Workman, Slash, and Stevie Ray Vaughan.

Lesson 13.4: Lead Technique Exercises

The following exercises will help you become fluent with these new techniques, first separately and then together. Concentrate on getting a smooth, fluid sound.

HAMMER-ON AND PULL-OFF

This exercise is in fifth position, with the first finger at the fifth fret. Consult the TAB to tell you where to find the notes in this position.

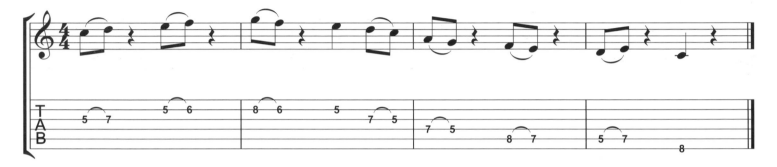

BENDS

Stay in fifth position for this exercise. The G-string bends should be played by the third finger and supported by the first two fingers. The B-string bends should be played by the fourth finger and supported by the first three fingers.

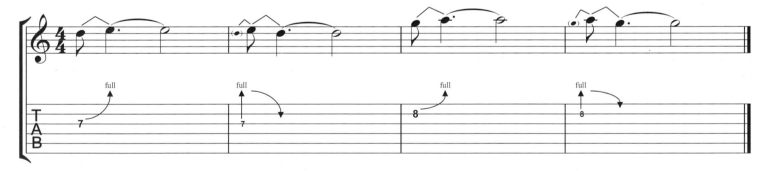

EXPERT'S TIP: Even tempo

It's important that when you are playing, the tempo stays even and you allow the music to flow smoothly. Not all musicians have a natural or perfect sense of timing. It may take months or even years of practice. Try counting evenly as you play, or tap the beat with your foot—or better still, use a metronome to improve tempo.

SLIDE

This exercise is organized into groups of three. Play the first note, slide up two frets, then slide back to the starting note. Try to keep the volume constant by maintaining pressure on the string and observing the written rhythm.

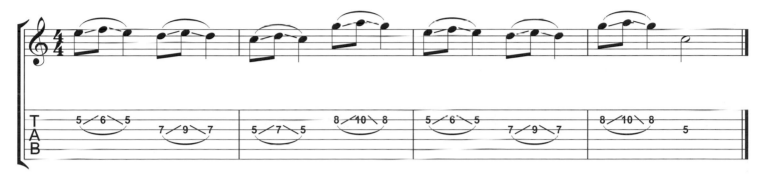

PUTTING IT ALL TOGETHER

This exercise uses bends, hammer-ons, pull-offs, and slides. The groups of three notes (marked *) involve both a hammer-on and a pull-off. Only the first note is struck.

Eddie Van Halen

1955–
GUITARS: VARIOUS

For many, Eddie Van Halen is the ultimate guitar hero. In an era characterized by big hair and little talent, his innovative two-handed tapping techniques, dazzling speed, and unparalleled rhythmic sensibility have set him apart from the crowd and influenced generations of guitarists.

Classically trained in piano from an early age, Van Halen started playing the drums while his older brother played guitar. However, when Eddie was out on his paper route, Alex would bang away at Eddie's drums and soon surpassed him in skill, so they swapped instruments. Eddie became obsessed with the guitar, even skipping school to play all day. By the age of 14, he had learned many of Eric Clapton's solos note for note.

Eddie and Alex began playing house parties and clubs around the Los Angeles area, where they met David Lee Roth, who joined the band —primarily so they could avoid paying to borrow his PA system. It was Roth who suggested that the group name themselves Van Halen. Van Halen signed to Warner Bros in 1977, and the band's classic eponymous debut album reached record stores a year later—the first of a string of multiplatinum albums and sold-out tours.

When heavy rock met R&B
Eddie Van Halen crossed over into pop territory when he was asked to play a guitar solo on the song "Beat It" on Michael Jackson's famous 1982 album *Thriller*. The combination of Jackson's voice and pop sound with Van Halen's guitar work melded several genres. Consequently, the Van Halen song "Jump" became popular in discos and R&B clubs.

Solid rock
While Eddie Van Halen is one of the most solid rock-rhythm players around, he has inevitably become known for his solo skills. The song "Eruption" from Van Halen's debut album provides a wonderful showcase of fret-melting finger work, outrageous "divebombs" (using a whammy bar to descend many octaves below the guitar's normal range), and two-handed tapping antics. Van Halen did not, in fact, invent the tapping technique, which involves using the picking hand to hammer-on and pull-off in combination with the fretting hand to produce blisteringly fast arpeggio patterns. Eddie credits Jimmy Page's solo from "Heartbreaker" (*Led Zeppelin II*) as his inspiration, but it has become Van Halen's trademark, making him perhaps the most imitated guitarist alive.

"Wonderful Tonight"

Words and Music by **Eric Clapton and Michael Kamen**

Here's a chance to put both your lead and rhythm guitar skills into practice with Eric Clapton's classic ballad "Wonderful Tonight." In the song itself, the lead guitar figure is shown using cue notes (small notes) on the vocal stave, but it's also written out in full here.

The main technique is the prebend and release; the final ascending phrase uses slides.

The rhythm guitar part is shown in full in the TAB and uses arpeggios. Although you may want to play this using your fingers in the manner of acoustic fingerstyle guitar, Eric (and most other electric players) plays it using a pick.

New chord

There is one new chord in this song: D/F# ("D *over* F sharp," or "D with F# in the bass.") This is an inversion, which means that F# is used as the lowest (bass) note instead of the root of the chord (D). This type of chord is very useful for joining other chords together while maintaining a melodic bass line.

LEAD PART

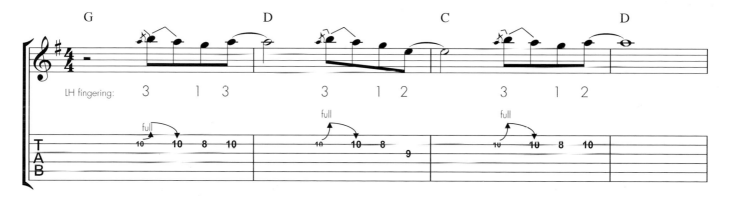

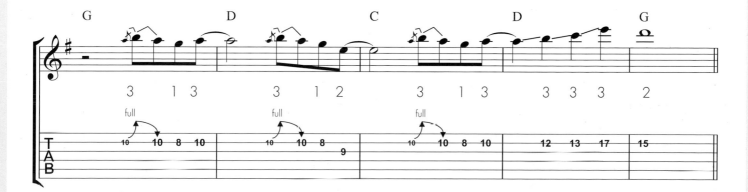

(continued)

1. It's late in the eve - ning,   she's wond-'ring what clothes
2. We go to a par - ty,   ev - 'ry-one turns

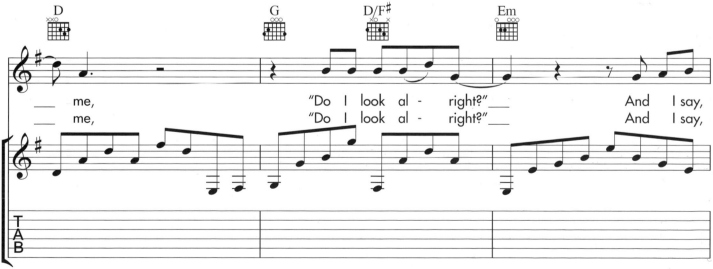

(continued)

1. "Yes,   you   look   won-der - ful___ to - night."
2. "Yes,   I   feel   won-der - ful___ to - night."

I   feel   won - der - ful,___   be -

lesson 14

Rocking Harder

More Power Chords

Trade Secrets

Rock Party Piece

In this chapter we'll look at some of the secrets of heavy rock guitar. You may think that this style is dominated by fretboard pyrotechnics way beyond the scope of this book, and this is true to an extent, particularly where lead guitar is concerned. However, the basics of playing heavy-rock rhythm guitar are fairly simple.

Lesson 14.1: More Power Chords

Crank it up

The two-note power chord reigns supreme in heavy rock. If you turn the "gain" on your amp up as far as it will go, it soon becomes apparent that full major and minor chords do not make a pleasant noise—in fact, they are completely unusable. Root-and-fifth power chords work wonderfully well, however, and have come to form the basis of most heavy rock/metal, from Iron Maiden to Marilyn Manson.

So crank up the distortion (and the volume) and try these simple power chord riffs.

GOTHIC CHUG

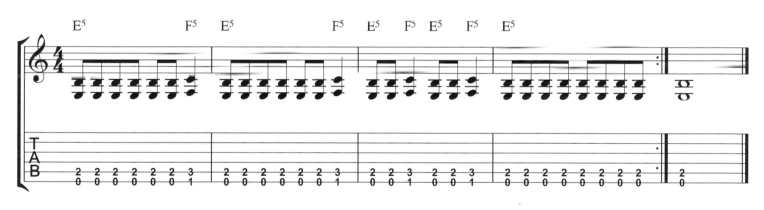

GREEN STEW

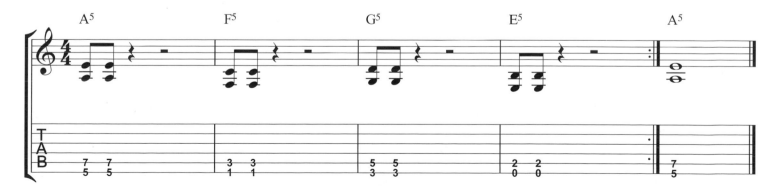

DOWN, DOWN, DOWN

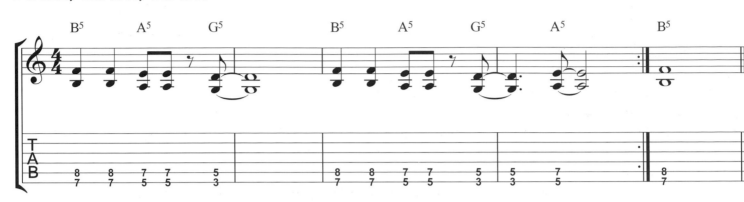

SMOKIN'

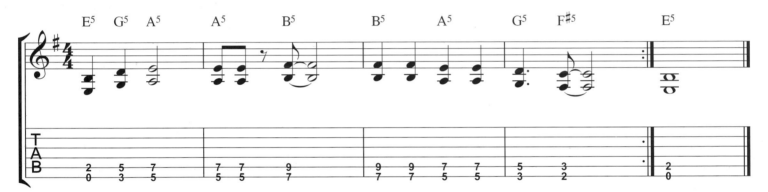

MAKE IT LAST

One of the joys of heavy distortion is that the guitar can be made to sustain much longer notes; this applies both to chords and lead playing. Try this:

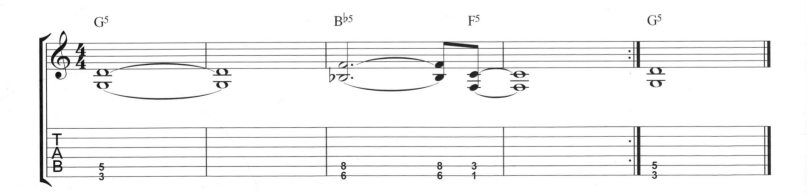

Steve Vai

1960—
GUITAR: IBANEZ JEM SIGNATURE

Recommended Listening:
Flex-Able
Passion & Warfare

Steve Vai has been hailed alongside guitarists such as Eddie Van Halen and Yngwie Malmsteen as one of the technical geniuses of modern electric guitar. Though he has been criticized for emphasizing showmanship over musical content, for every critic there is a fan attracted to his quirky, angular sound.

Experimental rock
Born in Carle Place, New York, Vai became interested in his teens in rock giants such as Jimi Hendrix, Alice Cooper, and Led Zeppelin. At Berklee College of Music, Vai took lessons from one Joe Satriani—the beginning of a lasting musical partnership. During college he became fascinated with the music of Frank Zappa and transcribed many of his most challenging pieces. When Vai sent Zappa one of his transcriptions, Zappa was so impressed that he hired Vai to transcribe his huge repertoire of experimental symphonic rock.

Vai toured the world with Zappa, who gave him the nickname Little Italian Virtuoso, and played on albums such as *Ship Arriving Too Late to Save a Drowning Witch* and *Them or Us*. On his departure from Zappa's band, Vai moved to California to record his first solo album, *Flex-Able*. In the following years, Vai was involved in collaborations with musicians such as Graham Bonnet

of Alcatrazz (replacing Yngwie Malmsteen), David Lee Roth, and Whitesnake. In 1990 he released his third solo album, *Passion & Warfare*.

Master of the seven-string guitar
Aside from his career as a recording artist and performer, Steve Vai has collaborated with Ibanez Guitars to create the JEM Signature Series, featuring the famous "monkey grip." He is a prolific producer and owns two studios. Vai is also credited with the revival of the seven-string guitar,

originally conceived in the 1940s by jazz guitarist George Van Epps.

Vai has also featured in various feature films, including *Bill & Ted's Bogus Journey* and the 1986 movie *Crossroads*, engaging in a guitar duel as the demonically inspired Jack Butler.

In a modern music scene dominated by garage bands and manufactured pop, Steve Vai is an example of a guitarist who has managed to combine technique and theoretical knowledge with a rock 'n' roll attitude.

"Walk This Way"

Words and Music by **Steven Tyler and Joe Perry**

Rock riffs don't come any catchier than Aerosmith's "Walk This Way," which was rerecorded and became a massive hit single in 1986 by Run DMC featuring Aerosmith. "Walk This Way" drives thousands of music store employees to distraction every Saturday afternoon as local kids, ostensibly "trying" guitars, crank this song out to impress each other.

It's such a great riff, in fact, that it simply stands on its own without lyrics, adding punctuation to the flow of the song.

THE RIFF

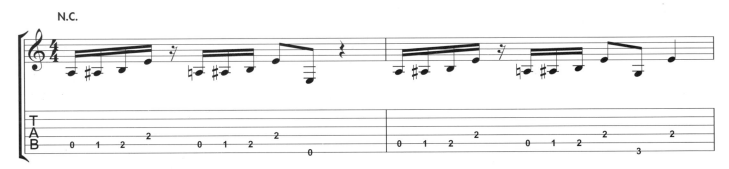

A5 chord

In the song, the main riff ends on an A5 power chord. This consists of the open A string, with the next two strings barred. If you extend the barre to the B string, you'll get a full A chord—this works fine too. This chord leads into the verse riff. The original is actually quite tricky, but this simplified version does the job well:

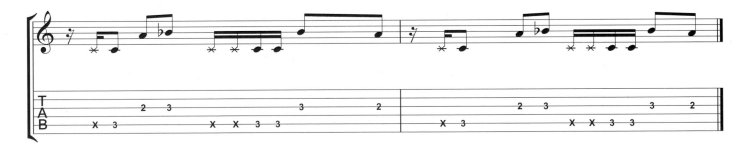

Muted notes

Feel free to add more muted notes instead of resting. This riff powers the verses, so there are no chord patterns in them. After the second verse the chorus uses simple power chords (C5 and F5) to the rhythm of the vocal line. Our simplified arrangement then returns to four bars of the main riff before ending on the A5 chord.

1. Back - seat lov - er   that's always un-der-cov - er, and I talked   'til my dad-dy say,   He said, you
2. She   start swing in' with the boys   in   school,   and her feet are fly-in' up in the air__   Sing in':

ain't   seen noth in' til you're down   on   a muf-fin then you're sure   to change_ your way.   There's a
Hey did-dle did-le with the   kit-ty in the mid-dle and you're swing-in' like you did-n't care.   So I

(continued)

Lesson 14.2: Trade Secrets

One of the trademarks of recent "nu" metal is the fast-moving power chord line—in other words, a fast melody harmonized in fifths.

Too many fingers

Beyond a certain speed, moving a standard power chord shape around fast (using the first and third fingers) starts to get clumsy, so we need some way of playing big, heavy power chords with just one finger.

"Drop D" Tuning

The only way to do this is to change the pitch relationship between the guitar's bottom strings by using an alternative tuning method. Dropping the pitch of the bottom string by a whole step to the note D (known as "drop D" tuning) puts the bottom strings a fifth apart.

Tuning to a D

This can be achieved either by using a chromatic tuner, by making the seventh fret (instead of the fifth) of the bottom string the same pitch as the open A string, or by playing the bottom string in unison with the open D (fourth) string. When these strings are both tuned to D, they will be an octave apart.

One-finger chords

A perfect octave gives a very pure sound, which is easy to identify, especially when using distortion—until they are perfectly in tune, these two strings will sound horrible when played together! Root-and-fifth power chords are then possible using just one finger. The exercises shown below use "drop D" tuning.

DROP D POWERCHORD 1

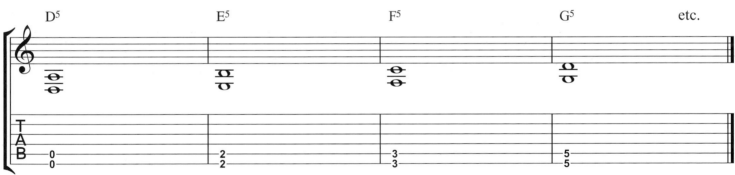

DROP D POWERCHORD 2

This is not really considered a barre, since only two strings are used. However, it's very easy to use a barre on the three bottom strings, adding the octave to the chord.

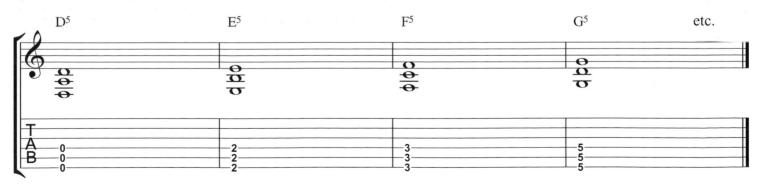

DROPPIN' IT

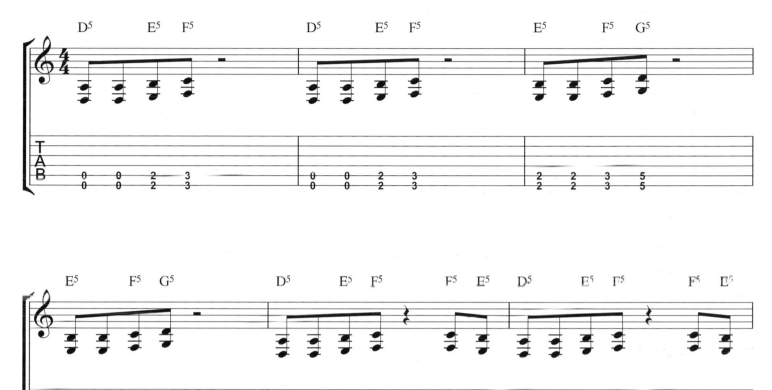

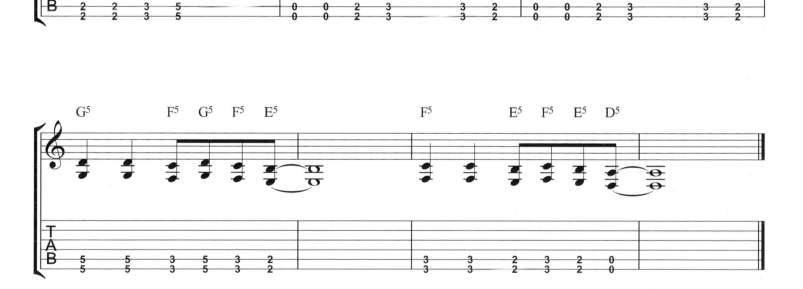

Lesson 14.3: Rock Party Piece

Here's a rock workout using a range of techniques seen in this book and some quintessentially "rock" chords. There's a new rhythm here too: the combination of two sixteenth notes and an eighth note, for example, in measure one, beat two. Where pairs of eighth notes can be counted as "1 and" or "2 and," in this combination the second sixteenth note comes between the beat and the "and." When counting this it can be helpful to say the second note as any vowel sound, typically "e." So, this rhythm can be counted: 1-e-and, 2-e and…

Getting
Funky

Sixteenths

Funk Practice

Minimal Funk

Let's now take a look at the funkier side of guitar playing. By "funky," we're talking about funk, disco, soul, and pop—a good slice of all the hit records of the last 30 years have featured funk guitar. All of these styles have a lot in common—the essential ingredients are sixteenth notes.

Lesson 15.1: Sixteenths

As you may have guessed, a sixteenth note is half as long as an eighth note. In 4/4 there are four sixteenths per beat (sixteen per measure).

Beat   1   2   3   4

The basic strumming technique for funky guitar is actually very simple, even when it sounds complex.

The "funk chord"

Before we delve into it, let's look at the funk chord. The ninth chord will sound instantly familiar if you have ever listened to the music of performers such as James Brown, Tower of Power, or Prince.

This shape may seem hard at first but it's worth persevering. We have already seen barre chords using the first finger. In this chord the third finger forms the barre. Actually, it's called a *half barre*, since not all of the strings are covered.

The E9 "funk chord" shape can be used at any position on the fretboard. Even though it is a half barre chord, it should be used in the same way as a barre chord.

E9

6th fret

Get into the groove

Almost all funk grooves involve a running right-hand movement in sixteenths. Rhythmic interest is added to this, but the right hand never stops strumming up and down!

If you have a metronome or drum machine, try this exercise with a click or drum pattern at around 80 bpm. There should be four strums (down, up, down, up) for each beat.

Keep this going until it feels natural and comfortable. Now try incorporating a slide into the pattern. Start with the E♭9 chord (one fret lower) on the first beat of the measure, then slide up to the E9 shape for the rest of the measure.

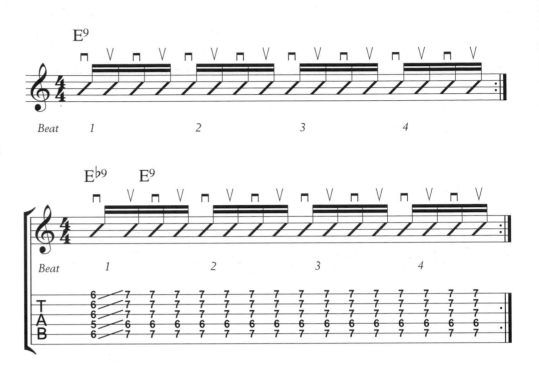

Nile Rogers (center), with his band Chic, fused distinctive funk-based guitar riffs with a disco beat and in the 1970s enjoyed great success on dance floors all over the world.

Rests

An almost infinite number of funky patterns can be derived from this simple groove, merely by inserting rests. The right hand still keeps moving in sixteenths, but some are "missed" rather than "hit." Try the variations below. Then, when you're feeling confident, invent some of your own, simply by deciding when to hit the strings and when to miss them.

FUNK VARIATIONS

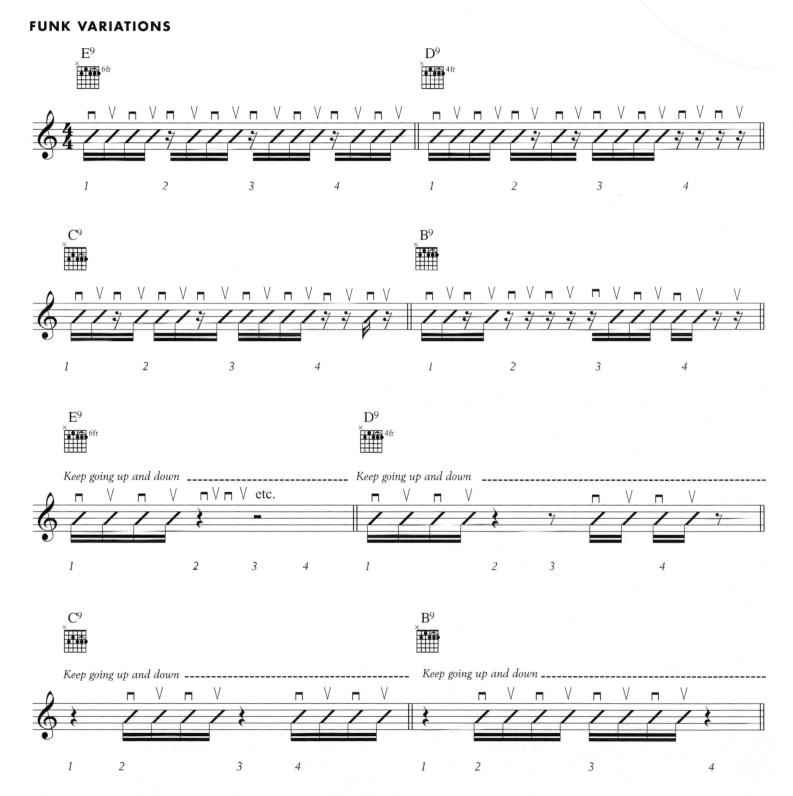

Lesson 15.2: Funk Practice

Lead fills

This practice piece combines the sort of sixteenth-note rhythm playing studied in this chapter with simple funky lead fills. Do you recognize the basic chord sequence? That's right, it's the 12-bar blues yet again—it's very common in this style too.

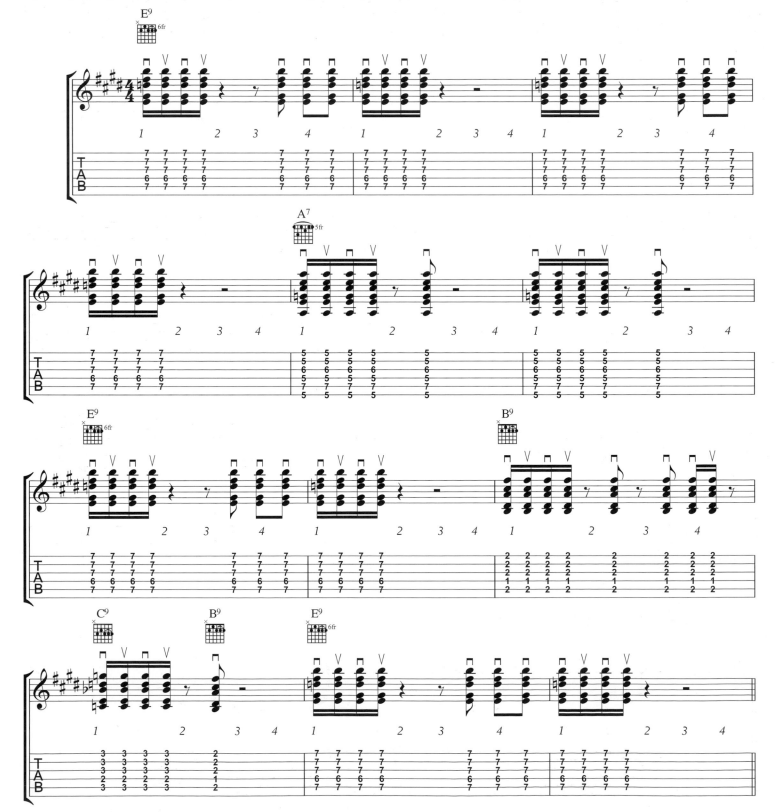

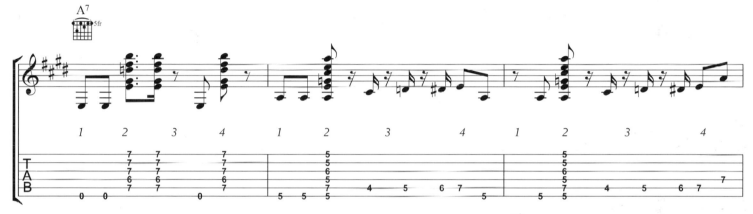

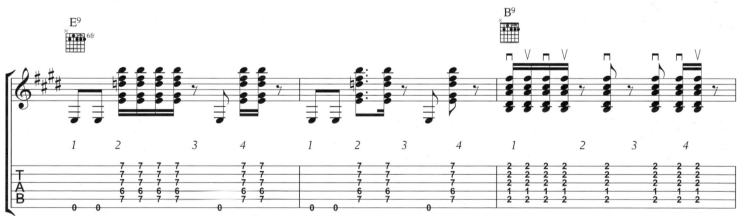

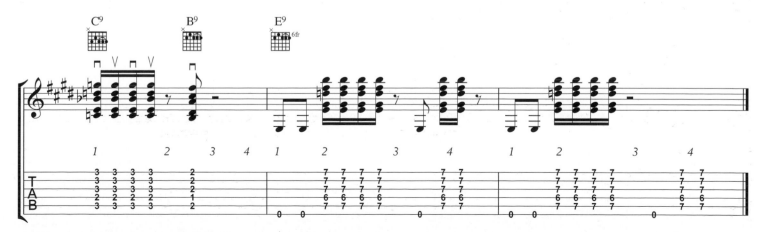

Lesson 15.3: Minimal Funk

Less is more

A lot of funky guitar parts are actually deceptively simple, once you have mastered the basic technique. One popular sound involves playing a repetitive single-note riff with palm muting. As with sixteenth-note strum patterns, it helps to keep the right hand moving in sixteenths.

THRILL ME

HAMMERED

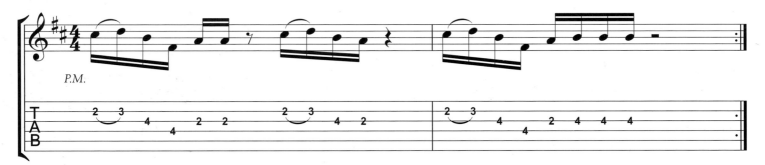

DARK FUNK

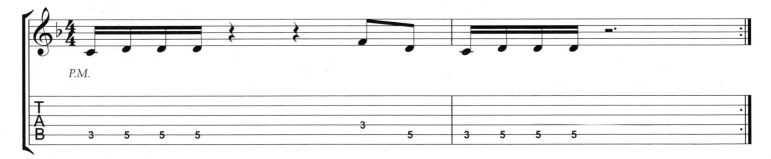

Prince

1958—
GUITARS: CUSTOM GUITARS, HOHNER TELECASTER COPY

Recommended Listening:

Purple Rain

Parade

Sign 'O' the Times

It's easy to forget that Prince Rogers Nelson, the man once known as "The Artist Formerly Known As Prince" (but now known as Prince), is a superb guitarist—possibly because it's only one of his many talents, and the one that he makes the least noise about. Many of his greatest records feature few other people.

Man with a mission
He's a pretty serious pianist, bass player, and drummer, as well as being perfectly at home behind the desk recording, producing, and mixing his own creations.

Prince is one of the music world's chameleons. Each of his records (particularly at his peak in the mid-to-late 1980s) declares a bold new direction for himself and—soon enough—the rest of the pop world.

Rock and funk hybrid
Prince's apparent influences are many and varied, the most obvious names being James Brown, Sly Stone, Jimi Hendrix, Stevie Wonder, and Joni Mitchell. His relentless musical experimentation is particularly reminiscent of Joni's equally adventurous output, and there are numerous references to her in his lyrics; however, the funk influence is perhaps the most musically obvious. Songs such as "Kiss" are now held up as classics

almost on a par with James Brown's "Sex Machine."

Among Prince's many talents there's an undoubted ability to rock, too, as evidenced in songs such as "Let's Go Crazy," with its blistering solo, and "Purple Rain."

In later years, Prince's musical and public personae have become even stranger (including changing his name to an unpronounceable symbol, and back), and the funk influence has moved to the fore once more.

191

Country Guitar

Country Bend

Fun with Tunings

The guitar has been just as central to the development of country music as it has to the blues. From the Carter Family and Hank Williams to the slick sounds coming out of Nashville today, the guitar has always been the sonic driving force in country music.

Lesson 16.1: Country Bend

There really isn't one single style of country guitar playing. Through the years country music has incorporated acoustic strumming, fingerpicking, slide guitar, electric "twang," and fast and furious "chicken picking" in the style of James Burton.

Let's take a look at a few of country's "signature sounds."

The double-string bend

This technique applies for the most part only to electric playing —you'll find it more or less impossible on an acoustic guitar. It involves bending a note on one string while playing a note on another (usually the adjacent string). The most popular double-string bend involves the G and B strings.

Position your third finger on the G string...

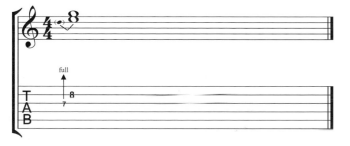

...and bend it, while the fretted B string rings out.

This example is in fifth position. The third finger performs a whole-step bend on the G string (7th fret) while the pinky plays the B string (8th fret). Once the bend is in place, the two strings are a minor third apart, forming a pleasing two-note chord (in fact, the third and fifth of a major chord).

This effect of sliding up to a chord simulates the sound of slide guitar or pedal steel.

193

"Proud Mary"

Words and Music by **John Fogerty**

Country fills

Country guitar blends many styles. From the acoustic guitars and lap steels of the Carter family to the hot licks of James Burton and Albert Lee, with a lot of other styles in between, it's hard to nail down a good definition of country guitar.

There are a few common threads, however. The division between rhythm and lead guitar is fairly sharp in most country music; rhythm parts usually involve simple strumming patterns on acoustic or clean electric guitar. This is often coupled with a separate lead part on electric guitar. Guitar solos are relatively common in country music; apart from his solo the lead guitarist usually interjects fills between vocal phrases. The lead guitarist must really "lead"—the point is to fill out the sound, complementing the vocal line and often playing phrases that seem to "answer" the vocal. You won't make too many friends among singers if your fills are too busy and get in their way, however.

Fills in practice

Let's take a look at a few fills you might use in the next song, the country-rock classic "Proud Mary." These fills are written along with the relevant sections of the melody but will often work elsewhere, too, so it's up to you to experiment with placing them in the song. You'll get the most out of this if a friend plays the rhythm part, or you record it and play along.

Double string bend in action

The fill below uses the double string bend—a staple of the country sound. This technique is described in detail on page 193; the version here is exactly the same, but two frets higher, putting us in the key of D. As shown, the pinky plays the B string, 10th fret, while the third finger (supported by the first and second) bends the G string, 9th fret, up a whole step.

The fill in the last measure is a very simple single note melody, answering the phrase "rolling on the river."

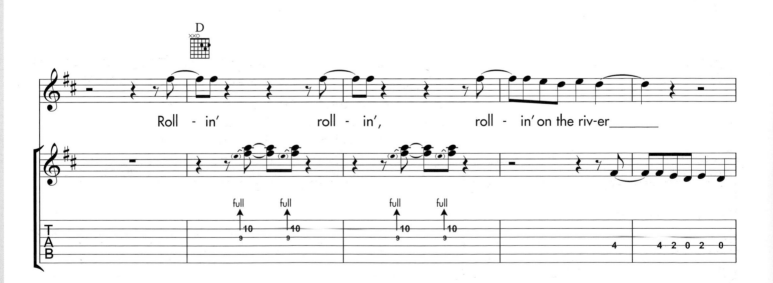

Four-note interjection

The next fill is a perfect, unobtrusive four-note interjection that can be used anywhere the rhythm part is playing the D chord (most of the song, in other words). It works particularly well after the first line of the verse.

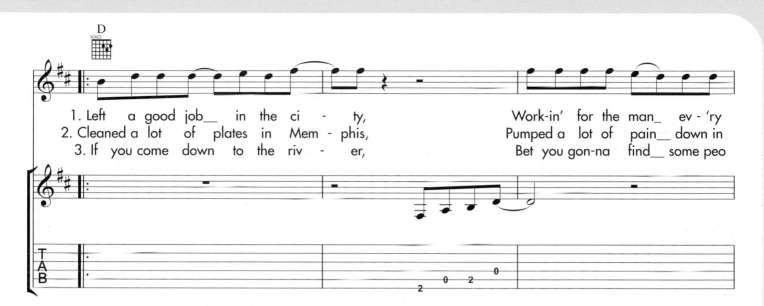

1. Left   a good job__   in the ci - ty,
2. Cleaned a lot   of plates in Mem - phis,
3. If you come down to the riv - er,

Work-in' for the man_ ev - 'ry
Pumped a lot of   pain__ down in
Bet you gon-na   find__ some peo

Hammer-on

This kind of simple fill can be given more of a country "twang" by simply adding a hammer-on (right). Here, a hammer-on is used before the first note of the fill; the hammered note (the open E string) is shown using a smaller "crossed out" note to show that it should be as short as possible, having no rhythmic value of its own.

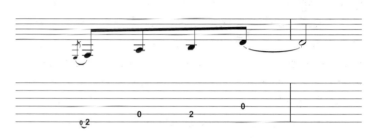

Descending run

Finally, try a simple descending run that works particularly well leading into the verse as shown (or back into the second verse).

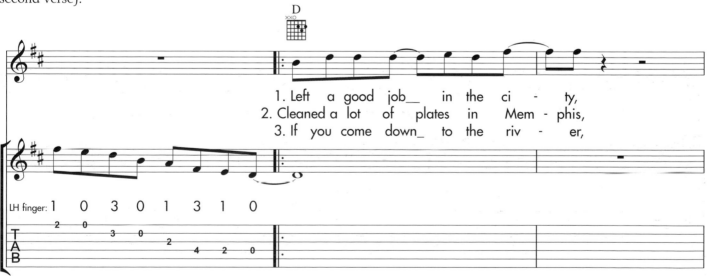

1. Left   a good   job__   in the ci -   ty,
2. Cleaned a lot   of plates in   Mem - phis,
3. If you come down_ to the   riv -   er,

LH finger: 1 0 3 0 1 3 1 0

You'll find this easiest in second position—in other words, the first finger is at the second fret, and plays any notes at that fret. The second finger plays the third fret, and the third finger plays the fourth fret. This is shown in the tab for clarity. Try adding hammer-ons to this one too!

(continued)

The whole song

Here's "Proud Mary" written out in full. We've used the top line format (see page 74), since the rhythm part is very straightforward. The intro uses the chords C, A, G, F, and D in the rhythm shown. For the rest of the song, relaxed eighth-note strumming (down on the beat, up on the off-beat) serves very well.

1. Left   a good job__ in the ci -   ty,
2. Cleaned a lot   of plates in Mem - phis,
3. If you come down to the riv -   er,

Work-in' for the man_ ev - 'ry night and day.
Pumped a lot of pain_ down in New Or-leans,
Bet you gon-na find_ some peo - ple who live

1. And I nev - er lost one min - ute of sleep - in',
2. But I nev - er saw the good__ side of the ci - ty,
3. You don't have to wor - ry, 'cause_ you have no mon-ey,

Worry-in''bout the way things might have been.
'til   I hitched a ride on a riv - er boat queen.
Peo-ple on the riv-er are hap-py to give.

Big wheel keep on   turn - in',   Proud_ Ma-ry keep on   burn - in'.   Roll-

To Coda

- in'   roll - in',   roll - in' on the riv - er_____

James Burton

1939—
GUITAR: FENDER TELECASTER

Recommended Listening:
Elvis Presley: *On Stage: February 1970*
Emmylou Harris: *Elite Hotel*

James Burton's list of credits is more impressive than most: John Denver, Ricky Nelson, Dale Hawkins, Emmylou Harris, Nat King Cole, Johnny Cash, The Byrds, Tom Jones, Waylon Jennings, Henry Mancini, Judy Collins, Frank Sinatra, Johnny Mathis, Buffalo Springfield, Ray Charles, and, of course, Elvis.

The King's guitarist
It is as Elvis's sideman, from his return to live performance in 1969 to the end of his career, that James Burton is best known. The King's band played two or three sets a night, seven days a week, during grueling residences in Las Vegas and tours across the length and breadth of the United States.

Pick and finger combination
Burton's distinctive picking style employs a regular pick between his thumb and index finger, with a fingerpick on the middle finger. He had already built his style around this technique when someone in a music shop told him it was "all wrong," but he went on to use it to great effect on hits by Dale Hawkins ("Suzy-Q," originally an instrumental written by Burton at the age of 15) and Ricky Nelson ("Hello Mary Lou," with its signature James Burton lick), with whom he would star for years on the *Ozzie and Harriet* TV show.

Session man
Burton went on to be the permanent lead guitarist on ABC's *Shindig* show from 1965, backing just about every major star of the era.

With an already huge range of experience, from radio and TV to the Louisiana Hayride and the recording studio, James Burton was the obvious choice for Elvis's live band in 1969. He also somehow managed to keep up a session career, as he does to this day, playing on a significant number of the records you might find filed under "country" in your local record store.

Lesson 16.2: Fun with Tunings

Playing with different tunings can be confusing, although ultimately fascinating and rewarding. Both the confusion and the fascination arise from the fact that the retuned guitar feels like (and essentially is) a completely different instrument. The more the tuning differs from standard tuning, the less its chord shapes resemble standard shapes, and the same applies to melodic playing. On the other hand, altered tunings open up new possibilities: Simple shapes and movements can create sounds that would be difficult or impossible in standard tuning.

A word of warning: raising the pitch of a string by more than a whole step from its conventional pitch, particularly on an acoustic guitar, can result in very high tension and, ultimately, in string breakage. If you want to raise a string beyond this, use a lighter string. Equally, lowering the tuning of a string by more than a third will often result in a flabby tone with little definable pitch—a heavier string will help here.

ALTERED TUNINGS

Let's take a look at a few of the most popular altered tunings in use.

Drop D Tuning

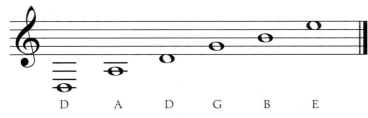

D   A   D   G   B   E

Drop D tuning is based on standard tuning. The only difference is that the bottom string is dropped by a whole step to the note D. This is particularly useful when playing in the key of D (or D minor) as the lower D makes rich, powerful D/Dm chords possible—the higher D string sounds a bit too high to provide a powerful bass.

It's possible to think in terms of standard chord shapes when playing in drop D tuning—just remember that the bottom string, if played, has to be fretted two frets higher than usual. Sometimes other fingers have to be moved around or the voicing changed in order to make this possible.

As we have seen, drop D tuning is also used extensively to enable playing power chords with one finger. Here are the shapes for E, E minor, and G:

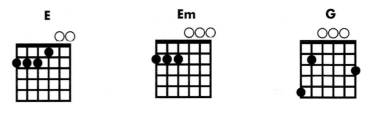

E A D G B D Tuning

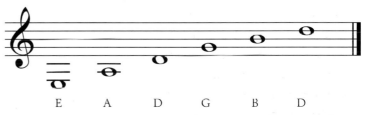

E   A   D   G   B   D

In this tuning, the top E string is dropped by a tone. This turns ordinary open major and minor shapes into some more advanced chords. Here are some useful chords in this tuning:

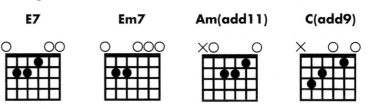

Double Drop D tuning

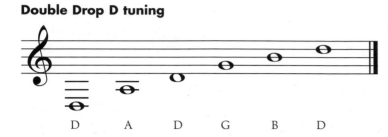

D A D G B D

This is like both of the previous tunings rolled into one—both E strings are lowered to D. This is mainly useful in D or D minor, resulting in a very rich, ringy sound.

OPEN TUNINGS

"Open tunings" are tunings where the strings of the guitar are tuned to the notes of a chord. These tunings are very popular among folk, country, and blues players. In a major key, tonic chords (for example: C in the key of C, D in the key of D) can be played without any fretted notes. The other major chord in the key can be played by barring at the fifth and seventh frets.

Try some of these tunings yourself.

Open G

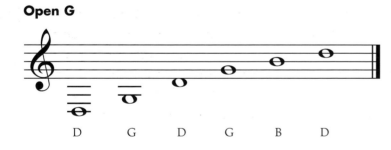

D G D G B D

Open A

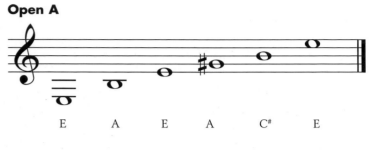

E A E A C♯ E

Open D

E A E A C♯ E

D A D F♯ A D

Open E

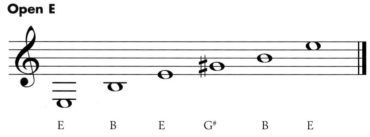

E B E G♯ B E

EXPERT'S TIP:
Tuning to different pitches

By far the best way to tune your guitar to varied pitches is to use an electronic tuner. Electronic tuners are widely available and come in many shapes and forms. Some effects boxes and pedals, and to a limited extent some amplifiers, also offer tuning capabilities. It is possible, too, to tune your guitar by ear, to a keyboard, a piano, or a tuning fork. Ultimately, your choice of tuning method will depend on your own sense of pitch and your ability to detect fine differences between tones and semitones.

Chet Atkins

1924–2001

GUITARS: GRETSCH CHET ATKINS SIGNATURE RANGE, GIBSON SPANISH ELECTRIC

Recommended Listening:

Guitar Legend: The RCA Years

Mark Knopfler & Chet Atkins:
Neck and Neck

Chester Burton ("Chet") Atkins was one of the most influential musicians of the last century, both in terms of the artists he worked with as a sideman and producer, and for his role in bringing country music to a wider audience.

Born in Luttrell, Tennessee, Atkins started playing fiddle at an early age but switched to guitar playing at the age of nine, after trading a rifle for a guitar. Ill health forced Atkins to move to Georgia and it was there that he became an accomplished guitarist.

After graduating from high school in 1942, Chet gained a wealth of experience playing guitar and fiddle in the house bands of radio stations across the South. Unfortunately, he was often fired for "not sounding country enough," since by now he was incorporating elements of the jazz styles of Django Reinhardt, Les Paul, and others.

Atkins's long association with RCA records began in 1947, in the wake of the success of Merle Travis's similarly sophisticated playing style. Although his early records as an RCA recording artist were not successful, involvement in recording sessions for other acts led to a deepening of the Atkins–RCA relationship, with Atkins producing many RCA sessions and, by the mid-1950s, running RCA's Nashville studio. Here Chet played on much of Elvis Presley's early RCA output.

A reorganization at RCA in the wake of Elvis's enormous success led to RCA putting Atkins in charge of the Nashville division in 1957. From this point, Atkins worked with fellow producer Owen Bradley to develop a new style of country music that could compete with the emerging Rock 'n' Roll—dropping old-fashioned fiddles and steel guitars and often adding the Jordanaires (Elvis's vocal quartet), to produce massive hits such as Jim Reeves's "He'll Have To Go" and Don Gibson's "Oh Lonesome Me."

From the 1960s onward, Atkins juggled a corporate career at RCA (he became vice president of their Country Division in 1968) with his own recording and performing career. The 1965 single "Yakety Axe" was a big hit, and Atkins brought many hugely successful recording artists to RCA, including Dolly Parton, Waylon Jennings, Jerry Reed, and Willie Nelson, often playing on their records, too.

The strain of Atkins's workload began to tell and he gave up some of his corporate responsibilities in the 1970s to concentrate on music. Fading health forced him to slow down, and he was eventually dropped as a recording artist by RCA executives, who would not agree to the jazzier direction Atkins wished to take. A long association with Gretsch guitars also ended, as Atkins chose to collaborate with Gibson to produce a signature model nylon-strung electric guitar.

Chet Atkins remained active in music until the end of his life; late albums included a collaboration with Mark Knopfler. His final tally of awards lists eleven Grammys and nine Country Music Association awards.

The World of Guitars

Guitar Types

There's a wide variety of guitars available—electric guitars especially. You may find that guitar magazines and music store assistants assume you have a certain level of familiarity. It can be embarrassing to admit you're not sure of the difference between a single coil and a humbucker, or exactly what a floating trem is. If that's the case, this chapter is for you.

Lesson 17.1: Guitar Types

The worldwide market in musical instruments is bigger today than ever. Most of the instruments available (except for the very cheapest) are made to very high standards, whether in the United States, Europe, or the Far East. Although there is a bewildering array of equipment available, it's also true that the majority (of guitars, at least) are based on a handful of classic designs originated by makers such as Gibson and Fender. Some of these guitars are discussed in detail elsewhere in this book. Guitars available today range from straightforward copies of these designs, which vary in quality but generally look the part, to more sophisticated and experimental versions. Of course, instruments of comparatively original design are also available (though even these generally use basic hardware such as pickups based on classic designs). True classic guitars are also generally still available.

The Gibson Explorer is distinctive in its angular body shape. Not the ideal guitar for a beginner, but more designed for rock star performance—with attitude!

ELECTRIC GUITARS

Let's take a look at some of the most popular and long-lived electric guitar designs, from such famous names from the 1950s and 1960s as Gibson, Fender, and Rickenbacker, to innovative modern designs like the Parker Fly and Steinberger.

Gibson Les Paul and SG

The Les Paul is seen by many as *the* rock guitar, and for good reason. The fat sound of a Les Paul through a Marshall stack at full tilt is a force to be reckoned with, but this guitar is capable of a full range of sounds, from crisp, clean funk to howling rock. It was particularly favored by blues and rock players of the late 1960s and 1970s. Before Eric Clapton discovered the Stratocaster, most of his output with Cream was played on a Les Paul or SG. Other names associated with this guitar include Carlos Santana, Jimmy Page (Led Zeppelin), Tony Iommi (Black Sabbath), Pete Townshend (The Who), and Paul Kossoff (Free, Bad Company).

The Les Paul is actually a very simple design. Various woods have been used through the years, but most Les Paul guitars feature mahogany for the body and neck and maple for the carved top. Most models feature two PAF (Patent Applied For) humbucking pickups with a three-way selector switch

Gibson Les Paul

Pickup type(s):	Two humbuckers
Body type:	Solid
Body wood:	Usually mahogany
Fretboard wood:	Usually mahogany
Number of frets:	22
Controls:	2-volume; 2-tone; 3-way switch
Tremolo or fixed bridge:	Fixed bridge

Gibson SG

Pickup type(s): Two humbuckers

Body type: Solid

Body wood: Mahogany

Fretboard wood: Mahogany

Number of frets: 22

Controls: 2-volume; 2-tone; 3-way switch

Tremolo or fixed bridge: Fixed bridge

(either, middle, or both). The bridge pickup ("lead") is trebly and is the one to use for screaming solos that cut right through the mix. The neck pickup ("rhythm") is good for both clean and crunchy rhythm playing, with greater depth to the sound.

The SG is essentially a stripped-down Les Paul that has a double cutaway. Production costs are reduced since there is no carved top; the sound and other features are generally similar.

Pickups

Most guitar pickups belong to one of two main types: *single coil* pickups and *humbuckers*.

Single-coil pickups generally have six poles (one for each string) with a coil of copper wire forming a single electromagnet around them. Each pole is aligned with one of the guitar strings; string movement translates into electrical impulses.

Single coil pickups are prone to electromagnetic interference (hum) from electrical equipment such as lighting circuits and refrigerators. "Humbucker" pickups (which cancel or "buck" the hum) were invented by Gibson in 1957. They solve the problem by placing two single coils out of phase—so interference, if picked up equally by each coil, is therefore completely eliminated.

Gibson Flying V/Explorer

In the late 1950s, Gibson responded to Fender's radical new designs with its own futuristic body shapes. Most of these were essentially Les Pauls in disguise (in terms of pickup configuration and controls), though some featured tremolo arms.

Though unsuccessful at the time, Gibson reissued these guitars in the late 1960s. Their popularity was boosted by Jimi Hendrix playing a psychedelic Flying V (when not playing his white Strat).

B. C. Rich guitars

The radical shapes of these guitars have inspired many other guitar manufacturers, notably B. C. Rich, whose outrageously shaped guitars (such as The Beast, pictured below) have been a mainstay of heavy rock videos since the early 1980s.

Gibson Flying V

Pickup type(s):	H-H Neck and bridge
Body type:	Solid Flying V
Body wood:	Korina or mahogany
Fretboard wood:	Rosewood or ebony
Number of frets:	22
Controls:	2-volume; 1-tone; 3-way switch
Tremolo or fixed bridge:	Tune-o-matic

Fender Stratocaster

Ask any nonmusician to draw an electric guitar, and chances are the result will look something like a Fender Stratocaster. "Revolutionary" is an overused word, but no other word will do—there was nothing remotely like this guitar when Leo Fender introduced it in 1954. Most electric guitars were simply acoustic archtops with a single primitive pickup. Even the Gibson Les Paul (launched only two years earlier) and Fender's own Telecaster owed a great deal to the traditional guitar shape, for all their departures. With the Stratocaster, Leo Fender threw the rule book out of the window and created a sculpted, asymmetrical body designed for maximum balance and comfort whether being played sitting or standing.

Various tremolo arm designs existed already, but all caused some tuning problems. Fender's spring-tensioned system solved the problem elegantly. Three pickups provided a previously unimaginable array of sounds, with "out-of-phase" sounds available by carefully positioning the switch halfway between two positions. (Today, a five-way switch has made these sounds "officially" available.)

Fender Stratocaster

Pickup type(s):	Three single-coil
Body type:	Solid
Body wood:	Alder or ash
Fretboard wood:	Maple or rosewood
Number of frets:	21
Controls:	Volume; 2-tone (neck pickup and middle pickup); 5-position blade; Tremolo arm
Tremolo or fixed bridge:	Synchronized tremolo

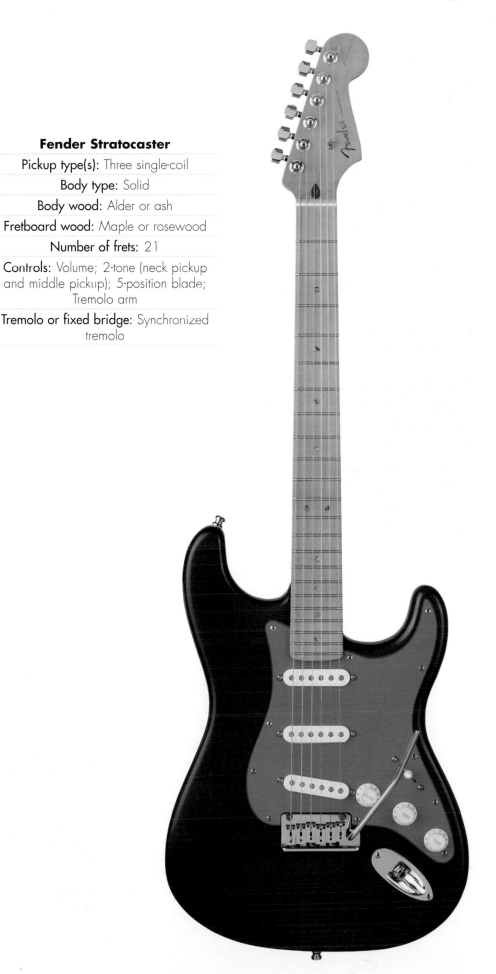

Fender Telecaster

If country music is your thing, you are likely to already own a Telecaster —such is the popularity of this instrument with country players and its close association with this style.

The Telecaster is a two-pickup version of what had been Leo Fender's first venture into guitar making, the Esquire. It is a simple instrument featuring two single-coil pickups, a three-way selector switch, and volume and tone controls. The neck is bolted to the body (a Fender innovation, now widely adopted, to keep costs down and simplify repairs). The bridge unit featured Leo Fender's first attempt at effective intonation adjustment, with three adjustable saddles, although modern Telecasters feature six.

The Telecaster has a large user base outside of country music too: its simple, gutsy tone is popular with blues, rock 'n' roll, funk, and even punk guitar players. James Burton, Bruce Springsteen, Albert Collins and Jon Buckland (Coldplay) are just a few of the players closely associated with this instrument. Various subsequent versions have featured humbuckers, three pickups, and tremolo arms, but none of these has threatened the popularity of the original, basic model.

Fender Telecaster

Pickup type(s):	Two single-coil
Body type:	Solid
Body wood:	Alder or ash
Fretboard wood:	Maple or rosewood
Number of frets:	21 or 22
Controls:	Volume; Delta tone
Tremolo or fixed bridge:	Fixed

Paul Reed Smith guitars

Paul Reed Smith started making guitars during college and hasn't stopped since. As a guitarist himself, he loved playing both Fenders and Gibsons, noting the strengths and weaknesses of each. Fender guitars are generally seen as bright and responsive, if a little "twangy" (although twang is exactly what's required for some styles of music), while Gibsons are thought of as sounding rich and warm but perhaps sounding a little "muddy." Paul Reed Smith set out to create a guitar with the strengths of both and the weaknesses of neither.

Early innovations included a rotary selector system enabling humbuckers to be split and used as single coils, wired in series, or parallel in many combinations.

Smith built his company (now one of the most highly regarded in the business) from nothing, often waiting hours at music venues to make friends with musicians on the road and to secure backstage passes in order to show his designs to star guitarists. Once established, he teamed up with long-time Gibson luthier and guitar guru Ted McCarty, himself a key figure in the development of the Les Paul, to produce the current line of PRS guitars. This includes solid and semisolid models in a variety of stunning exotic woods and finishes. Unsurprisingly, many of these are very expensive, but in recent years cheaper ranges of guitars have been developed and they benefit from the same painstaking research process.

Paul Reed Smith McCarty

Pickup type(s): Treble and bass

Body type: Solid

Body wood: Maple with mahogany

Fretboard wood: Rosewood

Number of frets: 22

Controls: Volume and push/pull tone control, with 3-way toggle pickup selector

Tremolo or fixed bridge: Tail piece bridge

Parker Fly DeLuxe

Pickup type(s): 2 H-H

Body type: Solid

Body wood: Poplar

Fretboard wood: Composite

Number of frets: 24

Controls: Mag volume and tone; Mag/Piezo 3-way selector

Tremolo or fixed bridge: Vibrato bridge

Parker Fly

Launched in the early 1990s, the Parker Fly was the most radically new design since the Fender Stratocaster.

The Fly features several unique innovations; the most well known one is the use of a wooden body with a thin outer shell made of carbon and glass fiber. This creates a guitar with a light, thin body and a smooth, seamless neck-joint that is nonetheless completely stable and rigid.

Other innovations have included the use of piezo transducers, giving access to a range of convincing acoustic guitar sounds. The piezo can be blended with magnetic pickups for various hybrid jazzy sounds too. In fact, the combination of the piezo and the use of humbucking pickups with coil split/tap switches enables them to be used as single coils and makes the Fly one of the most versatile guitars on the market today. Not surprisingly, the top-of-the line Parker guitars are not cheap, but various budget models have been very successful in recent years.

Steinberger guitars

Steinberger guitars are among the most radical ones of the past 20 years.

The original Steinberger design is a classic piece of 1980s minimalism that dispenses with all references to the traditional guitar body shape. These guitars are known as "headless," because the strings are anchored to the end of the neck and tuned using fine-tuners at the bridge, giving improved tuning stability and accuracy. The neck is made of a woven graphite composite—a technology borrowed from the world of sports equipment. Steinbergers are light and ideal travel guitars, but they are also capable of serious sounds, particularly for those with modernist or avant garde leanings.

Famous Steinberger players have included Mike Rutherford of Genesis, Reeves Gabrels (Tin Machine), and Curt Smith (Tears For Fears).

Steinberger GS72A Scepter

Pickup type(s):	EMG
Body type:	Solid
Body wood:	Poplar
Fretboard:	Synthetic reinforced fiber
Number of frets:	24
Controls:	Volume, tone
Tremolo or fixed bridge:	S-Trem system

The classic Steinberger "headless" bass

Line 6 Variax

Pickup type(s):	No pickups
Body type:	Solid
Body wood:	Basswood
Fretboard wood:	Maple
Number of frets:	22
Controls:	Volume; tone and five-way switch
Tremolo or fixed bridge:	Tremolo bridge

Line 6 guitars

Given Line 6's success in the field of amp- and effects-modeling (see Lesson 18), it was inevitable that this company should turn its attention to the ultimate source, the electric guitar itself.

Line 6 Variax

The Variax, unlike a conventional electric guitar, does not have magnetic pickups at all. Instead, six separate piezo transducers feed their signals to a processor—essentially an onboard computer—which uses physical modelling technology to emulate the response of magnetic pickups. The Variax can be set to emulate a number of sounds produced by models including classic Stratocasters, Telecasters, Les Pauls, acoustics, and even banjos.

This model uses a rotary switch; a conventional 5-way switch enables access to variations within the basic guitar model, usually corresponding to pickup selection.

Though some players feel that this technology has some way to go before it feels and sounds entirely "real," there is no doubt that the sheer variety of sounds accessible from one instrument presents excellent value.

SEMI-ACOUSTIC GUITARS

Gibson drew the template for the modern semiacoustic guitar in 1958. Until then, there were essentially two types of electric guitar. The first were hollow-body archtops with pickups, such as Gibson's ES series (favored by jazz players and essentially acoustic guitars with pickups). The second type were the new solid-body electrics such as the Les Paul, Telecaster, and Stratocaster.

Existing semiacoustic guitars suffered from feedback problems on stage as the thin, hollow body would resonate in sympathy with the sound from the amplifier, creating an unpleasant howling noise. Players would combat this by stuffing the guitar with cloth to dampen the resonance. It was this problem that Les Paul was addressing with the creation of a solid-body instrument.

Gibson ES-335

The ES-335 was, and remains, the perfect compromise. A solid center-block dampens excessive resonance. The body is hollowed out around this, adding depth to the sound and preserving the "feel" of a big-bodied instrument. This type of guitar is more correctly described as "semi-solid."

The 335 has always been a particular favorite with blues players, and together with closely related models such as the ES-345 and ES-

Gibson ES-335

355, is a great rock 'n' roll instrument, too. Chuck Berry's "duck walk" (and Michael J. Fox's superb imitation in *Back to the Future*) just wouldn't look right with any other guitar.

Semiacoustic or electroacoustic?

These two terms are easily confused. *Semiacoustic* refers to electric guitars (guitars with magnetic pickups) that have a hollow, or semisolid, body.

Electroacoustic guitars are usually standard acoustic guitars in every respect (body size, shape, string gauge, and so on), but they are also capable of direct connection to an amplifier or PA system. Though early models used magnetic pickups, modern electroacoustics generally use *piezoelectric transducers*, which pick up vibrations from the body of

the guitar and give a more faithful reproduction of the acoustic guitar sound. Some guitars combine this with a microphone inside the guitar, which picks up airborne sound.

Most electroacoustics feature an on-board battery-powered pre-amplifier ("preamp"), allowing control over volume, pickup balance, and equalization.

Rickenbacker guitars

If you've ever heard a guitar riff described as "chiming," there's a very good chance it was played on a Rickenbacker. Since the late 1950s, Rickenbacker has made some of the most distinctive guitars around, both sonically and visually.

Adolf Rickenbacker, one of the true fathers of the electric guitar, started making instruments in the 1920s, but the features that instantly identify a guitar as a Rickenbacker did not arrive until some 30 years later.

The company's big break occurred quietly, when John Lennon purchased a model 325 in Hamburg, Germany,

in 1960. The Rickenbacker was to become a defining part of both the look and the sound of The Beatles—George Harrison, too, eventually moved over from his trusted Gretsch to a Rickenbacker 425.

Rickenbacker is also responsible for popularizing the twelve-string electric guitar. In 1964, George Harrison took delivery of one of the very first 12-string model 360s. This was physically as compact as a Rickenbacker six-string, owing to its innovative headstock design—the machine heads for each pair of strings are set at right angles.

The Rickenbacker "chime" has powered many hit records since the 1960s, from The Beatles' own "Ticket To Ride" and The Byrds' "Mr. Tambourine Man," to numerous hits by artists and groups as diverse as Tom Petty and The Jam.

Rickenbacker 325 C58MG

Pickup type(s): Three vintage single-coils
Body type: Semi-hollow
Body wood: Alder
Fretboard wood: Rosewood
Number of frets: 21
Controls: Four
Tremolo or fixed bridge: Kauffman Vibrola

Gretsch guitars

There's something about a Gretsch guitar that proudly proclaims, "I'm different." In fact, many things set most Gretsch guitars apart from the field—like Rickenbackers, they were never intended to emulate the sound or style of either Fender or Gibson guitars.

The Gretsch company was formed in the 1880s in New York, and much of its early history was associated with the banjo—at the time a more popular instrument in America than the guitar. Apart from a few electric lap steels and electrified jazz archtops, it was not until the 1950s that Gretsch entered the electric guitar arena in a big way. Popular early models included the 6120 Chet Atkins model and, famously, the White Falcon. This was an expensive, white-finished semi-acoustic with gold-plated trimmings and an ostentatious "G" logo.

Although originally aimed at the country market, Gretsch guitars quickly found a following among rock 'n' rollers, too, most notably Eddie Cochran and two British guitarists he undoubtedly influenced: Pete Townshend and George Harrison. In 1964 George Harrison played his Gretsch Country Gentleman on the Ed Sullivan show and sales went through the roof—at one point the company was a year behind with orders.

Gretsch guitars rapidly became less popular in the late 1960s, as the Stratocaster and Les Paul became fashionable, but they have seen a renaissance in recent years, with modern versions of their Gretsch classic models being made available once again.

Gretsch 6120 Chet Atkins

Pickup type(s): 2 DeArmond Dynasonics

Body type: Hollow single cutaway

Body wood: Maple

Fretboard wood: Ebony

Number of frets: 22

Controls: Volume for each pickup; master volume; tone and pickup selector switch

Tremolo or fixed bridge: Compensated aluminium Bigsby

ACOUSTIC GUITARS

Martin Guitars

C. F. Martin & Co. was established in 1833 and has remained a family-run business to this day.

Frustrated with the restrictions imposed by Austrian guitar craftsmen's guilds, the original Christian Frederick Martin emigrated to the United States. His company originally made Spanish guitars, but they introduced a few important innovations, notably their system of "X bracing"—thin strips of wood glued to the underside of the top of the guitar which greatly increased the stability and strength of the instruments.

By the early 1900s many manufacturers were making steel-strung instruments in increasing quantities, and C. F. Martin was no exception. The rise of folk and country music led to a demand for louder guitars. In 1916 Martin introduced the "dreadnought" shape, which soon became the standard shape for acoustic guitars. Martin also started the practice of joining the body and neck at the fourteenth fret (instead of the twelfth), allowing easier access to higher notes, which is now the norm.

The company currently produces around 180 different models. Martins still set the standards by which other acoustic guitars are judged.

Martin D1

Pickup type(s): None
Body type: Hollow
Body wood: Mahogany
Fretboard wood: Rosewood
Number of frets: 20
Controls: None
Tremolo or fixed bridge: Fixed bridge

National Resonator

Acoustic guitars were simply not loud enough to cut through the volume produced by the emerging big bands and dance bands of the first quarter of the twentieth century. Before the invention of the electric guitar, National Guitars designed their own solution to the problem. Resonator guitars feature a resonating cone of thin aluminum inside the guitar, protected by a circular cover that looks like a speaker grille. Sound is transmitted to the cone from the bridge and then projected forward.

Resonators are actually only a little louder than most acoustic guitars, but their ability to cut through the band is boosted further by their metallic tone. This sound has found favor with slide guitarists in particular—most resonators are now set up for slide playing—but also with fingerstyle folk and bluegrass players. Mark Knopfler's intro pattern on the Dire Straits hit "Romeo and Juliet" is a perfect example of the resonator tone. Knopfler boosted the instrument's public profile by using it on the cover of Dire Straits' multi-platinum album *Brothers in Arms* (1985) as did Paul Simon the following year with the first line of his hit "Graceland": "The Mississippi Delta was shining like a National guitar...."

National Resonator Custom

Pickup type(s):	NA
Body type:	Hollow
Body wood:	Nickel-plated Brass
Fretboard wood:	Ebony
Number of frets:	20
Controls:	NA
Tremolo or fixed bridge:	Fixed bridge

Kurt Cobain

1967–1994

GUITARS: FENDER JAGUAR, MUSTANG, STRATOCASTER

Recommended Listening:

Nevermind

In Utero

As the lead singer and guitarist of Nirvana, the American grunge band, Kurt Cobain was hailed as the "spokesperson" for Generation X, and his thoughtful if depressing lyrics struck a chord with legions of disillusioned teenagers of the 1980s and 1990s.

Cobain's interest in music came early on. It started with The Beatles—he once claimed that John Lennon was his greatest idol—and led to his involvement with heavier music. In interviews Cobain would often talk about his love of obscure bands such as the Melvins and The Vaselines. Stylistically, Cobain was undoubtedly most influenced by punk bands such as Black Flag and The Sex Pistols, although he later made a habit of covering songs by bands such as KISS and Led Zeppelin—artists that hard core punks would have derided as pompous "dinosaurs."

However, Cobain's parents divorced when he was seven and this was possibly as influential a factor as his musical heroes. The event had a profound impact on him, triggering a depression that would hound Cobain for the rest of his life and undoubtedly affected his music. Songs such as "Lithium" and "Something in the Way" portray the sense of tired hopelessness that permeated Nirvana's music.

Kurt's uncle gave him his first guitar when he was 14 and he immediately tried to start bands with his friends, playing rough covers of AC/DC and Led Zeppelin songs. In high school he met fellow punk fan Krist Novoselic, who after much persuasion agreed to join Cobain in what would become Nirvana. After trying out a number of drummers, including Chad Channing, with whom they recorded the album *Bleach,* they settled on Dave Grohl. With Grohl, Nirvana went on to release the timeless album *Nevermind*.

Major success followed, solidified by worldwide touring and the albums *In Utero* and *Incesticide*, but Cobain was ill-equipped to handle this largely unlooked-for fame.

On April 8, 1994 Kurt Cobain was found dead in the greenhouse of his home near Lake Washington, after escaping his rehab clinic in California. A suicide note was found beneath an overturned flowerpot, ending with the Neil Young lyric, "It's better to burn out than to fade away." An autopsy report concluded that Cobain had died on April 5 as a result of a self-inflicted shotgun wound to the head. Cobain was cremated, with one third of his ashes scattered in a Buddhist temple in Ithaca, New York, another third in the Wishkah River in Washington State, and the rest left in the possession of his widow, Courtney Love.

Kurt's legacy has continued long after his death, and every generation of teenagers has its fans of Nirvana. Numerous books have been published since his death, including the controversial *Who Killed Kurt Cobain?*, which alleges that he was murdered; and what many see as Cobain's definitive biography, Charles R. Cross's *Heavier Than Heaven*. Many feel that Nirvana changed the face of rock music forever, and Kurt certainly championed alternative music, helping many unheard of bands such as The Jesus Lizard gain recognition.

Eight years after Kurt Cobain's death, Nirvana's last studio recording, "You Know You're Right" topped charts worldwide—a tribute to a songwriter who captured the mood of an entire generation.

Guitar Gear

Amps

Tremolo and Vibrato Systems

Effects

Amp Modeling

and Virtual Guitar

As you will have discovered, the electric guitar makes virtually no sound on its own. The sheer variety of sounds available when you plug it in depends as much, if not more, on the other equipment used as the type of guitar itself. In this lesson we'll explore some of the most important and interesting pieces of equipment that make this world of sound available, from amps to effects boxes and recent electronic innovations.

Lesson 18.1: Amps

The original aim of guitar amplifiers was, as the word implies, to amplify the guitar's sound. The acoustic guitar is a very quiet instrument compared to the drum kit or brass instruments such as saxophones and trumpets.

As the dance bands of the 1920s and 1930s expanded in size, the guitar became relegated to providing a rhythmic accompaniment and, even in this role, was often barely audible. Early electric guitars and amplifiers simply aimed to raise the guitar's volume to a level that could be heard within these bands. There was generally little control over the sound beyond a simple volume control.

The resulting sound had little in common with the sound of an acoustic guitar with no amplification. The early amplification circuits and speakers were very crude by the standards of today's hi-fi components, and the pickups were basic devices.

Early adopters of the new technology managed to make it their own, however. Charlie Christian, playing with Benny Goodman's small groups in the late 1930s, epitomized the new breed of guitarist. In Christian's hands, the guitar was emancipated from the back row, becoming a lead instrument as capable of fluid solo playing as the sax or trumpet. Gradually, the "flaws" in the emerging technology were forgotten and accepted as an integral part of the electric guitar sound. By the 1950s Gibson and Fender were making solid-bodied guitars that abandoned any attempt to sound like acoustic guitars.

Gibson began manufacturing amps in the 1950s, but never achieved the same success as their arch-rival Fender.

Fender amps

As a leading guitar maker, Leo Fender was in a prime position to develop amplifiers to complement his guitar designs, and that's exactly what he did. The standard in the 1950s, in the United States at least, was set by Fender amps such as the Showman and the Bassman. These tweed-covered classics set the standard that Fender and others built on in later decades and have provided the inspiration for many of today's retro-styled designs.

Tubes vs. transistors

Until roughly the mid-1960s, all guitar amplifiers—as well as domestic audio equipment—used thermionic tubes (generally known as "valves") as their main components. The glass tube was the forerunner of the transistors and microchips found in much of today's electronic equipment.

When they first appeared, transistors were seen as generally superior to tubes, as indeed they were for such things as portable radios and hi-fi systems. Tubes were comparatively expensive, large, fragile, and unreliable, yet they provided the foundation of the sound we expect from the electric guitar today.

Transistor-based designs (known as "solid state" amps) sounded poor by comparison, at least at first, though they have greatly improved over the years. Surprisingly, solid-state amps were something of an "emperor's new clothes" phenomenon—it took some years for many guitarists and the major manufacturers to discover that this bright, shiny, exciting new technology really didn't sound as good as the old tube amps.

Fender classic

The standard for clean, bright—yet powerful—amplification, particularly for players of bright and twangy Fender guitars, was set in the 1960s by the Fender Twin Reverb amplifier.

This 100-watt tube amp featured Fender's own spring reverb and two 12-inch (30-cm) speakers, providing enough power for all but the biggest venues.

Distortion by design

During the 1960s, rock 'n' roll and blues players realized that guitar amplifiers could make sounds not envisioned even by their designers. Most amplifier circuits, if fed a suitably "hot" signal and turned to full volume, will produce a certain amount of distortion.

**Fender Amps
Recommended Listening:**

Beach Boys: *Pet Sounds*

The venerable Fender Twin amp, first produced in the 1960s, is still a popular choice for musicians. Many amplifiers today still use tubes (above) rather than the cheaper and more reliable transistor.

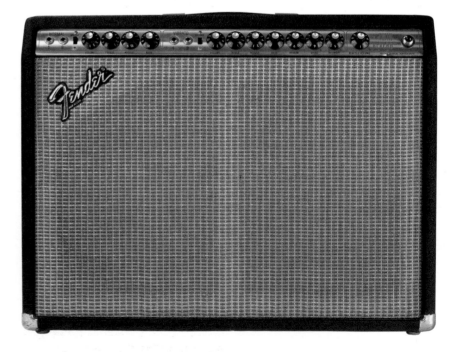

**Marshall Amps
Recommended Listening:**

Jimi Hendrix: *Electric Ladyland*

Led Zeppelin: *Led Zeppelin II*

Considered by many to be the definitive rock amp, the Marshall SL Plexi head was used in stacks by legendary 1960s guitarists including Jimmy Page (Led Zeppelin) and Jimi Hendrix.

Combo amps such as this Marshall AS100D, designed for amplifying acoustic guitars, combine controls and speakers within the same unit.

Solid-state distortion often sounds harsh and unpleasant, but tube amps tend to give a warmer, more pleasant distortion, and soon guitar players discovered that they liked it. In the early days, amplifiers had only one volume control—the only way to produce distortion was to crank the amp up to 10.

Marshall amps

One amp that became popular for its distortion characteristics was the Fender Bassman. British amp maker Jim Marshall became aware of this and based his Model 1959 on this design. Marshall amps became a crucial part of the emerging rock sound. The 1959 (known as a Plexi because the back panel was made of plexiglass) is regarded by many as the definitive rock amplifier, powering classics by Cream, Led Zeppelin, and Jimi Hendrix.

Power output

Amps fall into two other broad categories: *combos* and *head/cabinet* combinations (also known as stacks).

Combination ("combo") amplifiers combine the amplifier circuitry, controls, and loudspeaker(s) within the same unit. Typically, this includes one or two speakers, which are often referred to by their size: often 10 or 12 in. in diameter (25 or 30 cm). The rated power of the amp is often quoted too, so a "100-watt 2 x 12 combo" is an all-in-one amplifier with two 12-in. speakers, rated at 100 watts. The rated output is not always a particularly useful figure—some amps, especially tube amps, can

Many guitarists consider the Boogie MkIV to be the ultimate combo amp. Though rather expensive when new, Boogie amps can often be found on the secondhand market.

the "gain" control) and, usually, separate channels for clean and overdriven sounds. These can be set up in advance to the player's taste, balanced in level, and selected on stage by means of a foot switch.

While large amps are fine for the loud environment of gigs, they can also be an excellent route to poor relations with family members and other people living nearby, and they are not the easiest things to carry to rehearsals or lessons. Practice amps are small, light and low-powered amplifiers that solve this problem neatly. Many feature quite passable distortion sounds, although they can sound a little like a wasp in a mason jar at high volumes.

Most practice amps include a headphone output for silent practice. There are also dedicated headphone practice amps with no speaker at all —these are often battery powered for ease of use when on the move.

Another innovation is the *JamBug FM*. This is a miniature FM radio transmitter. Inserting this into the guitar's output jack enables any FM radio within a short range to be used as a wireless practice amp.

be louder than others with higher ratings—but it gives a general idea.

Beyond a certain size, speaker cabinets ("cabs") get rather heavy, even without the weight of the amplifier circuitry and transformers. For this reason, the biggest guitar amps tend to be made as two separate units: the "head" contains the amp itself, which is then paired

with one or more speaker cabinets: the classic rock stage setup is two 4 x 12-in. (30 cm) cabs.

Amplifier controls
Nowadays, most amplifiers have a master volume control, allowing the overall output volume to be controlled separately from the amount of distortion (controlled by

Lesson 18.2: Tremolo and Vibrato Systems

Tremolo and vibrato, although they might sound similar, actually produce quite different sounds. Vibrato is a periodic variation in pitch. This is often produced by string players, including guitarists, by "wobbling" the left-hand fingers along the string. Tremolo, on the other hand, is a periodic variation in volume, and this effect is available on many amplifiers and effects units.

The two terms have generally been confused, at least among guitarists, since Leo Fender named his vibrato bar system a tremolo arm when he introduced the Stratocaster.

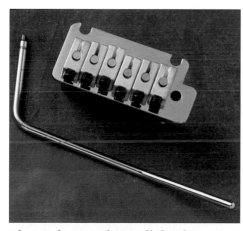

The Fender tremolo is still the classic design, standard on most guitars.

Floyd Rose tremolos are the favorite of heavy rock players.

Vibrato arms

The vibrato arm was originally invented by Paul Bigsby—a motorcycle manufacturer, racer, and guitar innovator—in the late 1940s, and consists of a spring-balanced arm attached to a rolling tailpiece.

Though still popular with some players, and often found on semi-acoustic guitars, the Bigsby design suffers from poor stability and was generally superseded by Leo Fender's design. This uses springs inside the body of the guitar that exactly balance the tension in the strings. The bridge is only attached to the

A Bigsby tremolo gives a retro twang.

guitar body at the front—the back moves up or down as pressure is applied to the arm. There is virtually no friction; the arm can be used for vibrato or string bending, and the strings will, in theory, always return to perfect tuning.

Floating tremolo

The zero-friction principle was taken further in the 1980s with the Floyd Rose floating tremolo. As the name implies, the bridge "floats," enabling wide bending of notes both upwards and downward. This design, generally coupled with a locking nut to improve stability and fine tuners at the bridge, is particularly popular with heavy rock players.

223

Lesson 18.3: Effects

Stomp boxes

You may have noticed a difference between the sound of a guitar connected directly to an amplifier—with or without distortion—and some of the sounds you hear from professional players on stage or recorded.

The basic electric guitar sound can be altered in many ways—both subtle and radical—with processes known as *effects* (or *FX*). There are many types of units for applying effects, either individually or several at once. Some amps have one or more built-in effects.

The longest-established and most popular of these devices are effects pedals—sometimes known as *stomp boxes*—which generally give access to a single effect, but can easily be chained together for multiple effects. The effect is set up in advance using knobs on the pedal, then simply switched on or off as required. Let's explore some of the most popular effects pedals available.

Overdrive/distortion

Technically, this is not an effect at all, but an integral part of the electric guitar sound. However, many amplifiers, especially practice amps, do not produce pleasant-sounding distortion, and players often need a choice of different types of distortion and overdrive—since using many different amps at one gig is simply not practical or affordable. Distortion pedals solve this problem by putting a pre-amp inside a pedal, giving players easy access to a wide range of distortion and overdrive sounds.

An overdrive/distortion pedal (above) allows the player to choose from a wide range of distortion sounds.

Chorus

Chorus is possibly the most popular effect in use. As the name implies, this effect simulates the sound of several instruments playing the same thing and works by splitting the signal, de-tuning it, and mixing the result with the dry (un-effected) signal. This effect is used to produce the rich, shimmering sound found on so many pop records from the 1970s to the present day. This sound is so common that, without it, the electric guitar can sometimes sound a little raw and unfinished to ears accustomed to the sound of chorus.

Delay

Delay is one of the oldest effects in use. Before the invention of the microchip, the effect was produced by feeding a loop of tape through a tape recorder. One of the machine's heads would record the incoming signal to tape while another would feed it back into the signal path. The

delay time was regulated by varying the speed of the tape. This is the "slap-back" delay effect found on many early rock 'n' roll recordings.

Dedicated sealed delay units (with a tape loop inside) made this effect portable and available to the live performer, but the possibilities of delay really opened up in the 1970s with the advent of digital processing.

Nowadays, very long delays are possible, as are complex rhythmic patterns resulting from multiple delay.

Reverb

Various methods of creating "reverb" (short for reverberation) to simulate the effect produced by playing in a large room or hall have been in use since the very early days of guitar amplification. The most common device, found in most guitar amps, is the spring reverb unit. The signal is fed to a magnetic transducer, which causes one or more springs to vibrate. This vibration is then picked up at the other end of the spring(s) and fed back into the dry signal.

Digital reverb offers a greater choice of sounds, ranging from simulations of spring reverb and other devices to complex imitations of the sound of a real room or hall.

Compression

Compression has been in constant use in the recording studio since the 1960s. Almost no pop recording has been made since then without using compression to some degree, and some production styles such as the 1980s "Big Drums" soft metal sound were built entirely on the use of heavy compression. Simply put, a compressor effect "squeezes" the audio signal to reduce the relative difference between loud and soft notes. This can be used to add smoothness to a performance. With some more extreme settings, compression can be used to create a very long sustain, so that a note, once played, dies away much slower than it otherwise would. This can be used equally well for long, sustained chords or screaming solos.

Wah wah

The term "wah wah" was originally applied to the sound produced by the use of the trumpet mute, which is held by a player's left hand and moved in and out of the bell of the trumpet to produce the characteristic "wah wah" sound.

A wah wah pedal emulates this effect by boosting the middle frequencies of the guitar signal. As the guitarist's foot rocks back and forth, this motion turns a potentiometer similar to a guitar's tone control,

which varies the frequency. The signal is often boosted so much that some distortion is also created; this is very much a part of the classic wah wah sound. Most rock players use wah wah to a degree. Listen to Jimi Hendrix on the intro to "Voodoo Chile" for possibly the most famous example.

Auto wah

Auto wah (or dynamic wah) offers various ways to produce a convincing wah sound without the constant use of the right foot. Some players find the necessary hand and foot coordination difficult, and it is impossible to move around a stage while using a conventional wah pedal.

Automatic wah generally uses the level of the guitar signal to generate the wah effect: in other words, as each note decays in volume, the wah sound changes. Other auto wah pedals simply "rock" back and forth electronically at a fixed frequency. The parameters can usually be set by the user to produce a convincing effect.

Multi-FX

Guitarists often mount their pedals on a board for live performances. This makes it easy to keep the pedals connected in the same way and minimizes setup time. Many pedal boards also double as handy carrying cases. If you can build up a collection of pedals and experiment with connecting them together, you will discover that they can often be joined in a number of different ways, with very different results. For example,

A vintage wah wah pedal gives a unique effect familiar from many hit songs.

wah wah sounds very different depending on whether it is placed before or after distortion; chorus sounds terrible if placed before distortion but adds a glossy sheen if placed afterwards. Changing the order of your pedals during a gig, let alone during the course of a song, is not generally practical, however.

Complex FX setups can also be noisy. An FX chain involving four different pedals typically involves four units of audio circuitry, up to four power supplies, five jack leads, and at least eight jack sockets. Each additional pedal (even when bypassed) adds more noise.

Multi-FX units provide a solution to some of these problems by assigning all the work to one processor. Each effects "block" is part of a virtual chain that can generally be rearranged as required. Typically, a multi-FX unit can store 100 or more programs, and each program consists of exact settings for each effect. In this way, it's possible to switch instantly from, for example, a clean sound with chorus, delay, and compression, to raw distortion with a rotary speaker effect. With individual pedals, this would involve five separate actions. With a multi-FX unit the two programs could be assigned adjacent numbers; one press of the "up" foot switch would take care of all of them!

Lesson 18.4: Amp Modeling and Virtual Guitar

One of the most exciting recent developments in modern audio technology as applied to the electric guitar has been the advent of *physical modeling*. The idea behind this is simple. One of the most exciting recent developments in modern audio technology as applied to the electric guitar has been the advent of *physical modeling*. The idea behind this technology is simple.

Amp modeling

Any electrical device, whether it's an amplifier, electric guitar, or a single component such as a tube, responds to a given set of inputs by producing a certain set of outputs. If this is analyzed in sufficient detail, a virtual "model" of the device can be programmed to run on a computer processor. Thus, a single unit can contain digital models of the sound of dozens of different amplifiers, speaker cabinets, reverb springs, and other effects.

While there is still a feeling among professionals that this technology still

The Line 6 Pod was the first unit to exploit the physical modeling idea, and has become a popular piece of equipment in studios worldwide.

has some way to go before the results are truly indistinguishable from the real thing, the advantages are significant. For the first time, the home-recording guitarist can at least come close to the sound quality that is associated with professional studio recordings and a selection of amps and cabs that was previously the stuff of fantasy.

Amp modeling equipment like the Line 6 Pod (above) has also found a following for live use. Transporting heavy guitar amps can sometimes be impractical, but the Pod can be connected directly to a PA system. The resulting sound, while perhaps lacking the exact feel of a top-of-the-line tube amp, comes in at a small fraction of the latter's cost and weight and is undoubtedly excellent value for the money.

Virtual Guitar

While Line 6 and others have until now kept the guitar and amplifier separate in their approaches to

Roland Virtual Guitar Recommended Listening:

Joni Mitchell: *Taming The Tiger*

Steve Vai: *Mystery Tracks Archives Vol. 3*

The Roland VG-88 is a remarkable machine, but you will still need to permanently attach a third pickup to your guitar for it to work.

modeling, the Roland Virtual Guitar system brings both together in one environment.

The Roland VG-88 works by attaching a "hex" pickup (that is, a pickup that "reads" each string separately) to any standard electric guitar. The signal from this pickup is fed to the VG-88's "brain," which models a particular guitar type from the vibration of the strings up, making it possible to switch virtually for example, from a Stratocaster played through a Marshall, to an acoustic 12-string, with just one press of a foot switch.

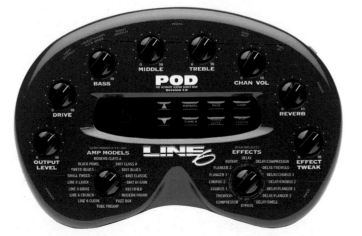

Jack White

1975—
GUITARS: VARIOUS

Recommended Listening:
White Blood Cells
Elephant

Along with bands such as The Hives and The Strokes, The White Stripes were pioneers of the garage rock revival of the new millennium. Jack White, as one-half of the minimalist rock duo, burst into the mainstream in 2001 with their third album, *White Blood Cells*. Emerging into a rock scene that was dominated by nu-metal boy-bands, the Stripes represented a breath of fresh air raw, straightforward rock 'n' roll. However, even with the deliberate simplicity of songs such as "Seven Nation Army," Jack White is a guitarist of deceptive depth and skill.

Despite their recording success, The White Stripes are first and foremost a live act. Clad in red, black, and white, their live shows are a spontaneous frenzy of improvisation, half gig, half jam session. The onstage chemistry between Jack White and his ex-wife, Meg, makes for a captivating performance that has won them headlining spots at some of the world's biggest festivals.

Blues, punk, and pop
As a songwriter, Jack White is capable of combining styles with ease. While blues and punk are the most obvious influences on his music —White has frequently referred to the Stooges' 1970 release *Fun House* as the greatest album ever—his deep love of country music lies just beneath the surface. Able to move from the fingerpicked folk blues of "Blind Willie McTell" to Kinks-style pop within the span of just two songs, White hides a myriad of influences beneath his cartoonlike public image.

Eccentricity is at the heart of Jack White's appeal—he is interested in taxidermy and collects stuffed animals and has spoken about his obsession with the number three. The band's idiosyncrasies and ever-present uniform make the White Stripes not just a musical duo performance but a truly involving experience.

Chord
Reference

Chord Charts

This section is a handy reference library of chord shapes. Though there are literally tens of thousands of possible chord shapes, those included here should see you through most musical situations where basic chords are required, up to an intermediate level of playing. If you're ever stuck for a chord when playing from a songbook with no chord boxes, you'll probably find something usable here. Also, don't forget to make use of movable barre chords, as detailed in lesson 9.

Lesson 19.1: Chord Charts

Understanding the chord charts

In these charts we've used gray vertical rules to represent the guitar strings. The black horizontal rules are the frets. The frets are numbered from the nut (guitar neck) downward. The letters at the top of each string represent the open string note, starting with bottom E (the lowest string) on the left to the top E (the highest string) on the right.

The suggested finger positions are color coded like this:

(1) = FIRST FINGER   (3) = THIRD FINGER

(2) = SECOND FINGER   (4) = FOURTH FINGER

The following symbols are sometimes used at the top of the strings:

[O] = OPEN STRING   [X] = DO NOT PLAY THIS STRING   ◯ = OPTIONAL NOTE

A Chords

 = OPEN STRING   ☒ = DO NOT PLAY THIS STRING   ⬤ = OPTIONAL NOTE

A
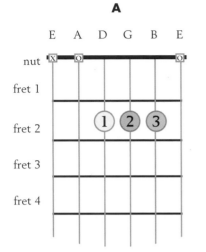

A (alternative)

A7
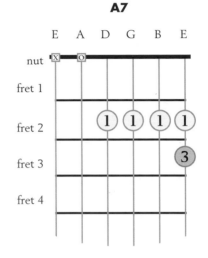

Amaj7
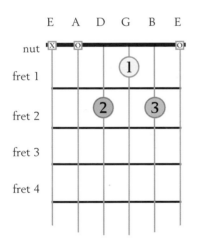

Am
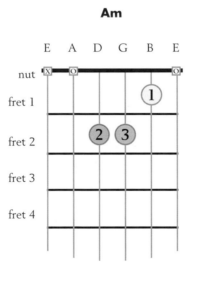

Am (alternative)

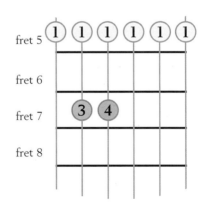

Am7

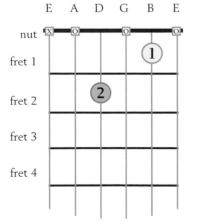

A6
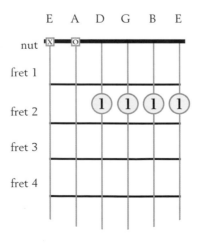

A9
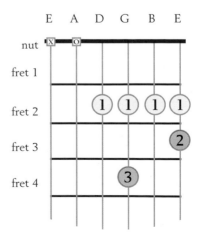

① = FIRST FINGER   ② = SECOND FINGER   ③ = THIRD FINGER   ④ = FOURTH FINGER

A♭

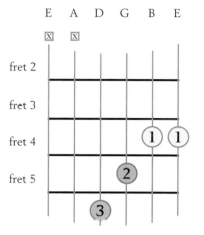

A♭ (alternative)

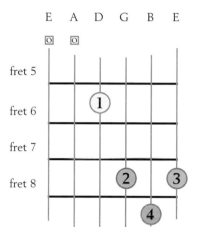

A♭7

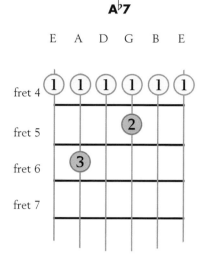

A♭maj7

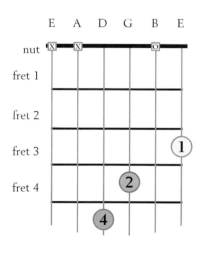

A♭m

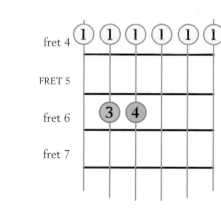

A♭m (alternative)

A♭m7

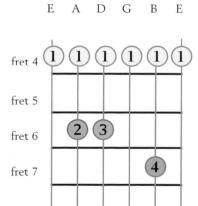

B Chords

 = OPEN STRING   = DO NOT PLAY THIS STRING   ⬤ = OPTIONAL NOTE

B

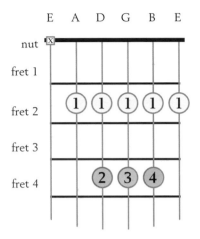

B (alternative)

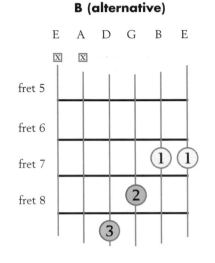

B (alternative)

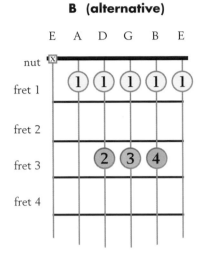

B7

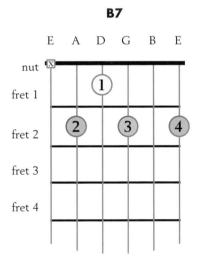

Bmaj7

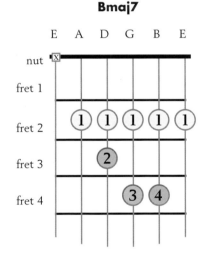

Bm

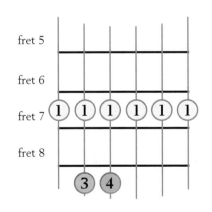

Bm (alternative)

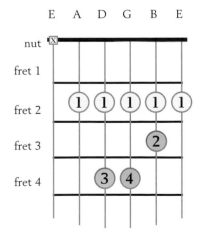

Bm7

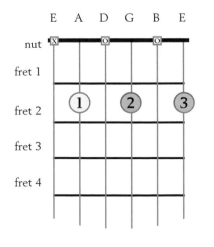

B♭

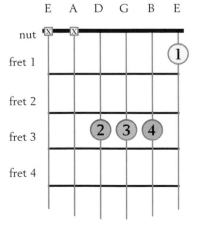

232

= FIRST FINGER   = SECOND FINGER   3 = THIRD FINGER   4 = FOURTH FINGER

B♭7

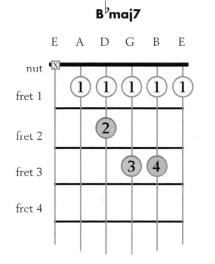

B♭maj7

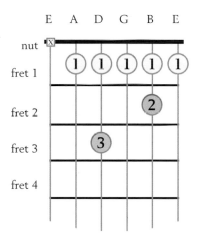

B♭m

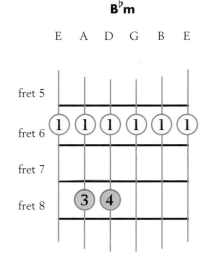

B♭m (alternative)

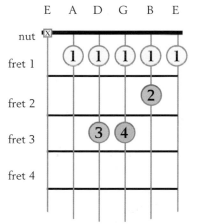

B♭m7

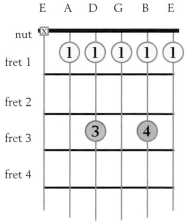

233

C Chords

 = OPEN STRING   = DO NOT PLAY THIS STRING   = OPTIONAL NOTE

C

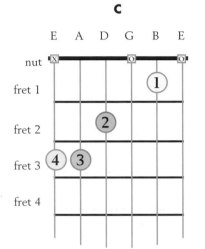

C (alternative)

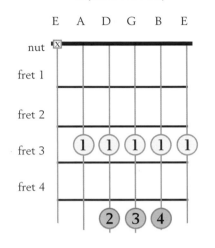

C7

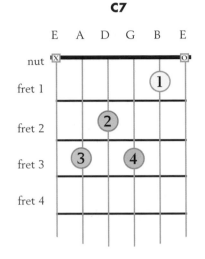

Cmaj7

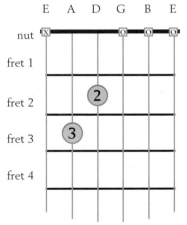

Cm

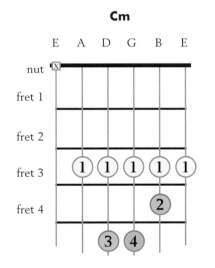

Cm (alternative)

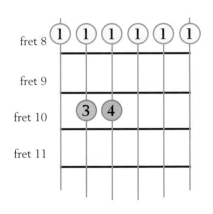

Cm7

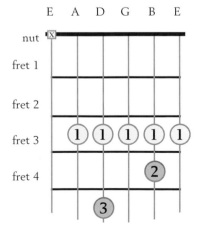

C6

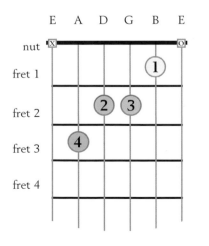

C9

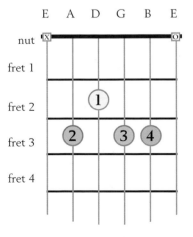

= FIRST FINGER   = SECOND FINGER   3 = THIRD FINGER   4 = FOURTH FINGER

C♯

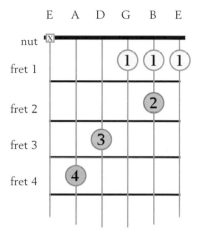

C♯ (alternative)

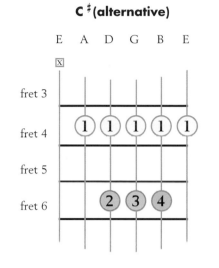

C♯7

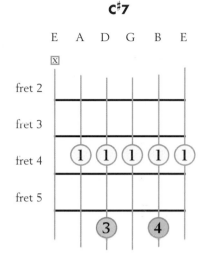

C♯maj7

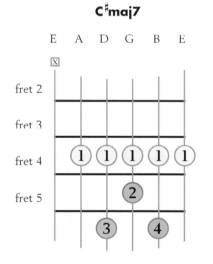

C♯m

C♯m (alternative)

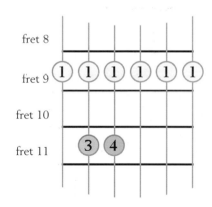

C♯m7

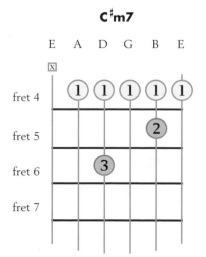

D Chords

D

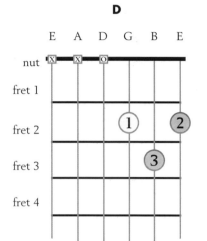

D (alternative)

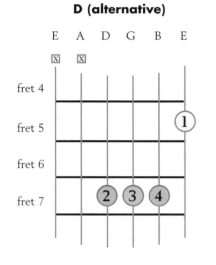

D7

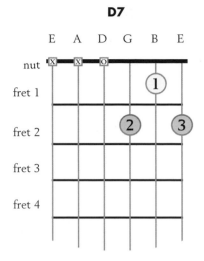

Dmaj7

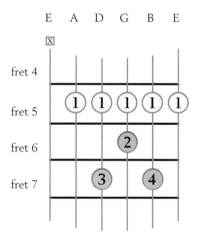

Dm

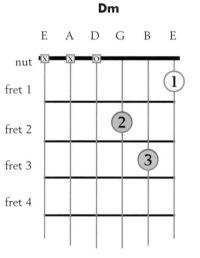

Dm (alternative)

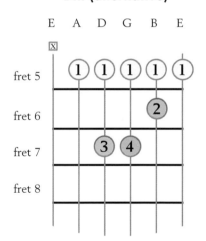

= FIRST FINGER   = SECOND FINGER   = THIRD FINGER   – FOURTH FINGER

Dm7

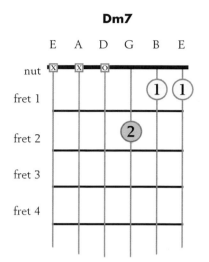

D6

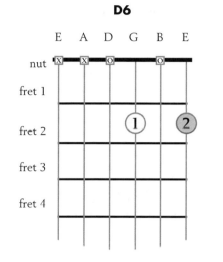

D9

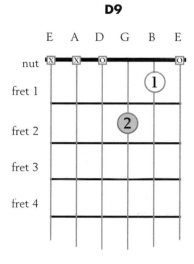

237

E Chords

 = OPEN STRING   X = DO NOT PLAY THIS STRING   ◯ = OPTIONAL NOTE

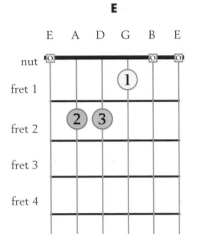

E

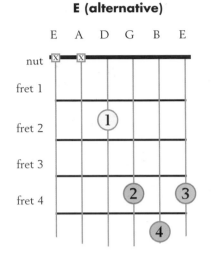

E (alternative)

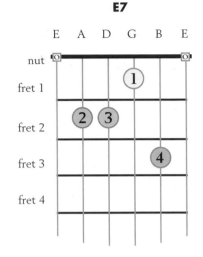

E7

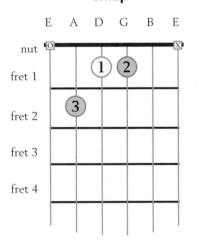

Emaj7

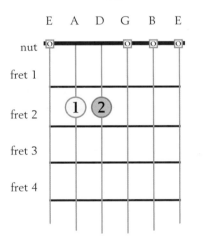

Em

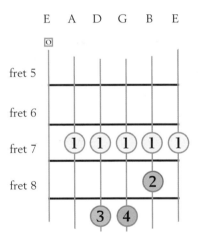

Em (alternative)

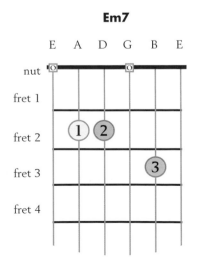

Em7

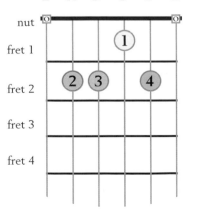

E6

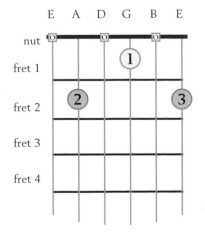

E9

238

① = FIRST FINGER   ② = SECOND FINGER   ③ = THIRD FINGER   ④ = FOURTH FINGER

E♭

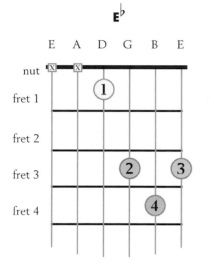

E♭ (alternative)

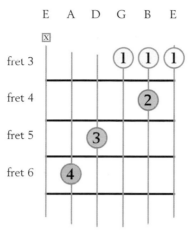

E♭7

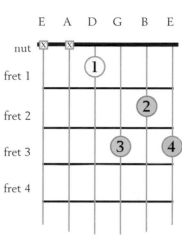

E♭maj7

E♭m

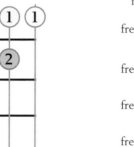

E♭m (alternative)

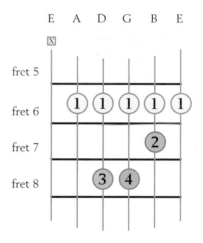

E♭m7

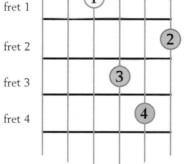

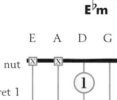

F Chords

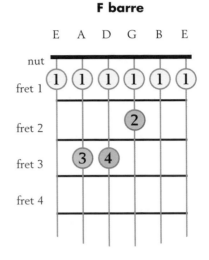

O = OPEN STRING	X = DO NOT PLAY THIS STRING
⬤ = OPTIONAL NOTE	

F

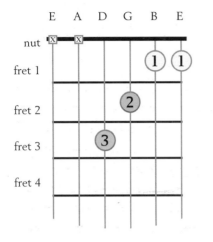

F (alternative)

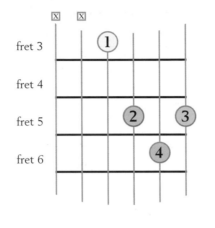

F barre

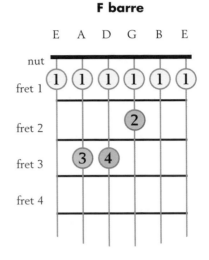

F7

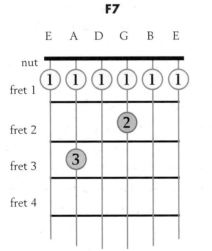

Fmaj7

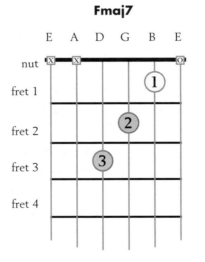

Fm

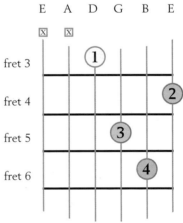

Fm (alternative)

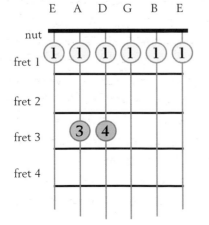

Fm barre

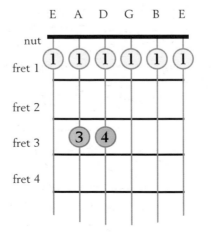

Fm7

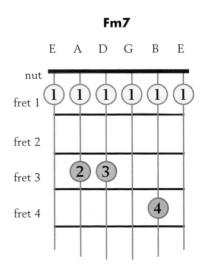

= FIRST FINGER   = SECOND FINGER   = THIRD FINGER   = FOURTH FINGER

F6

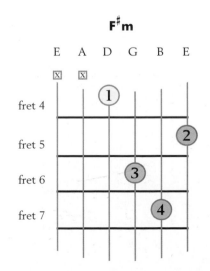

F9

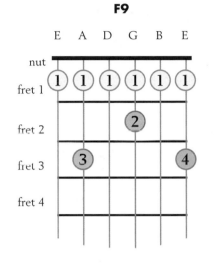

F#

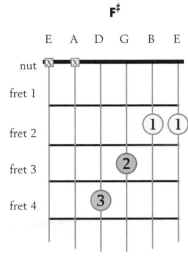

F# (alternative)

F#7

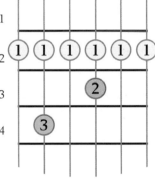

F#maj7

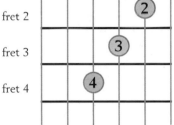

F#m

F#m (alternative)

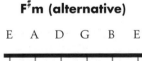

F#m7

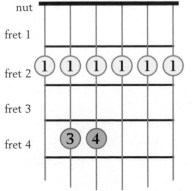

G Chords

 = OPEN STRING   X = DO NOT PLAY THIS STRING   ◯ = OPTIONAL NOTE

G
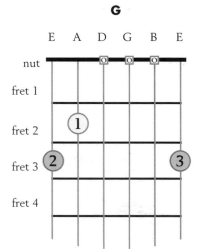

G (alternative)
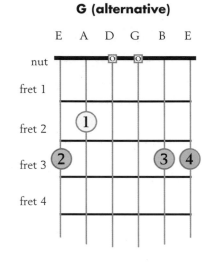

G barre
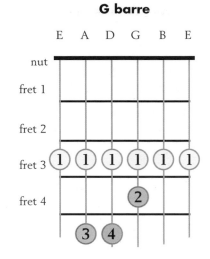

G7
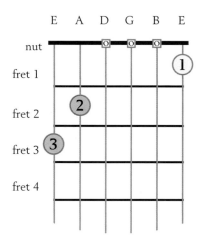

Gmaj7
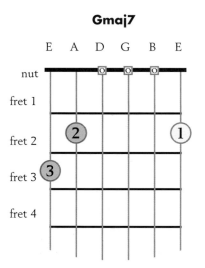

Gm
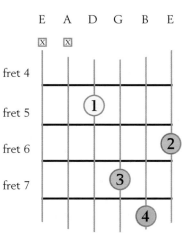

= FIRST FINGER   = SECOND FINGER   = THIRD FINGER   = FOURTH FINGER

Gm (alternative)

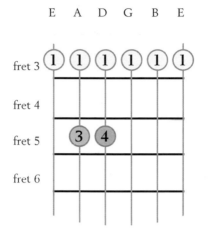

Gm barre

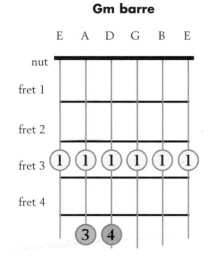

Gm7

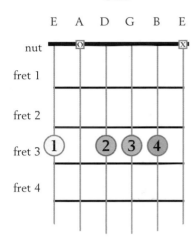

G6

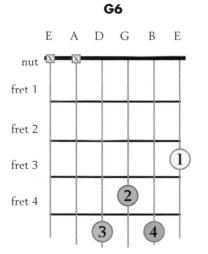

G9

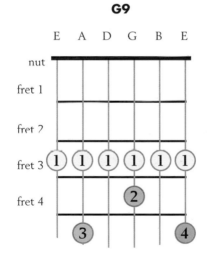

Practicing with
Scales

Scales Practice
Major Scales
Minor Scales
Blues Scales

During this course, we've highlighted a few scales and noted their usefulness in gaining greater fluency as well as fretboard knowledge. If you're going to get serious about learning the guitar, or any instrument for that matter, you will at some point want to practice scales. The scales in this section provide you with a starting point and introduce some useful shapes that can, of course, be moved around the neck to play in other keys.

Lesson 20.1: Scales Practice

To become familiar with scales, just start practicing but don't worry about getting them absolutely perfect at this point. The scales here have been kept in the lower frets and use open strings wherever possible. The resulting shapes provide a good basis for transferring this knowledge all over the neck at a later stage. If you like, you could work though them in this order: C, F, G, D, A, E, B, and then the rest in any order you wish. This way you'll be concentrating on the most common (and therefore most useful) scales first.

You'll notice that some of the "black" notes (sharps and flats) have different names depending on the scale type. For example, D♭ and C♯ are the same physical note, but D♭ is much more frequently encountered than C♯ as a major key, and vice versa for the minor.

C MAJOR

C MINOR

C BLUES

D♭ MAJOR

C# MINOR

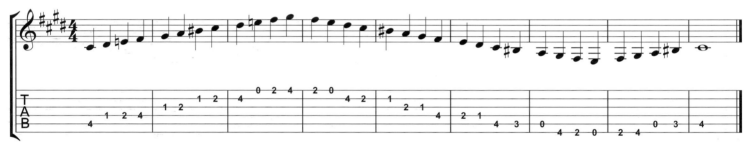

D♭ BLUES

D MAJOR

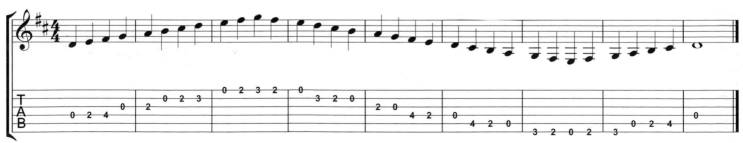

D MINOR

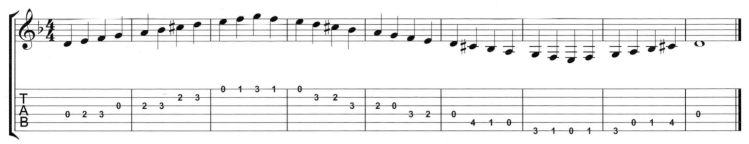

D BLUES

E♭ MAJOR

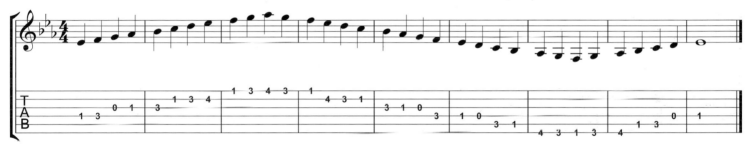

E♭ MINOR

E♭ BLUES

E MAJOR

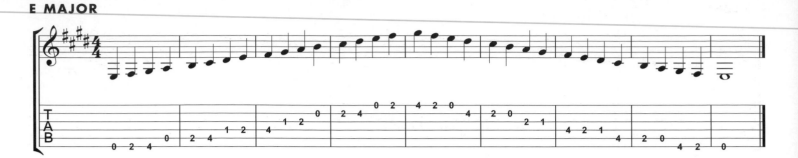

E MINOR

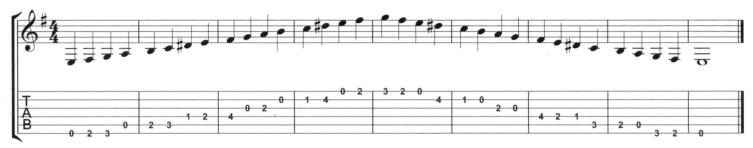

E BLUES

F MAJOR

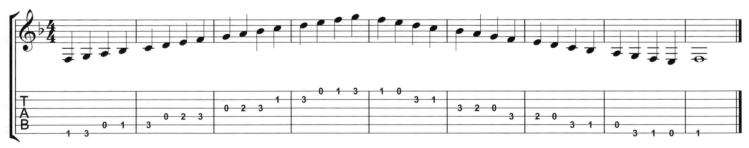

F MINOR

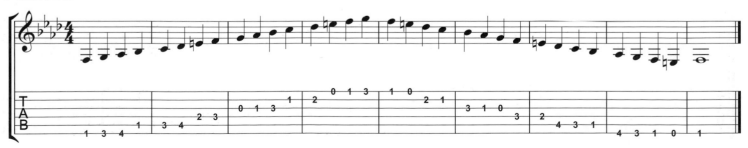

F BLUES

G♭ MAJOR

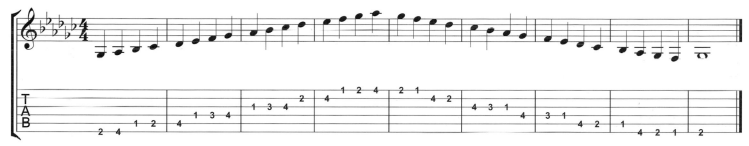

F♯ MINOR

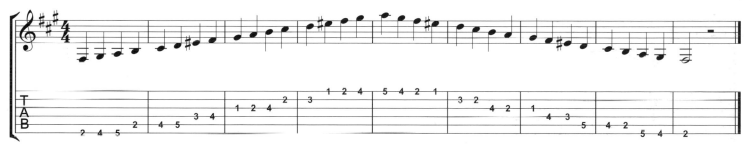

G♭ BLUES

G MAJOR

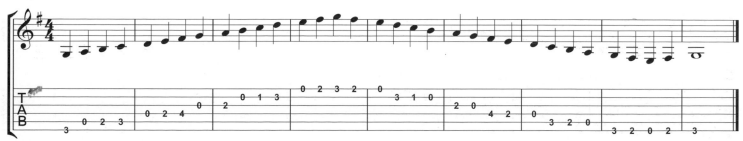

G MINOR

G BLUES

A♭ MAJOR

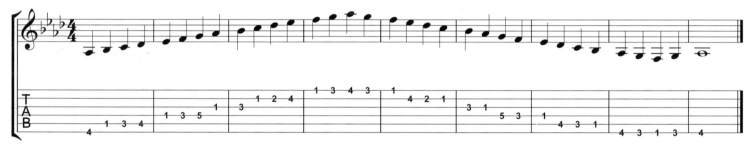

G♯ MINOR

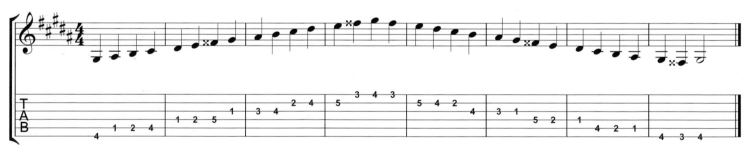

A♭ BLUES

A MAJOR

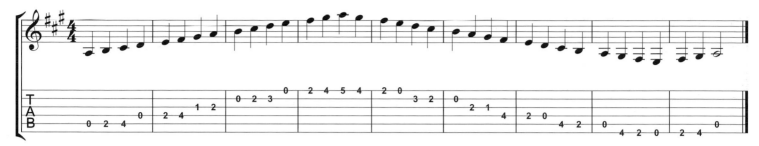

A MINOR

A BLUES

B♭ MAJOR

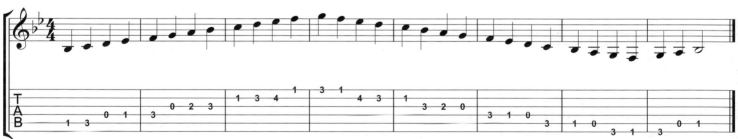

B♭ MINOR

B♭ BLUES

B MAJOR

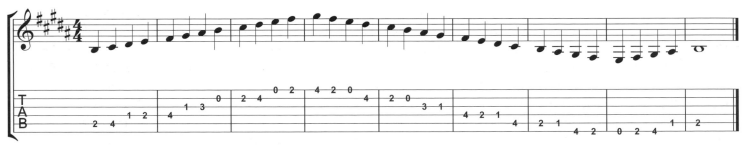

B MINOR

B BLUES

Index

References in **boldface** indicate music for playing. *Italic* references indicate photographs.

A

A♭ blues scale, 250
A♭ major scale, 250
A blues scale, 251
Accessories, 24–25
A chords
    A, 27–28, 30–31
    A5, 101, 176
    A6, 101
    A7, 78
    Am, 73
    Am7, 74
    charts, 230–31
Acoustic guitar, *11*
American acoustic guitar, 47
    changing strings, 16
    choosing, 11
    fingerstyle, 133
    makers, 215–16
    twelve-string guitar, 135
Action, 10, 11
Aerosmith, 176–79
After the Goldrush (Young), 80
Air travel, 14
All Things Must Pass (Harrison), 61
Altered tunings, 199
A major key, 143
A major scale, 251
American acoustic guitar, *47, 47*
A minor pentatonic scale, 146
A minor scale, 70, 251
Amp modeling, 226
Amps, *13*, 219–22
    Boogie amps, 222
    choosing, 13
    combo amps, 221–22

Fender amps, 121, 220
head amps, 221–22
Marshall amps, 121, 221–22
practice amps, 222
volume and gain, 87, 222
Appetite for Destruction (Guns N' Roses), 99
Are You Experienced? (Hendrix), 163
Arpeggios, 123, 139
Asher, Peter, 128
Atkins, Chet, 201, *201, 214*, 214
Auto wah, 225

B

B♭5 chord, 90
B♭ blues scale, 252
B♭ major scale, 251
B♭ minor scale, 251
"Bad Moon Rising" (Fogerty), **34–35**
Baker, Ginger, 151
Bar lines, 31
Baroque era, 39
Barre chords, 113–19
Barrett, Syd, 56
Bass/chord accompaniment, 140
Bass guitars, 121
Bassman, 121
Bass notes, 129
Bass/strum, 125
B blues scale, 252
B chords
    B5, 90
    B7, 78
    B barre, 114
    charts, 232–33
B. C. Rich guitars, 206
Beach Boys, 108
Beams, 60
Beatles, The, 61, 128, 151, 213
Beauchamp, George, 67

"Be-Bop-A-Lula" (Vincent)", 102
Berry, Chuck, 102, 103, 108, *108*
"Black" and "white" notes, 58
Blocks, 74
Blue notes, 145
Blues, 145–55
blues scale, 70, 152
    end phrases, 155
    improvisation, 152, 154
    keys, 104
Bluesbreakers, 150
"Blues Party Piece," **160–62**
"Blue Suede Shoes" (Perkins), 61
B major scale, 252
B minor scale, 252
Boogie amps, 222
Boogie MkIV, *222*
Boogie pattern, 101–5, 107, 160
"Born on the Bayou" (Fogerty), **94–97**
"Bottom" string, 31
Bream, Julian, *137*
Bruce, Jack, 151
Buckland, John, *59, 59*
Buffett, Jimmy, 71, *71*
Burton, James, 198, *198*

C

C♯ minor scale, 246
Cables, 24
Capos, 25, 81, *81*
Care, 14
C blues scale, 246
C chords
    C, 42
    C5, 90
    C7, 78, 125
    charts, 234–35
Chic, *186*
Chiming riffs, 213
Chords, 27–35, 73–74

barre chords, 113–19
changing chords, 31–32
chord boxes, 27
chord charts, 229–43
chord shapes, 27
    exercises, 32
    finger position, 28
    minor chords, 79
    power chords, 88–92
    rock chords, 182
    roots and fifths finder, 125
    sevenths, 78–79
    strumming, 30
    thumb position, 29
Chorus, 224
Christian, Charlie, 67, 219
Chromatic tuners, 19
Chugging patterns, 89
Clapton, Eric, *150*, 150–51, 204
Classical guitar, *10*, 137–43
    bass line, 139–41
    changing strings, 17
    choosing, 10
    finger positions, 138
    notation, 138
    origins, 39
    sitting position, 137
Clean channels, 87
Cleaning, 14
C major scale, 57, 84, 145, 245
C minor pentatonic scale, 145
C minor scale, 245
Cobain, Kurt, 80, 217, *217*
Coldplay, 59
Combo amps, 221–22
Compound time, 109
Compression, 224–25
Concept albums, 56
Concert pitch, 21
Country fills, 194
Country guitar, 193–97
Crazy Horse, 80

Cream, 151, 204
Crickets, The, 69
Crosby, Stills, Nash and Young, 80

D

D♭ blues scale, 246
D♭ major scale, 246
"Dark Funk", **190**
Dark Side of the Moon, The (Pink Floyd), 56
D blues scale, 247
D chords
    charts, 236–37
    D, 30
    D5/D6 pattern, 102
    D7, 78
    D barre, 114
    D/F♯, 167
    Dm, 73
Delay, 224
Descending runs, 915
Distortion, 87–88, 162, 174, 220, 224
D major key, 84
D major scale, 246
D minor scale, 247
Dotted notes, 109
Double drop D tuning, 200
Double-string bends, 193, 194
"Down, Down, Down," **174**
Dreadnoughts, 47
Drop D tuning, 180, 199, 200
"Droppin' It," **181**

E

E♭9 chord, 186
E♭ blues scale, 247
E♭ major scale, 247
EADGBD tuning, 199
E blues scale, 248
E chords
    charts, 238–39

E5/E6 pattern, 102
E7, 78
E9, 185
E chord, 30
Em, 42
"Edelweiss" (Rodgers and Hammerstein), **62**
Effects, 224–25
Eighth notes, 60, 182
Electric guitar, *12*
  changing strings, 15
  choosing, 12
  makers, 204–12
  origins, 47, 67
Electric pianos, 121
Electro-acoustic guitars, 213
Electronic tuners, 19, *19*, 24, 200
Em7 chord, 74
E major scale, 248
E minor key, 139
E minor scale, 248
European instruments, 38–39
Everly Brothers, 108
"Every Good Boy Deserves Favor," 49

F

F# minor scale, 249
F#5 chord, 90
FACE, 49
Fan-braces, 39
F blues scale, 249
F chords
  charts, 240–41
  F5, 90
  F barre, 114
  F chord, 73
Fender, Leo, *120*, 120–21
Fender amps, 121, 220
Fender Rhodes electric piano, 121
Fender Stratocaster, *93*, 93, 151, *207*, 207
Fender Telecaster, *85*, 85, 120–21, 208, *208*
Fender tremolos, 93, 223, *223*
Fender Twin amp, *220*, 220

Final Cut, The (Pink Floyd), 56
Finger picks, 123
Finger positions, 28, 229
Fingerstyle, 123–35
First position, 51–53, 58
Flack, Roberta, *74*, 74
Flat notes, 57
Flattened fifth, 152
Flex-Able (Vai), 175
Floating tremolo, 223
Floyd Rose tremolos, 223, *223*
F major key, 84
F major scale, 57, 248
F minor scale, 248
Footrests, 25
4/4 time, 37, 60
France, 38–39
Fret buzz, 11
"Frying pans", 67
Fugees, *77*
Funk, 185–91
Funk chord, 185

G

G♭ blues scale, 249
G♭ major scale, 249
G# minor scale, 250
Gain controls, 87, 173
G blues scale, 250
G chords
  charts, 242–43
  G5, 90, 104
  G6, 104
  G7, 78
  G chord, 41
  Gm, 114
Gear, 219–26
Gibson, Orville, 47
Gibson amps, *219*
Gibson ES-335, 212–13, *213*
Gibson Explorer, *203*
Gibson Flying V, 206, *206*
Gibson Les Paul, 110–11, *111*, 204, *204*
Gibson SG, 205, *205*
Gibson pickups, 67
Gilmour, David, *56*, 56

G major key, 84, 105
G major scale, 249
G minor scale, 250
Goodman, Benny, 219
"Gothic chug," **173**
Grapelli, Stephane, 48
"Greensleeves," **130–31**
"Green Stew," **173**
Gretsch 6120 Chet Atkins, *214*
Gretsch guitars, 214
Guitars, origins of, 38–39
Guitar types, 9–12, 203–17
Guns N' Roses, 99

H

Half notes, 36
"Hammered," **190**
Hammer-on, 158, 164, 915
Hancock, Herbie, 121
Harmonic minor scales, 70
Harmony, 36
Harrison, George, 61, *61*, 81, 151, 213
Harvest (Young), 80
Hawaiian guitars, 67
Head amps, 221–22
"Heart of Gold" (Young), 80
"Helter Skelter" (McCartney), 118
Hendrix, Jimi, 93, *163*, 163, 221
Hendrix chord, 162
"Here Comes the Sun" (Beatles), 81
High fidelity, 13
Hill, Lauryn, *77*
Holding the guitar, 22–23
Holly, Buddy, 69, *69*
Howlin' Wolf, 153
Hudson, Paul, 99
Humbuckers, 205

I

Ibanez JEM Series, 175
Improvisation, 152, 154
Intonation, 11, 12
Inversions, 167

J

Jagger, Mick, 106
JamBug FM, 222
Jazz style, 124
Jimi Hendrix Experience, 163
"Jingle Bells", **55**
"Johnny B. Goode" (Berry), 102
Johnson, Robert, *153*, 153

K

Key signatures, 84
"Killing Me Softly" (Fox and Gimbel), **74–77**
King, B. B., *159*, 159
King, Ben E., 44, *44*

L

"Layla" (Clapton), 151
Lead guitar, 51–63
  first position, 51–53
  Hendrix chord, 162
  rhythm, 60
  scales, 57, 70
  sharps and flats, 58
  string bending, 157–58
  tablature (TAB), 66
  techniques, 157–71
  upstrokes, 43, 44, 65, 68
Ledger lines, 49
Left-hand damping, 119
Left-handed playing, 17
Left hand position, 138
Lennon, John, 33, 61, 67, 213
Licks, 152, 154–55
Line 6 guitars, 212
Line 6 Pod, *226*, 226
Line 6 Variax, *212*
Live8, 56
Living and Dying in 3/4 Time (Buffett), 71
Louis XIV, 39
Lutes, 39
Luthiers, 39, 47

M

McCartney, Paul, 118, 128
"Make It Last," **174**

Marshall, Jim, 121
Marshall amps, 121, 221–22
Marshall AS100D, *221*
Marshall SL Plexi, *221*
Martin D 1, *215*
Martin D-18, 47
Martin guitars, 47, 215
Mayall, John, 150
Measures, 31
Melody, 36
Metronomes, 24, *37*, 54
"Michael Row the Boat Ashore," **54**
Mingus, Charlie, 132
Minor chords, 79
Minor pentatonic scales, 145–46
Minor scales, 70
Mitchell, Joni, *132*, 132
"Moochin," 147
Movable power chords, 90
Moving bass line, 139
Multi-FX, 225
Music stands, 25
Music theory, 36–37, 109
Muted notes, 176

N

National Resonator Custom, *216*
National Resonator guitars, 216
Natural symbol, 70
Neck, 11
Nevermind (Nirvana), 217
Nirvana, 217
Noise, 12
Note names, 46, 49
"Nu" metal, 180

O

Octave pairs, 135
One-finger chords, 180
Open tunings, 200
Organized Crime, 106
Overdrive, 87–88, *224*, 224

P

Page, Jimmy, 221
Palm muting, 119
Parachutes (Coldplay), 59
Parker Fly Deluxe, *210*
Parker Fly guitars, 210
Paul, Les, *110*, 110–11
Paul Reed Smith guitars, 209
Paul Reed Smith McCarty, *209*
Perkins, Carl, 61
Pick and fingers, 127
Picking, 23, 24, 123–24
Pickups, 67, 205
Piezoelectric transducers, 213
Pinched notes, 141
Pink Floyd, 56
Posture, 137
Power chords, 88–92
    distortion, 173–74
    drop D tuning, 180
    exercises, 89, 92, 98
    higher frets, 104
    movable power chords, 90
    root notes, 91
Practice amps, 222
Presley, Elvis, *33*, 33, 198
Prince, *191*, 191
"Proud Mary" (Fogerty), **194–97**
Pull-off, 158, 164
Pulse, 36
Punk rock, 80
Purple Rain (Prince), 191

Q

Quarter notes, 36
Quintette du Hot Club de France, 48

R

RCA, 201
Reinhardt, Django, 48, *48*
Relative tuning, 21
Rests, 60
Reverb, 224
Rhythm, 36, 60, 182
Rhythm guitar, 27, 119

Rhythm slashes, 79
Richards, Keith, 106, *106*
Rickenbacker, Adolph, 67, *67*
Rickenbacker 325 C58MG, *213*
Rickenbacker guitars, 67, 213
Riffs, 94, 176, 213
Right-hand position, 138
Rock chords, 182
Rock 'n' roll, 101–11
    in any key, 104
    rock 'n' roll pattern, 101–5, 107
    swing/shuffle, 107
    Twelve-Bar Blues, 103, 105, 188
Rock opera, 118
"Rock Party Piece", **182–83**
Rogers, Neil, *186*
Roland VG-88, *226*
Roland Virtual Guitar, 226
Rolling Stones, 106
Root notes, 91, 125
A Rush of Blood to the Head (Coldplay), 59

S

Safety, 14
Santa Monica Flyers, 80
Sanz, Gaspar, 39
Scales
    blues scale, 70, 152
    C major, 57, 84, 145
    C minor pentatonic, 145
    F major, 57
    harmonic minor scales, 70
    A minor, 70
    A minor pentatonic, 146
    playing, 58
scales practice, 245–52
Segovia, Andrés, *142*, 142
Sellas, Giorgio and Matteo, 39

Semi-acoustic guitars, 212–14
Sevenths, 78, 107
Sharps and flats, 58
Shuffles, 101, 107
"Shufflin", 148
Simon, Carly, 128
Single coil pickups, 205
Sitting position, 137
Sixteenths, 185–87
Sixth chords, 101
Slash, *99*, 99
Slash noteheads, 79
Slide, 32, 61, 158, 165
"Smokin'," **174**
Soap-bar pickups, 67
Sound, 11
Spain, 38–39
Spanish guitar, 10, 47
Staff/stave, 46
Standard notation, 66
"Stand by Me" (King, Leiber, Stoller), **43**
Stands, 25
Static bass, moving chords, 140
Steel strings, 135
Steinberger GS72A, *211*
Steinberger guitars, 211
Stomp boxes, 224
"Straight," 107
Straps, 24
Stray Gators, 80
String bending, 157–58, 164, 193, 194
Strings, 24
Strings, changing, 15–17
String winders, 15, 25
Strumming, 23, 74, 185–86
Struts, 39
Sunrise (Presley), 33
Supergroups, 151
Sweet Baby James (Taylor), 128
Swing, 107
Symbols, 27
Syncopated rhythm, 94

T

Tablature (TAB), 66

Tárrega, Frances de, 39
Taylor, James, *128*, 128
Tempo, 164
"That'll Be the Day" (Allison, Holly and Petty), **82**
The Who, 118
3/4 time, 37, 60
3/8 time, 143
Thriller (Jackson), 166
"Thrill Me", **190**
Thumb picks, 123
Thumb position, 29
Ties, 109
Time, 31
Time signatures, 36–37
Top line and chords, 74
Torres, Antoni Jurado de, 39
Townsend, Pete, 118, *118*
Transposition, 81
Traveling Wilburys, 61
Treble clef, 46
Tremolo arms, 223
Triplets, 109
Tubes/transistors, 220
Tuning, 18–21, 180, 199–200
Tuning forks, 19
Twelve-Bar Blues, 103, 105, 188
Twelve-string guitar, 135, *135*
"Twinkle, Twinkle, Little Star," **55**
Twin Reverb, 121

U

Unison triplet, 160
Unplugged (Clapton), 151
Upstrokes, 43, 44, 65, 68

V

Vai, Steve, *175*, 175
Van Halen, Eddie, 166, *166*
Verboam, René, 39
Vibrato arms, 223
Vincent, Gene, 101, *102*
Virtual guitar, 226
Vocal lines, 74

Voices, 141
Volume controls, 87

W

"Wade in the Water," **149**
Wah wah, *225*, 225
"Walk This Way" (Aerosmith), **176–79**
Wall, The (Pink Floyd), 56
"Waltz in A" (Carulli), **143**
" Water is Wide, The," **133–34**
Waters, Muddy, 153
Waters, Roger, 56
"While My Guitar Gently Weeps" (Harrison), 151
White, Jack, 227, *227*
White Album (Beatles), 151
White Blood Cells (White Stripes), 227
A White Sport Coat and a Pink Crustacean (Buffett), 71
White Stripes, The, 227
Whole notes, 36
Williams, John, *141*
Wish You Were Here (Pink Floyd), 56
"Wonderful Tonight" (Clapton and Kamen), **167–71**

X

X & Y (Coldplay), 59

Y

Yardbirds, 150
Young, Neil, 80, *80*

Z

Zappa, Frank, 175

Music credits

Bad Moon Rising
Words and Music by John Fogerty. Copyright © 1969 Jondora Music. Copyright Renewed. This arrangement Copyright © 2006 Jondora Music. International Copyright Secured. All Rights Reserved.

Stand By Me
Words and Music by Jerry Leiber, Mike Stoller and Ben E. King. © 1961 (Renewed) JERRY LEIBER MUSIC, MIKE STOLLER MUSIC and MIKE & JERRY MUSIC LLC. This arrangement © 2006 JERRY LEIBER MUSIC, MIKE STOLLER MUSIC and MIKE & JERRY. MUSIC LLC. All Rights outside the U.S. and Canada Controlled by JERRY LEIBER MUSIC, MIKE STOLLER MUSIC and TRIO MUSIC COMPANY. All Rights Reserved.

Edelweiss
From THE SOUND OF MUSIC. Lyrics by Oscar Hammerstein II. Music by Richard Rodgers. Copyright © 1959 by Richard Rodgers and Oscar Hammerstein II. Copyright renewed. This arrangement Copyright © 2006 by WILLIAMSON MUSIC. WILLIAMSON MUSIC owner of publication and allied rights throughout the world. International Copyright Secured. All Rights Reserved.

That'll Be the Day
Words and Music by Jerry Allison, Norman Petty and Buddy Holly. © 1957 (Renewed) MPL MUSIC PUBLISHING, INC. and WREN MUSIC CO. This arrangement © 2006 MPL MUSIC PUBLISHING, INC. and WREN MUSIC CO. Peermusic (UK) Limited. Used by permission of Music Sales Limited (UK). Rights Reserved. International Copyright Secured.

Killing Me Softly with His Song
Words by Norman Gimbel. Music by Charles Fox. Copyright © 1972 Rodali Music and Fox-Gimbel Productions, Inc. (P.O. Box 15221, Beverly Hills, CA. 90209 USA). Copyright Renewed. This arrangement Copyright © 2006 Rodali Music and Fox-Gimbel Productions, Inc. (P.O. Box 15221, Beverly Hills, CA 90209 USA). All Rights on behalf of Rodali Music Administered by Sony/ATV Music Publishing, 8 Music Square West, Nashville, TN 37203. International Copyright Secured. All Rights Reserved.

Walk This Way
Words and Music by Steven Tyler and Joe Perry. Copyright © 1977 Music Of Stage Three. Copyright Renewed. This arrangement Copyright © 2006 Music Of Stage Three. All rights Reserved. Used by Permission.

Born on the Bayou
Words and Music by John Fogerty. Copyright © 1968 Jondora Music. Copyright Renewed. This arrangement Copyright © 2006 Jondora Music. International Copyright Secured. All Rights Reserved.

Wonderful Tonight
Words and Music by Eric Clapton. Copyright © 1977 by Eric Patrick Clapton. Copyright Renewed. This arrangement Copyright © 2006 by Eric Patrick Clapton. All Rights for the U.S. Administered by Unichappell Music Inc. Used by permission of Music Sales Limited (UK). Copyright Secured. All Rights Reserved.

Proud Mary
Words and Music by John Fogerty. Copyright © 1968 Jondora Music. Copyright Renewed. This arrangement Copyright © 2006 Jondora Music. International Copyright Secured. All Rights Reserved.

Picture credits

All pictures © Amber Books except the following:

Corbis: 38 (Arte & Immagini srl); 39 (Geoffrey Clements); 71 (John Atashian); 106 (Neal Preston); 108 (Lynn Goldsmith); 118 (Neal Preston); 128 (Henry Diltz); 132 (Henry Diltz); 142 (Erich Auerbach); 150; 175 (Contographer); 191 (Neal Preston); 201 (Neal Preston)
Dorling Kindersley: 47; 211(r); 220(t)
Fender Musical Instruments Corporation: 12; 85; 93; 121; 207; 208

Getty Images: 33 (Frank Driggs Collection); 44 (Mike Putland); 48 (Frank Driggs Collection); 77 (Frank Micelotta); 159 (Kevin Winter); 166 (Scott Harrison); 227 (Bertrand Guay)
Gibson Guitar Corporation: 111; 135; 203; 204; 205; 206(r); 213(t); 219
Line 6: 212; 226(t)
Marshall Amplification: 221(both)
National Reso-Phonic Guitars Inc.: 216
Photos.com: 20
Popperfoto: 61
Redferns: 59 (Diana Scrimgeour); 80 (Richard Aaron); 99 (Ebet Roberts); 110 (Andrew Lepley); 137 (David Redfern); 152 (David Redfern); 153 (Deltahaze Corporation); 186 (Ebet Roberts); 198 (Jon Super); 209 (Steve Catlin); 210 (Steve Catlin); 211(l) (Steve Catlin); 214 (Steve Catlin); 215 (Steve Catlin); 220(b) (Richard Ecclestone); 223(r) (Steve Catlin)
Rex Features: 56 (Brian Rasic); 74 (Robert Legon); 102 (Everett Collection); 141 (Clive Dixon); 163 (Marc Sharratt); 217 (Roger Sargent)
B. C. Rich: 206(l)
Rickenbacker International Corporation: 67(both); 213(b)
Roland Corporation: 224, 226(b)
Stock.Xchng: 225 (Ed Desyon)
Topfoto: 69

256